DEUS EX MACHINA

THE UPGRADE SERIES #6

WESLEY CROSS

JOIN THE UPGRADE SERIES

To receive free books, get behind the scenes stories, and be the first to hear about new releases—sign up for the newsletter.

See the back of the book for details.

PUBLISHER INFORMATION

This is a work of fiction. Names, characters, businesses, places, events, and incidents are either the product of the author's imagination or used in a fictitious manner. Any resemblance to actual persons, living or dead, or actual events is purely coincidental.

Published by
Cerberus Prints
PO BOX 90399
Brooklyn, NY 11209

1

Rigel Compound, Upstate New York

Jason Hunt watched the main computer terminal over Poznyak's shoulder.

The lights at the lower level of Silo 1 blinked as the generator kicked in and then returned to full brightness. The rhythmic breathing of an open dilution refrigerator superimposed over the hum of high-energy cables snaking away from the quantum computer seemed to fill the round chamber with nervous energy. In the middle of the room, surrounded by rolling desks with monitors and electronic equipment, stood a table holding a sarcophagus. The normally transparent plastic was now frosted from the inside, the intricate patterns of ice hiding the nude body of Rachel Hunt. A large monitor running the entire side of the bed was dark at the moment, except a single word in the middle.

Initializing.

There were some changes to the giant container since Jason Hunt had seen it last. A black box was bolted on top of the surface right above Rachel's face, with thick, multicolored woven wire cables running from either side. The wires were fed through the vacuum-sealed ports drilled in the plastic lid, where they disappeared at the back of Rachel's head. A new-generation cranial implant was going to be installed when the body was sufficiently rewarmed. Once active, it would communicate with a small army of nanobots that would remain in Rachel indefinitely after the procedure and direct them to repair any remaining damage.

"Want to do the honors?" Steven asked him and stepped back from the terminal, gesturing at the sarcophagus. "Whenever you're ready."

"Okay." Jason exhaled, startling himself as his breath rustled loudly through the closed space of the helmet. He took a step forward and stood in front of the monitor. "JC?"

"Yes?"

"You may proceed."

The AI didn't answer, but the monitors around the sarcophagus came to life all at the same time. An outline of a female body colored in the lightest shade of blue appeared on the main display on the side of the bed.

"Systems are normal," Schlager said, looking at one of the monitors. "We are at twenty-three percent capacity and climbing at the moment."

"Same on my end," Helen said from another corner of the room.

A warning popped into Jason's internal vision. His heart rate was spiking. He took a slow breath and rolled his shoulders back.

"Relax," he heard Poznyak's voice, and a gloved hand patted him on the back. "It's going to work. We've run the sims a million times."

"Sims aren't the same as the real deal."

"True." Poznyak made a gesture as if he was trying to scratch his nose, only to bump his fingers against the bubble of his helmet. "Crap. Why does it always itch when I have this on?"

Jason smiled despite the nerves. Poznyak had the same effect on people as baby pandas—it was impossible not to feel better in his presence.

"Forty-two percent," Schlager said. "Holding steady."

The faint-blue lines on the display took on a slight shade of pink, with a cluster of warm colors appearing at the base of Rachel's skull.

"Neurolink established," he heard Helen say.

"We are going from the head down," Poznyak said to him. They'd discussed the process a thousand times, but Steven continued to play a doctor with good bedside manners, explaining things as they went. "The bots have now established a bridge between the implant and the brain. Naturally, the brain is the most important part of the rewarming procedure, and also the most energy hungry. It'll take us four times longer to be done with it than we are going to spend on the rest of the body. The vast majority of bots remaining in Rachel after the procedure will stay in her head as well."

"Neurolink steady," JC announced through the speakers. "Implant is active and communicating. Neural activity is adequate for suspended animation."

Jason blew out a long breath. Poznyak and the techs tiptoed around their explanations when they discussed the process, but it sounded like the initial connection was the first step where things could go catastrophically bad. Or, to be more precise, where they could discover it *had been* catastrophically bad all along. There was a fine line between death and extremely deep sleep, and Rachel had been on the right side of it.

"So far, so good." Poznyak grinned through the glass of his helmet, as if reading his thoughts. "That's a big one."

"Still steady at forty-two," Schlager echoed. "A great sign."

"Why is that?"

"No obvious damage," Poznyak said. "It means the bots aren't encountering anything unusual that requires more work. And the same amount of work translates into roughly the same computing power requirements."

The back of the head on the monitor was now a solid pink, with streaks of it stretching down the spine and then smaller streaks still deeper into the body.

"Are you sure there's no chance cancer can spread from her lungs?"

"There's no guarantee, but I think the blockade should hold until the implants are in." Poznyak waved at a small table at the back with two thermal containers. "That's why we won't be rewarming the lungs to the same degree as the rest of the body. Only enough to perform the surgery."

"I wish we didn't have to do a heart transplant," Jason said, his eyes darting between the computer-generated outline of Rachel's body and one of the containers.

"Me too," Poznyak said. "It will put some extra stress on the body, no doubt. But after years in suspension, I'm afraid it's too big of a risk not to. The last thing you want is for the heart to fail after she's up and about and is somewhere away from urgent care. I think the rewards outweigh the risks."

"I see."

"Don't worry about the implants." Poznyak looked up at him and lightly tapped Jason on the chest plate of his pressurized suit. "We've perfected the procedure by now. Yours is working like a clock. It's an upgraded version of what Mother Nature gave us. If, God forbid, she's out of our care and something happens, whoever is helping her doesn't need to do anything different. Chest compressions, defibrillators…everything works the same way. Besides, the mainframe that goes in with the heart and the lungs solves the problem of a power source for her right from the start. Any future augs will be a plug-and-play kind of a setup. We won't have to reinvent the wheel like we had to with you. I wish we had this tech when you got your first augmentations. We wouldn't have to do so much backtracking and rewiring over the years."

"Getting an arm chopped off wasn't on my wish list, either," he said, a slew of horrifying images flashing in his mind. A dirty holding cell. The face of Johnny the Butcher contorted in a blind rage. He shook his head, willing the memories to disappear.

"I get it," Steven said. "I do. But this is akin to the argument whether we should send a spacecraft to the nearest star now or wait for a better engine. Any future generation tech will be so much faster, it'll get there before the original. At least in this instance, we don't have to philosophize. The tech is here. We'll do the lungs first. The heart will work on its own while we are using the heart-lung machine. Then, once we get the lung augs in and everything works properly, we'll swap the heart, too."

"Still stable at forty-two," Helen said. "All systems are normal. How are we doing, JC?"

The entire silhouette on the screen was now glowing a faint pink, with the back of the head and the spine taking on a deep-scarlet hue.

"JC?"

"Neural matrix is at seventy-six percent," the AI replied after a slight delay. "No material damage present."

"When integration of the matrix is complete," Poznyak said, his eyes beaming, "the rest should be easy."

Jason watched in a trance as the minutes on the internal clock ticked by and the picture on the main monitor that had started as a thin outline filled with deeper shades of color. He thought his eyes tricked him, but as the time passed by, he became certain that Rachel's cheeks lost their ghostly grayish hue.

"Integration's complete," JC said, and a round of cheers and applause rang in Jason's speakers, reverberating inside of his fishbowl helmet.

"This is it." Poznyak grabbed his elbow and shook it. "We've done it, buddy. We've done it!"

Jason found himself wearing a manic grin and slowly walked around the station and next to the sarcophagus. The frost was mostly gone from the transparent plastic. His wife's face looked peaceful, as if in a deep sleep. A warning screeched and another amber alert popped in his internal vision, but he ignored them, his breath shallow as the tips of his bionic fingers touched the smooth surface of the plastic. He longed to rip the lid open and pick her up. To bury his face in her black hair. To smell her skin. To feel the touch of her hands.

"How long?" He stopped and cleared his throat, suddenly finding himself unable to speak. "How long until she wakes up?"

"I'd say about a week?" Poznyak responded, respectfully keeping distance. "We should be able to do the transplants tomorrow. It'd be best if she stayed in a coma for a few days afterward. It'll give her a chance to recover. In the meantime, we'll run some diagnostics and make sure everything is ticking the way it should be. By this time next week, she should be fully alert."

A loud beep made him jump, and he swerved, wildly looking around the lab. There was another beep and then another. He panicked, searching for the source of the sound, until he caught Steven's eyes glimmer through the plastic of his shield.

"It's her heart, Jason," Poznyak said, and Hunt felt his cheeks stretch into a grin. "Your wife is alive."

2

The Oval Office, Washington, DC

Alexander Engel stood by the window and watched an American robin hop on the South Lawn. The curious bird was small, almost a chick. It made its way closer to the bulletproof glass, stopped for a moment, turned this way and that, as if showing off his orange-red breast, and then took flight, disappearing over the bushes. Engel wondered if Roger, a black stray cat that had been living on the grounds for the past several weeks and got befriended by the Secret Service agents, was nearby. The feline tried to catch some birds on the lawn, but so far hadn't been successful.

"You haven't answered my question," he heard Susan say and Alexander turned back, pulled the chair out and sat down, resting his elbows on the famed Resolute desk.

"I haven't?"

Susan didn't answer, just raised her eyebrows. She sat at the edge of the cream-colored couch, the palms of her hands pressing down on her knees. She wore a smart gray pantsuit and a plain white blouse, and her hair fell down in layers. The look he liked so much. As proper as ever. Too proper.

"Come here." He beckoned.

"I don't think so," she said, without moving.

"Come on."

She ignored him, her feet firmly planted on the dark-blue rug.

He sighed. Elevating her to his chief of staff made sense and was one of the best decisions he'd made since he moved into the White House, and yet it also seemed to be the worst. Although Susan had been de facto occupying the role already, there were dozens of people who lobbied him for the post in the weeks leading to his official move: senior management types from within his own company, Victor Ye's emissaries, professional politicians. Most were qualified to fill the role. Some were better than others. None knew him like she did. He resisted them all and gave her the role a week before moving into the West Wing.

While necessary, the new power dynamic created a tangible distance between them, further not helped by the fact that most days she would start working while most of the personnel was still asleep, and stay up, long after the vast majority of his staff retired for the night. Above all, Susan absolutely refused to be anything but a professional in the Oval Office or move into the West Wing with him. If he didn't know better, he'd assume she was waiting for him to make their relationship official. Like her predecessor, she commuted to the most recognizable address in the country every morning and left it at the end of the night. Which meant that at the end of each day, Engel had to retreat into the empty king-sized bed in the presidential bedroom on the second floor of the White House.

On a few occasions they shared the bed, she'd run off as soon as she could, as if the very walls of the room were pressing down on her.

He could hardly blame her. Even after a few months at the White House, he still wasn't used to it. The entire place was imbued with such power, it was almost palpable. Every little detail, from the dark-blue hand-woven rug on the floor of the Oval Office, to the hand-polished wood floors, to the stately drapes framing the windows, made anyone who entered stand straighter, like a soldier at attention.

If the West Wing made you stiffen your posture, the Oval Office took it to another level. Even the smell was different in the place that housed the most powerful man in the world. A mixture of the wax polish and fresh flowers that were delivered to his desk every morning. The smoke from the fireplace on the northern side of the room and a slight scent of lime that lingered after the regular cleanings. He found the cocktail intoxicating. If it could be bottled, he thought sometimes, it would sell like crazy.

"You don't think it's a good idea?" he said.

"No. Not at all. And I thought you weren't convinced, either. That's why you wanted to sleep on it."

"Well," his fingers drummed on the polished surface of the desk, "the more I thought of it, the more it made sense. While Hunt's forces are getting bogged down in cities and towns across the country, if we could decapitate the movement in one decisive strike, the rest of them would scatter into the wind. His supporters might claim they want Darius Price in my place, but Hunt is who they follow."

"That's what you said before." She shuffled her feet ever so slightly. "And yet you hesitate. You know it's a mistake. We have an advantage here. And the longer we maintain the status quo, the harder it's going to be for Hunt and Price to maintain their momentum and keep people who support them invested in their cause. You sit in the Oval Office, for God's sake. We control the media. Eventually, we can shape the public opinion about them. They will turn from rebels into terrorists. We can highlight atrocities and attribute them to Orion's forces. Civilians caught in the crossfire. Kids dying. We can mold the narrative until even the most active supporters turn against them. The resistance will smolder for some time, but it will die out."

"All true." He watched the curve of her back as she shifted on the couch. Despite the seriousness of the topic, he found himself distracted. Running a country, as he discovered, was a lonely business. For a second, he contemplated locking the doors and taking her right on the couch. He dismissed the urge. It would not happen. She'd only get angry.

"So why not stick with the plan?" she asked, interrupting his wandering thoughts.

"Because I'm not sure the fire will go out as easily as you say. And the longer it goes on, the harder it will get for people to reconcile. Nobody wants a long civil war. People have families to feed. If we can finish it quickly and they can go back to their jobs, by Christmas no one will remember why we were fighting in the first place, and they'll thank us for it. And most importantly—"

"You don't think he'll use Project Thor?"

"No." He shook his head. "I don't think he will. For all his bluster, he knows the optics would be terrible. He'd win the battle but lose the war. We'll have every drone and every TV station crew on standby to cover the use. It'll be all over the evening news. The pushback will be momentous."

Susan leaned back on the couch and crossed her legs.

Engel's cheeks grew hot with anger. She clearly didn't agree with him but kept her opinion to herself. "What do we have with Black Arrow in the Northeast?"

She pulled out a tablet and scrolled through the notes before answering. "We have two infantry brigades. Fourth and Fifth. The Fifth is tied up in Connecticut. Resistance has been stiff up there."

"And the Fourth?"

"They are camping near Buffalo, with not a lot of action as of late. Mostly available. Some skirmishes with local guerrilla fighters, but nothing that would prevent them from being deployed. We can move them toward the silos within forty-eight hours."

"How much manpower does Hunt have?"

"The last satellite imagery showed about two thousand troops. They have a few howitzers and a few old, decommissioned tanks. We saw them set up some new fortifications, too. A network of trenches and bunkers. But it's all volunteer force. From the reports, it seems like they are well organized and have vets of various ranks in key positions, but they are not as cohesive as Black Arrow. The Fourth Brigade should be able to overwhelm them."

"Okay." He stood up and went to the window again. The robin was nowhere to be seen. "Send the order out. Have the Fourth positioned for a direct attack on the Rigel compound in the next forty-eight hours."

"Don't you want to discuss it with Rodney Graham first?" she said, referring to his military advisor. "I can set up the meeting."

"No." He shook his head. "The decision's been made. But I want to talk to him. We need to discuss how to press our advantage once Rigel falls. We'll have to be quick and decisive. It's time to end this farce."

"Will do." Susan stood up and picked up her notebook. "Would there be anything else, Mr. President?"

He glanced at her over his shoulder. "Will you consider staying tonight?"

"Not tonight, I'm afraid. My last meeting is scheduled for ten o'clock and after that, I'd rather just get home and grab some sleep."

"You could sleep here." He waited for a response, but none came. For a moment, he thought about asking her to find him a few companions for the night. To punish her for not staying. But watching her calm professional demeanor, he reconsidered. Susan was a lot of things. Jealous wasn't one of them. "All right. That'll be all then."

"Thank you."

He heard her departing steps and then the sound of the closing door. Engel stood there for a few more seconds, watching the garden. Then he went back to the desk and fired up his computer. There was much work to be done. Sooner or later, he'd tighten his grip on the country. And once it was under his control, there'd be new frontiers to look at. A new world order was finally coming.

3

Jay Mountain Wilderness, Upstate New York

Jason Hunt hugged the ground as the sounds of the patrol grew closer. The earth under his fingers was wet and mossy and smelled of withered leaves and rotten grass. He could hear the rumbling of the engine reverberating through the dark, sleepy woods and the gruff laughter of two soldiers. A passive sonar presented him with a ghostly outline of a pickup truck on a dirt road a couple of hundred yards to the north, moving in his direction. He surmised the shadowy mass in the truck's bed was the two men talking, but there could have been more. An active radar would have given him a much clearer picture, but Hunt didn't want to risk it.

He frowned as the engine grew closer and crawled backward, pushing himself deeper into the woods and behind a trunk of a fallen tree. A few seconds later, the high beams of the truck, bobbing up and down, sliced through the dark shadows, and the vehicle with Black Arrow markings rolled into view.

The picture in his view was colored in bright green of the infrared.

From this distance, he could see there were five men—two in the cabin, and three in the back. One, a short, stocky man, was manning a mounted machine gun. Another man sat leaning against the cabin. The third mercenary lay along the left side of the truck, sleeping or resting.

"You are so full of it, dude," the gunner said as the long barrel swept the woods in a slow arc. "Both of them? At the same time? In your dreams."

"Yes, sir." The man leaned over the side of the truck and spat into the night. "Both of them. They had a good time, if you must know."

Jason lifted his head, judging the distance to the approaching truck. He had no doubt he could take them on, but wasn't sure he could do it quietly. He tensed like a coiled spring, ready to pounce as the truck rolled in front of him, but then froze as the barrel swung in his direction. It was too much of a gamble, he decided. A firefight would alert other patrols in the area and compromise his mission.

"Which one did you like more?"

"Sarah for sure," the man said and clicked his tongue. "Much bigger tits."

The truck rolled away into the woods, its taillights glowing red through the trees for some time like the eyes of a mythical beast.

Jason stood up and brushed himself off as he listened to the fading sounds of the engine. When the forest became quiet again, he headed for the road.

He left the silo compound right after midnight, sneaking past the guards and then his own militia patrolling the outskirts of the defensive area, like a saboteur trying to get away after a mission. He trusted them, maybe most of them, at least. There were a mixed bunch. Some were former military, and some were just hardened men and women of different walks of life, who came to support Darius Price and him as an extension of what they saw as a legitimate government. A few groups had formed right after the assassination attempt during Price's inauguration ceremony. A trickle first, more and more people poured in, joining their ranks all over the country as the conflict grew.

It's strange how civil wars played out, he thought. No number of riots or civil disobedience can prepare the average citizen for the amount of violence that spills into the streets once it reached critical mass. And once it did, it seemed so sudden, so overwhelming when former neighbors picked up arms against one another, and block parties gave way to barricades and Czech hedgehogs. Before long, the stability of peace and normalcy seemed like things of the distant past, and burnt-out buildings and bullet-ridden vehicles didn't shock anyone anymore.

With the patrol out of the immediate vicinity, Jason risked a quick burst of a short-range active radar. The pulse illuminated a 3D map in his internal vision, like an expanding shock wave, with him as the epicenter. There seemed to be no threats nearby, the woods still in the predawn silence, save for a few birds, and he picked up speed, his bionic legs stomping into the trail with a precise mechanical efficiency of a robot. As Jason followed the path on autopilot, just occasionally checking the map against the satellite images, his mind wandered.

The meeting was of utmost importance. As he got closer to his destination, he knew he should have been thinking of nothing else but how to convince Leonard Freeman to join their cause. And yet, as the distance to the virtual glowing dot on top of Jay Mountain grew brighter, Jason found himself unable to keep his mind off the images of the lower level of Silo 1 and the sound it took him a few long seconds to recognize—his wife's beating heart.

He was happy, of course. But if he had been honest with himself, he wasn't prepared for it. Quite the opposite. He'd done everything in his power to make it happen. And yet, despite the mountains of work and Poznyak's unwavering dedication, there was a moment, as he stood in the middle of the room, receiving congratulations from ecstatic friends, when he realized he had been preparing for something else. He was steeling himself for a spectacular failure. And now, when only a few days separated him from the long-awaited reunion, he found himself at a loss.

He wanted to share this with someone, anyone, but what was he supposed to say? That he thought it'd be easier to mourn the wife who he hadn't seen in years, rather than meet her face-to-face?

Face-to-face, he thought. *That was going to be something else.* The face she remembers, the round cheeks and the long hair, and the face he wore now could have belonged to two different people. What was she going to think when she saw him for the first time? The artificial arms fused into the internal chassis. The legs, where thighs transformed midway into a gray silver of metal. The wet-wired weapons and armor implants on his torso. And to top it all off—the multitude of cranial implants governed by a CPU more powerful than anything she could get her hands on while she was still alive. His heart, his liver, his kidneys, his lungs—most of his internal organs had been replaced with artificial implants and then supplemented with more implants still. Would she even think he kept his humanity? Did he?

He wanted to believe none of that mattered, and Rachel would look past the body modifications and see the man who pushed through the years full of fire and brimstone to bring her back. But what if she couldn't? What if all she saw was a cybernetic freak who took her husband's place and smuggled her from an imperfect but stable present into a bloody and violent future? He tried to imagine how he would feel had their roles been reversed. He couldn't.

Jason reached into his backpack and pulled out a thermos. A few milligrams of caffeine made no difference to his artificially balanced system, where several stimulants picked from an implant could be pumped directly into his blood, but the habit remained, and he found it comforting. The hot, bitter liquid stung his tongue as he took a few greedy sips and it ran down his throat, helping push the thoughts of Rachel away.

In some other time, in a different life, he would have enjoyed this hike, he thought, as the trail became steeper. He'd work up some sweat and appetite by the time he reached the summit. For now, as his power cell took care of most of the walking and a sprinkle of leptin delivered by his hormonal implant suppressed his hunger, Jason felt almost nothing as he cleared the woods and stepped onto the stony surface on the top of the mountain, looking for the other party.

It was a magnificent view. A series of rolling hills in every direction and a sparkle of water on the east side of the mountain in what looked like a small lake or a pond. Light, puffy clouds, still dark on the top, were tinted pink and yellow on the bottom by the first rays of the rising sun.

Yeah, Hunt thought, *I would have enjoyed this hike.* As he stood there, looking at the woods below, the beauty of the surroundings was spoiled. He made the journey for nothing. The summit was empty. He'd stay here for another hour or two just to be certain, he decided, but there was no doubt in his mind. Leonard Freeman wasn't coming. Leonard Freeman stood him up.

He drew a deep breath, looking at the hills. Freeman's no-show was worrisome, but Jason wondered if it was a sign of something more troublesome to come. An early demonstration that the support for the rebellion was waning. If that was true, their long-term odds had never looked bleaker.

4

Rigel Compound, Upstate New York

"Neural matrix is at one hundred percent and stable," Jason Hunt heard the androgynous voice say. JC had been monitoring the post-procedure vitals and made announcements of what she considered being newsworthy out loud. He should be used to them by now, but somehow, they always took him by surprise, making him jump. No matter how much he knew about the AI or how many times he talked to it, he couldn't bring himself to accept it for what Helen and Max, and even Steven, claimed it to be—a live being. Even saying *she* felt weird and forced, and after unsuccessfully trying to train himself, he gave up and continued to refer to JC as *it*, except for the time he had a direct conversation with the AI. Then, he tried his best to avoid any pronouns altogether.

There was another reason he couldn't bring himself to accept JC as a sentient being—its help in Rachel's revival. If the AI was just another tool, he didn't have to think about the role it had played during the procedure or worry about an ulterior motive it might have had to sabotage the process in some ways. Or worse—if it was indeed a *she*, then Jason owed her an enormous debt for bringing the revival to its successful completion, which without JC wouldn't be possible for a long time, if ever.

Now, with JC's role reduced to a minimum, he pushed the thoughts of the AI's involvement to the back of his mind. All he cared for at the moment was the woman with a ghostly pale complexion in front of him.

They still kept Rachel Hunt at the lower level of Silo 1 after the transplant, but now as both the revival and the triple-implant surgery procedures were complete, they had moved her out of the sarcophagus and onto the med bay platform. Her body was covered up to her waist by a sheet of white linen and her torso sported a multitude of sensors and wires. An IV dripped steadily on the stand next to the bed, but the lung tubes had already been removed. Unlike people with normal lungs, who needed a ventilator while in a coma, Rachel's artificial organs could deliver oxygen to her body on their own, stimulated by the independent commands of the CPU.

Jason could see a red, angry-looking scar run across Rachel's chest just below her breasts and there was some fairly extensive bruising on her rib cage. A few octagon-shaped metal splice connectors glistened on her skin—a pair on each shoulder and one more in the middle of both of her collarbones. The flesh around the metal was slightly raised and inflamed as well, though not as much as the scar from the surgery.

She had a long way to go before her body was back to normal, but considering the operation took place less than twenty-four hours ago, the recovery had been going at a blistering, almost miraculous pace.

While her body remained in a medically induced coma, the nanobots, controlled by JC through the newly built-in cranial implant, accelerated the healing process by leaps and bounds. Steven Poznyak, taking pains to make complicated terms as simple as possible, explained to him that the army of miniature bots had been more active when Rachel was unconscious or sleeping, but their activity had to be reduced to a minimum when she was awake. Even the tiniest electric charges that were carried by the bots could interfere with normal neural activity of the body.

"I know you're itching to talk to her," the scientist said. "But she needs to do a lot of sleeping in the beginning. But we'll keep waking her up for longer and longer intervals and, sooner rather than later, she should be back to normal. Then whatever updates and patching up that will happen during her natural sleep cycle will be enough to keep everything in top shape."

Now Poznyak was busying himself watching the readings on his monitors and giving commands to a couple of nurses.

"How much longer?"

"Just a few more seconds," Poznyak said, giving a nod to one of his assistants and watching her press a few buttons.

"Okay."

"Remember. When she comes to, she'll be alert for less than a minute. We also don't know if she'll be able to see you or understand what you're saying, but you should talk to her, anyway. Many studies have shown that hearing the voice of their loved ones helps patients recover. It doesn't matter what you say, just keep talking."

"Okay." Something touched his shoulder, and Jason shuddered, startled, only to see Poznyak's hand.

"There's no reason to be alarmed now," he said. "The hardest part is behind us. Now we just need to be patient and help her back to the real world, bit by bit."

Hunt nodded, unable to find the words. The debt he owed to the perpetually cheerful scientist was bigger than he'd ever be able to repay. The least he could do was listen to the man and do what he said.

"I'm detecting a sharp spike in neural activity," JC announced. "The patient will be conscious in five seconds."

He watched Rachel's eyelids flutter for a moment, the smallest of motions, almost imperceptible. Then she grimaced, a few areas of her face independently moving in a tic-like fashion, almost as if her muscles were trying themselves out, to make sure everything was working as intended before committing to bigger movements.

"Rachel?"

She frowned with one side only, the left corner of her mouth drooping and momentarily sending him into panic mode as the images of stroke victims flashed in his mind. But the moment passed, and her lips parted and then pursed together in a childlike fashion.

"Rachel? It's Jason. I'm here."

Her eyelids fluttered again, more noticeable this time, and she slowly opened her eyes. They were bloodshot and unfocused at first but then there was a glint of recognition.

"It's me, baby." He reached out and touched her arm with his fingers. "You're back. I know you might be confused, but everything is fine. You are safe. I'm here, and Steven, too."

Her lips moved as if trying to form words, but no words came. Then her eyes lost focus, her lids closing again.

"What's going on?" Hunt turned to face Poznyak, a sudden tightness in his chest. "Something wrong?"

"Not at all." Poznyak gave him a reassuring smile. "The girl needs more sleep, that's all. I've warned you. This is going to be a process for the first few days. In and out. This was just perfect. JC? How's it looking?"

"Neural activity dropping within normal parameters," the AI said. "The subject is entering suspension."

"See? Nothing to worry about."

Jason watched Rachel's chest rise and fall. The rhythm of the artificial lungs was too slow for a normal pattern, but he knew the implanted devices, besides being more efficient than a regular pair of lungs, also had a built-in storage that worked like a battery: it accumulated the excess oxygen and released it, supplying the blood to what the CPU deemed to be an optimum level.

"What now? How long does she need to sleep?"

"Eight hours," Poznyak replied. "Give or take. I'll keep on monitoring her and will make a call when she's ready. Then we will wake her up for about five minutes. Depending on how she feels, that'd be the first time you'll be able to exchange a few words. Then she'll sleep for another eight hours and after that, we'll wake her up for an hour.

We need to walk a fine line between speeding up her recovery and making sure her cognitive abilities are functioning. We have to let the bots do their work and repair whatever lingering damage she might have from the cryogenic sleep and the surgeries."

"How long until she can function normally?"

"We don't have a reference point." Poznyak's smile was apologetic. "Nobody does. We are breaking new ground here. But if I had to take a guess, in about a week, she'll be able to hold a somewhat normal circadian rhythm. The bots are doing a lot of heavy lifting. I'd say in two weeks she'll be on her feet."

"That's...incredible." He paused, searching Poznyak's face as the man squinted, as if deciding whether to say more. "What? I feel like there's a *but* coming."

"I don't want to make you worried any more than you already are," Poznyak began. "And I have no reason to think this is anything but a giant success. But we are in uncharted territory. Her brain activity seems to be normal. If anything, it seems more active than normal. But we won't know if the cryogenic suspension has affected her cognitive abilities. We'll get a pretty good picture of what state we are in, once she's up long enough for a sustained conversation, but we won't know for sure for months, if not years, because certain things might take awhile to develop."

"I understand."

"However," Poznyak raised his voice slightly, "the next two weeks are crucial. If anything is seriously wrong, it'll most likely manifest itself then. It's a steep curve. The further we are from the awakening, the less chance anything can go wrong."

Jason looked back at the woman on the sheets. Her face was still pale, but her features were relaxed. Peaceful. He drew in a long breath. It was going to be the longest two weeks of his life.

5

Rigel Compound, Upstate New York

"Can I talk to you for a minute?"

Jason Hunt looked up from the tablet to see Schlager's head poking out of the stairwell. "Sure. Since when are you asking for permission? You usually just barge in here and tell me whatever you've got on your mind."

Schlager made an unintelligible noise, climbed up the stairs, and took a seat on the other side of the table, avoiding Jason's stare.

"Is everything all right?" He watched as his friend fidgeted in his chair. "You look mighty uncomfortable."

"I hear Freeman stood you up," Schlager said, ignoring Jason's question. "Have you heard anything from Leonard since?"

"Nope. Complete radio silence." Jason scrolled to the bottom of the document, a depressingly short list of food supplies available to the silo, and read Poznyak's note detailing his calculations for the current rations. As it stood, they were reduced to fourteen hundred calories per day, a number that was perilously close to what would be considered starvation. Getting some volunteer troops to patrol the area gave the compound some breathing room to bring in supplies and fend off Black Arrow's ambushes. At the same time, it added almost two thousand mouths to feed to the already ballooning roster of permanent silo personnel. The net effect was hardly noticeable enough to make anyone happy.

The meeting with Leonard Freeman could have given them enough manpower to drive the mercenary force far enough from the silos to establish a proper supply route. He was a vet, a paratrooper colonel in his previous life, who became one of the first known political and military movers and shakers to publicly question the disbandment of the army and the legitimacy of the Black Arrow's reign of terror when the civil war broke out. A charismatic leader, within the first two weeks of resistance, he gathered enough troops together, most of them former military themselves, to push back the mercenaries from his native Albany and the surrounding suburbs. But he stopped short of calling Alexander Engel's presidency illegitimate.

There were plenty of other successful pockets of resistance all over the country, but they all lacked the central command and organization of Black Arrow. Darius Price and Jason Hunt didn't agree on a lot of things, but they both acknowledged the need to fold the helter-skelter brigades under the same flag. Freeman and Price knew each other well, but until now, the former colonel hadn't proclaimed support, and limited his activities to protecting his hometown and neighboring areas from being terrorized by the mercenaries. Jason hoped to change that and bring Freeman into the fold. The man carried a lot of weight. Others would follow.

It was easier said than done, of course, as most of the leaders of the different groups were distrustful of anyone outside of their own and reluctant to relinquish newfound power. Jason had been hounding Freeman for a few weeks, trying to understand what made him tick until the man relented and agreed on the meeting, only not to show up to the rendezvous.

"Do you think something happened to him? An ambush or a coup within his own ranks?"

"I don't think so." He turned off the tablet and put it facedown on the table. "We can still see the movements of his regiment, but I couldn't get in touch with him or his lieutenant. From what I can tell, they are pulling back to Albany. My guess is they want to reinforce the western flank of his hometown against the potential attack from Black Arrow's brigade up in Buffalo. It looks like he's blowing me off. At least for the time being. I don't understand it. Why agree on a meeting and then not show up?"

"Because he didn't want the meeting to begin with," Schlager said, his voice low, almost as if he was talking to himself.

"How do you figure?"

"Isn't it obvious? You bullied him into this meeting," Schlager said, this time louder. "You kept pushing and pushing until he figured it was easier to just agree with you and then not show up than embarrass you on a video call with multiple people watching."

"Why didn't you say something? You were on that call."

"I don't know," Schlager said, visibly frustrated. He stood up and paced the small place back and forth, his hands stuffed into his pockets. "What the hell was I supposed to say? Don't go because he might not show up? How would that look?"

"Okay." Jason leaned back in his chair and stretched his legs. Schlager made a few more trips back and forth across the room, seemingly trying to bring his emotions under control. Then he returned to the table and stood in front of it, facing Jason. His outline glowed orange in Jason's view, which meant his EMU unit was just a shade away from considering Schlager as a threat. "I've never seen you so upset. Why don't you tell me what's on your mind? You're glowing orange."

Schlager only huffed in response, grabbed a chair, and straddled it, facing Jason. "I'm not going to jump you, if that's what you're afraid of."

"Pal." Hunt reached out over the table and put his hand over his friend's arm. "I would never think you're capable of hurting me. All I'm saying is I can see you're frustrated. Believe it or not, I am sufficiently human to distinguish between anxiety and hostility regardless of the colors my CPU is painting you with."

Schlager slumped, his shoulders relaxing, and took a long breath. "I'm sorry."

"No need to apologize. Just tell me what you came here to tell me."

"All right." His friend locked his bloodshot eyes with Jason, a look of resignation on his face. "I'm sure you've heard the phrase *possession is nine-tenths of the law?*"

"Of course."

Schlager rubbed his hands over his face. "We are losing the war, Jason. And it's not because Black Arrow is impossible to defeat, or because we can't find enough volunteers to fight them. We are losing it because our support is slowly disappearing. I know we can argue until we are blue in the face about what to do, but we are past the point of no return. On the current trajectory, we will be defeated, our forces around the country disbanded or slaughtered, and everyone in this silo will end up in jail for the rest of our lives. Or worse."

"So why fight, then?" Jason's face remained calm, but he could see the spike of adrenaline going up in his vision. "Should we just give it to Engel on a silver platter?"

"No. We can still turn the tide. But not by fighting random battles. Engel is coming to wipe us all out. I don't even think Project Thor will stop him. But the longer he stays at the White House, the more legitimate he'll look to the masses. If he stays long enough, people will eventually forget how he ended up in the Oval Office. They'll just know he's there. Possession is nine-tenths of the law, remember? Those shoes you wear are presumed to be yours unless proven otherwise."

"Then what do you suggest we do?"

Schlager looked down, examining his fingers. He stayed quiet for so long, Jason was about to repeat the question when his friend looked up, a burning fire in his eyes. "Something we should have done a long time ago. We kill Engel's right hand—Victor Ye. And then we kill Engel."

"I agree," he said quietly. Almost in a whisper.

"Enough of this—" Schlager started and then stopped, uncertain. "Wait, what? You agree?"

"I do." Jason drew a long breath. "I've been beating myself up about this. We should have listened to Connelly when he said it."

"Maybe." Schlager nodded. "But it's easier said than done. What do they say? Everything is fair in love and war? I supported you before, not to go through with this idea. It's one thing to kill someone in self-defense. It's quite another to put a hit on somebody's head. To become the judge, jury, and executioner. No trial, no due process, nothing. And yet, here we are, considering the very thing we had sworn not to do."

"Right. Now that we agree it's a necessity, we must find the way to do it. But not at the White House."

"You don't think we can pull it off?"

"That's only a small part of it. The White House grounds are guarded like nothing else, of course, and I heard they've been beefed up with sentinels. Victor Ye's supposedly brought quite a few of them from Hong Kong. But it's all irrelevant. It's not about pulling it off," Jason said. "Let's say we can overwhelm his defenses. Think about the optics. What are we going to do—storm the White House? Hit it with heavy artillery? Just imagine this playing out on national television. Charred windows of the building. Debris and bodies strewn all over the North Lawn. Collapsed iconic columns. We'll go from heroes and revolutionaries to villains and terrorists in a split second in the public's view. We can't defeat Engel if we lose public support. There are many people in this country who support us in principle but aren't exactly ready to take up arms. And if we push them away, then we will lose in the long run."

"We can't leave him there either. Possession is nine-tenths of the law, remember? Catch twenty-two."

"I understand." Hunt leaned forward and tapped his bionic finger on the surface of the table. "We need to find the way to lure him out of the White House. Preferably far enough from its ground defenses. Get him out in the open somehow. Then all bets are off."

"There's something else."

Jason looked at his friend, a quizzical look on his face. "What?"

"Before we bring down Engel, we need to take care of his biggest and most powerful supporter. We need to take care of Victor Ye first."

"You're right." Jason straightened and took a deep breath. "It's time to go all in."

6

Rigel Compound, Upstate New York

The top level of what used to be a control center of a ballistic missile silo was quiet, apart from beeping sounds coming from a medical monitor. A tall LCD lamp standing in the corner filled the space with a soft, almost comforting glow. There was a lingering smell permeating the room—a strange mixture of mechanical oil and rust, punctuated by a sharp note of disinfectant.

The chair squeaked under Jason as he shifted his weight, startling him, and he moved it closer to the bed.

Rachel Hunt, dressed in gray cotton pajamas, lay on a sturdy aluminum cot, her cheeks pale but with an unmistakable slight hint of pink, her chest rising and falling as she breathed. A small medical station was set up next to the bed, with an IV drip snaking down the stand and into her arm.

"She's ready," Poznyak said, checking her vitals again. "I can wake her up now."

Jason nodded, not trusting his voice. He watched Poznyak push a few buttons and the spikes on the heart monitor started to slowly accelerate.

"I'll leave you two," Steven said, retreating toward the stairwell. "I'll be just below with Max if you need me."

"Thank you, Steven."

Jason moved the chair closer to the bed, watching Rachel's face. After what seemed an eternity, her eyelids fluttered and then opened.

"Where…" she struggled. She cleared her throat and tried again. "Where am I?"

"Home," he said, bringing a cup of water to her chin, lifting her head, and helping her take a few sips through a straw. "At least what we call it these days. How are you feeling?"

"Hungover and sore, but otherwise fine." She blinked a few times, seemingly bringing her eyes into focus, and then gasped as she looked at him. "Your hands. What happened to you?"

"Argh." He leaned back, the chair squeaking in protest. "There've been a few changes since you saw me last."

"I thought," she murmured almost inaudibly, "when I briefly woke up, I saw you, but I thought it was just a dream. Short hair, sunken cheeks, and shiny arms…I was convinced I was dreaming."

"No." He reached out and took her hand in his. She stiffened as their fingers touched and, for a moment, he thought she'd yank her hand back, but she stayed. "It wasn't a dream. I was thinking a lot recently about that conversation we had in Fort Lauderdale while celebrating your offer. How I mocked your research. Now I've embraced the technology beyond anything you could imagine back then. Not all of it was my choice, but still."

"I'm sorry." She squeezed his hand. "It sounds like you've been through a lot while I happily slept. Can you feel that?"

"Yes." He smiled and squeezed her hand back. "Just like you said I would. It's…better than the original."

She smiled too, a tear running down her cheek. "I wish I had been there for you. It's been years, hasn't it?"

"Yes. But you are here now," he said and wiped her face with the back of his hand. "That's all that matters."

They stayed in silence for a few moments, watching each other. Getting accustomed to each other's presence.

"What happened while I was out?" she finally asked. "And where exactly is *home?*"

"Oh boy. I don't even know where to start."

"Start from the beginning." She gave him an encouraging smile. "That's usually a good place."

"It's a long story. We are in Upstate New York. For now, we live underground, in a former nuclear missile compound. Don't worry," he added as he saw a shadow of horror cross her face, "there hasn't been a nuclear war. At least not yet. No zombies either. But there is a civil war, and not just here. In a few countries, too. The cabal, a network of people and corporations that had been ruling the world from the shadows, is trying to step into the light. We have been fighting it. It's been tough lately."

She pushed her pillow up and sat up in bed, waving off Jason's protests. "I'm fine. I'm guessing we are helping the government to fight against the *cabal?*"

"No." He smiled, almost apologetically. "The government now *is* the cabal."

She rubbed her face. "It's just hard to process all this information."

"Wait until I tell you who the current president is."

"Please. Tell me everything."

He started from the beginning, his thoughts rushing back to the fateful night when he watched the cryogenic tank fill up with yellow liquid, covering his wife's body like amber over a prehistoric fly. The days and years that followed.

As he talked, Rachel sat straight, listening to the tale that spun many years, not taking her eyes off him, her cheeks flushed.

Jason tried to sound impartial at first, but as he took her through the series of painful defeats and sweet victories, it all came crushing down on him like an avalanche. Slow and insignificant in the beginning, a few loose pebbles running down a steep slope. Only to turn into an unstoppable force, destroying everything that stood in its path.

Rachel was taken by the story, and he lost himself in it as her face reflected each chapter of the past few years. There was the horror on her face when he described how he had lost his limbs. The curiosity of a scientific mind as he talked about numerous implants he and his team had installed over time. She wept as he told her about an unexpected friendship with Mike Connelly and the man's ultimate sacrifice in the desert. It surprised him when she reached out and cleaned his cheek. Apparently, he had been crying too. But there were good moments too, and she laughed as he told her how Poznyak and Schlager bickered about who needed to push the button to slice a piece of skin off her toe and then went to great lengths to find a way to tell him about it without making him angry.

"I'm so grateful Steven is here with you," she said when he finished. "Max and Helen and Chuck…it seems like you've got a good team on your side."

"I do."

"We can't lose," she said, giving him a crooked smile. "Not with the mighty cyborg, Jason Hunt, at the helm."

"It'll be two cyborgs soon." He returned the smile. "Your heart and your lungs are working. And your cranial implant for now is autonomous, but Steven will help you integrate it and have your interface running in the next few days."

She reached with her hand and gingerly touched the base of her head.

"Does it hurt?"

"No." She turned her head this way and that. "It's sore, but not painful. But it is weird."

"Weird how?"

"I don't know." She frowned. "It's almost like there's a room with a locked door in my head. I know it's there, but I can't see into it. Gives me the creeps, to be honest."

"That's normal," he said. "It takes some time to get used to, but by now it's a pretty standard procedure. And yours is the most powerful prototype yet. When it goes live, you'll get a bunch of icons floating in your inner vision you can customize once you know what you want.

Some prefer more, some less. I've seen Max's inner interface when he connects to an external display for tuning, and it's a miracle he can see anything past all those graphs and charts floating in front of his eyes. I keep it clean, with only essentials running at all times and bringing up other apps if I need something specialized. As for the control, it's easy. All you have to do is to visualize some simple action like clicking a button or turning a dial, or swiping from left to right. You'll feel clumsy for a few days, but then it'll become second nature."

"Amazing. It's so weird to wake up in the future." She gave a small shrug. "Although it feels like I just saw you yesterday, on some level, I *knew* it's been years even before I opened my eyes for the brief moment when Poznyak brought me out of the cryo-sleep."

"You did?"

"Yeah. It's impossible to quantify, but somehow I was aware of the passage of time. I'm sure it would make a great conversation topic with a therapist, but it sounds like, at the moment, the world is a little short on leather couches from where you can talk about abstract things that bother you to a nice, attentive doctor with a PhD."

"It may be true, but it doesn't mean you have nobody to talk to."

"Thanks." She glanced at the medical bay. "Do you know if I'm allowed to walk around yet? I'm anxious to see the place and everyone in it."

"Not today, I believe. You know how Steven is. He wants to run some diagnostics on you before he gives you a clean bill of health. As it is, we've been talking for longer than he gave me permission for. But he said if everything checks out, you should be able to walk around tomorrow."

"Okay." She sighed. "I've slept for many years, so I guess I can wait for one more day."

"Rest now." He stood up and leaned over for a kiss, but at the last moment she turned her head ever so slightly, giving him a cheek instead of her lips. He smiled, trying to hide his disappointment, and stepped back. "I will see you tomorrow."

7

The Bronx, New York

"I didn't realize this used to be a bus depot," Helen said as she watched the large building. Their minivan, an unremarkable gray Ford, was parked at the end of a quiet, tree-lined cul-de-sac. A small park with a baseball diamond separated the street from Victor Ye's warehouse. Over the past few weeks, with the help of JC, Helen had analyzed a huge amount of data, looking to locate where the head of the Red Dragon gang and Engel's right hand stored Daimyo cyborgs.

With the looming showdown, the Daimyo army was the wild card. The new company Victor was getting ready to launch, Ares Industries, was supposed to mass-produce the deadly machine. For now, nobody knew how many cyborgs had been built or were ready to be assembled. Finding the existing stock and destroying it could mean the difference between winning the war and losing it.

So far, the gangster proved to be a tough nut to crack, the location of most of the new-generation cyborgs still unknown. But the search wasn't unfruitful after all. They had uncovered a few previously unknown storage facilities, the place in the Bronx being their most promising lead. According to JC's calculations, there was a ninety-two percent chance the place was used to stockpile unfinished energy batteries for Daimyo units. It was a juicy target that, if hit successfully, could disrupt Victor's supply and delay mass production. When their forces had been spread thin and the primary stronghold threatened, the rebels couldn't afford anything more than a surgical strike. Max and Helen volunteered to run a reconnaissance mission to make that possible.

The building was a massive rectangle hidden behind the barbwire, its long side running along I-95. In the front, there was a checkpoint with a yellow-and-black boom gate and two machine-gun nests stationed on tripods behind the piles of sandbags. A large sentry, its long, spindly legs clanking over the concrete, walked in circles in front of the gaping main entrance to the warehouse. The short, stubby barrels of the energy weapons swung back and forth, covering most of the yard at all times.

From their position, Helen could only see two grim-looking Black Arrow mercenaries leaning against a pickup truck. But two Humvees in the front parking lot and a military truck in the back suggested there was a strong Black Arrow presence inside of the building.

"That was when we still had a semi-functional government that occasionally attempted to make the lives of ordinary folks tolerable. Those days are over," Schlager said. "Nobody even pretends anymore."

"Mass transport is a luxury nobody appreciates until it's gone," Helen said. "I can't tell you how many times I complained the subway was disgusting."

"That's right. At least, unlike the buses, it's still running."

She nodded as she continued to watch the building.

"Judging by the amount of the firepower Victor dedicated to protecting this place, I think JC was right about the batteries. You are ready for the drone?"

"Hang on." Even before they arrived at the Bronx, Helen tapped into the servers of the local utility company. Now, a window on her internal screen looked like a pulsating maze of bright colors—the fat red veins of power lines getting from the grid to the substation, the slimmer pink lines branching out into the building, and the thin bright-yellow lines of the internal power blueprint. "Okay, send her up."

There was a buzzing sound from the roof of the van, and then it was quiet again. Helen switched to the drone feed as the quadcopter gained altitude. When it reached a quarter mile, she scanned the air over the warehouse, checking for enemy drones, but the skies seemed to be clear.

"So far, so good," Schlager said. "Ready when you are."

She launched a mapping sequence, and the drone started the slow circle over the building as its sensors probed the structure below in different modes.

"Jesus," Schlager said. "Are those the batteries?"

"Looks that way." She looked at the rows of small, dark, rectangular shapes. The pile took most of the vast area on the first floor. "There must be thousands of them. If they make it to the production floor, we are done."

"Let's make sure they don't. Six exits on the first floor. I've counted twelve guards and two sentinels. We can do the underground level now. The layout matches the old blueprints you pulled from the archives. Doesn't seem like they've built anything new here."

Helen switched the drone's frequencies, and a new ghostly picture filled in the 3D image on her internal screen.

"Two elevators," Schlager said under his breath. "Two staircases. Two more sentinels, eight more guards. Lots of crap, but I don't see more batteries. Nothing out of the… Wait a second. Oh, shit."

"Yeah." She looked at eight motionless humanoid figures stationed next to the elevators, four at each door. Unlike the guards, who appeared as bright, glowing reddish outlines, or sentinels that were colored in solid blue, the outlines were faint purple, almost invisible. "Daimyo cyborgs. That's going to be a little tricky."

"That's not tricky," Schlager said. "This is outright impossible. Five sentinels and eight of those freak shows? I don't think Jason and

Martin can take them. Not without too much risk. I wish we had more Thor missiles. This would have been a perfect target."

"It wouldn't be." Helen disagreed. "It's too close to the highway and other buildings. But it's irrelevant. We don't have another missile."

"Christ." Schlager struck the palm of his hand with a fist. "Can't catch a break, can we?"

She didn't answer, keeping the drone circling around the facility. There was a shadow of an idea somewhere in the deep corner of her mind, like a slippery eel in dark waters she tried to catch by its tail.

"You have the look," Schlager said.

"Sentinels."

"Yeah?"

"They have energy weapons. Maybe we could use them somehow." She trailed off, her mind racing. "It's a long shot, but a simultaneous blast of all the sentinels on those stacks could overwhelm their safety margins and potentially even create a chain reaction."

Schlager scratched the week-old stubble on his chin. "Okay. Say we took over the sentinels. How are we going to line up all five of them to blast at the batteries? Those Frankenstein monsters in the basement will go apeshit and cut them to pieces."

She thought about it for a moment. Daimyos would perceive the sentinels as a threat if they changed their behavior. And so would the mercenaries. The odds of all five machines making a simultaneous blast in that scenario would be next to zero, and she wasn't sure one or two would cut it.

"Okay," she said out loud. "We need to keep them convinced the sentinels are still on their side while lining up for a shot. How are your drone flying skills?"

"You want to use it as bait?"

"Yes. Sentinels communicate to each other, but only when they are in the immediate vicinity. I can tap into the one at the front gate through the drone. Once it's ours, you'll buzz the soldiers and then head straight to the warehouse. I'll pretend I'm chasing it with the sentinel as well, and when I'm inside, I'll be close enough to grab the other four and bring them to the first floor."

"What if they shoot it down?"

"Try to not let it happen." She grinned. "But I have an idea for that, too. If you make a beeline for the batteries and keep the drone flying over the pile, they might be reluctant to shoot you for the fear of damaging their precious batteries. Maybe even wait for the cyborgs to come up and try to cut you down without blasting the entire place. If you can maneuver for a few seconds without getting shot, I'll bring the sentinels from downstairs and zap this place to kingdom come."

"If this doesn't work out, Victor will bring an entire army here. We only have one shot at this."

"Don't we always?"

She handed the drone controls to Schlager and uploaded the audio file. It worked for the first time in Hong Kong when she used a sound wave to hack into a sentinel. Once the program took over, she could establish a link with the machine, allowing her direct control.

Since then, the sentinels had gotten multiple upgrades, but their core programming remained the same. Helen tried to use the back-door sparingly, as it remained one of the few reliable vulnerabilities of the sentries.

"I'm ready when you are."

"Go slow," she said. "You need to get close enough for the impulse to be picked up by its microphone, but not too close for the guards to hear the drone."

She watched the ground drift closer in a minimized window. The guards steadily grew until they morphed from tiny figures into full-sized people. The view shifted as Schlager maneuvered the drone to stay over the roof, trying to shield the sound of the rotors.

Helen pinged the sentinel once and waited for two seconds, the time it would take the program to override the machine's defenses. Her interface, save for the drone view, remained empty.

"Nothing," she said. "You've got to get closer."

"All right. I think I have an idea just crazy enough."

Before she could reply, the view shifted, and the sentinel filled the screen. There was a clanking sound as the drone landed on top of the metallic plate and then the screech of servo motors as the sentinel reared like a wild horse, trying to shake off the intruder. A second later, the shouting of the guards joined the mayhem.

"Gotcha," she breathed, as a relay window popped in her screen. She moved the sentinel this way and that, keeping it on its hind legs. While it strained Schlager's ability to keep the drone on top of the machine, it also kept the quadcopter hidden away from the Black Arrow mercenaries, whose rifles went up and down, looking to take a shot. "On my mark, go!"

She lowered the machine, and the drone darted into the dark entrance of the warehouse. Then, before the guards took aim, the sentinel galloped after it as if in pursuit, eliciting a round of curses and yelling as it blocked their shots again.

"Come on, suckers!" Schlager yelled as the quadcopter zipped over the stacks of flat battery packs. The drone soared up to the ceiling, weaving through the exposed beams as the shots hit the steel next to it and then zoomed back to the pile. "Give me your best shot."

"I got all of them," Helen shouted. The view transmitted from a drone flipped and swayed, making her dizzy. A few shiny figures appeared, dashing into the ground floor, curved swords at the ready. "And now."

There was a brilliant flash as all sentinels fired, followed by a bang. The view from the floor stabilized long enough for her to see a mighty arc of electricity jumping from one stack to another and getting thicker.

"Shut down your augs!" she yelled at Schlager, simultaneously powering off her own. A moment later, the ceiling of the warehouse buckled upward and then collapsed, a large blue bubble of shimmering energy expanding outward like a shock wave. It hit the van, rocking it, slow rivulets of electricity running over the vehicle's hood, and then disappeared.

Helen waited for a few more seconds and then powered up her augmentations. She let out a sigh of relief when a few icons appeared in her internal vision.

"That was something," Schlager said, pressing the Start button on the dashboard. "We better be going."

The vehicle remained dark.

"Looks like the EMP fried the van," she said. "I doubt anything survived inside of that building. But we better get going. There's a gas station a few blocks from here. We can catch a taxi there."

They got out of the car and started walking. As she glanced over her shoulder, there was a large column of smoke rising above the warehouse. The war was far from over, but at least for now Victor Ye's shiny new company had a serious supply issue.

8

Rigel Compound, Upstate New York

The wail of a siren jerked Helen Chen out of a drowsy slumber, and she sat up with a start in her chair, scrambling around in the dark for the alarm button to press and knocking things off the desk.

There was none. The piercing, bloodcurdling sound was coming from the PA speakers throughout the silo compound.

She flipped the switch of a table lamp and squinted against the harsh light at the chaos of papers, maps, and electronic gear strewn across her working surface. An empty aluminum mug was lying on its side near the edge of the desk, a thick line of dark-brown liquid gleaming where the rim of the cup met the table. She picked it up and put it upright, giving the dried coffee stain at the bottom a longing look—the silo had had no real beans in weeks, and this was the last cup of instant powder she salvaged from the bottom of a can that morning. The prospects of getting more in the foreseeable future weren't great.

The battle for Rigel was in its third day, and she slept less than two hours in the past seventy-two, alternating between logistics support for the troops within the silo and watching the movements on the battlefield from the ever-shrinking fleet of stealth drones. The uneasy truce between Engel's forces and Orion's stronghold came to a violent end when Black Arrow's Fourth Brigade, after a quick march from Buffalo, came bearing down on the compound, pounding Rigel's positions with artillery strikes and mortar rounds. Four howitzers stationed around the silo's perimeter were destroyed in the first few minutes of the barrage, and so were the two decommissioned Abrams tanks, but not before annihilating most of the attackers' heavy artillery. The hodgepodge of an air defense the silo's crew had rigged up in the early days of its existence was still holding up, protecting the silo from direct hits, but it would not last.

The bulk of the Fourth Brigade's infantry units, supported by a few groups of sentinels, attacked the defensive positions from the northwest, hoping to crush the resistance in one fell swoop. But the outnumbered and outgunned defenders stood their ground, digging deep into the trenches and keeping pressure on the enemy. Jason Hunt, defying calls to stay behind, with the help of Martin, destroyed most of the sentries, robbing the attacking force of their most significant advantage.

After the first two hours of a fierce battle, the advancing troops had stalled and fell back to regroup and reorganize. The next forty-eight hours saw them establish trenches of their own, building fortifications, and digging in for what seemed like a prolonged siege.

The mood in the silo turned dark. With no reinforcements in sight that would help them break through the blockade, the fate of the compound seemed all but sealed. Already struggling with food and supplies, within days they would face a stark choice—surrender or die.

"Helen," Hunt said in a secure video link during the last lull. A sheen of sweat and dust covered his face, making his eyes look too bright, almost manic. There was a fresh cut above his right eyebrow and a trickle of blood going down his temple, culminating in a dirty smudge on his cheek. "How long do you need to activate Project Thor?"

"Let's see," she said, swallowing hard. She opened the screen, tracking the positions of two Thor satellites. "We have at least two visible most of the time. Depending on when we want to fire, it'll take about three or four minutes to feed the coordinates and launch it. The feed itself is quick, but the system then needs to send a confirmation request and when it does, it takes some sweet time to process it. This is ancient tech. Not much I can do to speed it up. Once it's launched, though, it takes another twelve to fifteen minutes until impact."

"Can you upload the data in advance? To save us some time?"

"Yes," she said. "But I can't keep them trigger-ready for too long. Thirty minutes, tops. It draws too much electricity. It'll deplete the batteries. When the US government put them up there, the solar tech wasn't exactly efficient."

"Okay. And if you don't keep them on high alert, how long does it take to launch?"

"The launch sequence itself is about forty-five seconds long, so it's not too bad. But it's not instantaneous."

"Okay then." He seemed to have made a decision. "One more question. I know you and Max crunched the numbers after the first attack. What's the closest to the silo we can hit without compromising the structural integrity of the compound?"

She studied his face for a few seconds before answering.

"Helen?"

"A quarter of a mile," she said. "It'll shake us good, but not hard enough to break anything. In theory, of course. But Jason, anyone outside of the silo will be dead. We'll wipe out our guys, too."

"I understand that." He frowned as a mortar round landed not too far from his location, showering him with dirt. "Let's hope it doesn't come to that. I want you to feed the nearest position northwest of Rigel into all Thor satellites, since we don't know which one will be available. Don't keep them trigger-ready. I guess I can live with an extra forty-five seconds of prep if the time comes. Let me know when it's done. And if we need to adjust the coordinates?"

"That shouldn't take more than a few seconds, as long as it's within five square miles."

"Sounds good. Hunt out."

The link disconnected before she could say anything back, and she sighed in frustration. Things were getting tough but hitting Black Arrow's units in the immediate vicinity of Rigel would put their own troops at significant risk. That seemed extreme. And no theoretical calculations could guarantee the silo wouldn't get damaged with a hit that close. There could have been structural damage after they had been struck the first time, hidden somewhere in the massive bulk of the underground building that would bury them all alive if they got hit again.

Helen drummed her fingers on the table and then pulled up the Thor interface. After all, she decided, this was Jason. There was no way he was going to kill his own. She had to trust there must be some kind of plan. She fed the data into the satellites and, after confirming it'd been accepted, she put them back into standby mode. Then she returned her attention to the drone fleet again.

She had started with fourteen, but by now her air force had shrunk to six and she ordered them to fan out, trying to cover as much ground as possible. An intricate net of trenches, like a spiderweb with its center at the silo, appeared in her internal vision. An occasional bright splash of fire appeared in different parts of the perimeter as the defending forces snapped at the Black Arrow's positions in the distance, pinning them down. With a mixture of satisfaction and frustration, she noted the lack of signatures for Hunt or Martin, their active camouflage systems making them invisible to the drone's sensors. If she couldn't see them, she hoped Black Arrow scanners couldn't detect them either.

She spent the next few hours switching from one bird's feed to another, tracking Black Arrow movement and updating the men on the ground. There wasn't a lot of fighting going on. Rigel forces lacked the firepower to break through, and Black Arrow didn't want to waste resources on what they saw as a matter-of-time outcome.

Chen's eyes grew heavy, and she shook her head, trying to focus. It didn't work, and she punched the icon of an intercom.

"Yes?" Molly was one of Poznyak's engineers and one of the few people at the silo with full augmentation capable of commanding the drone fleet.

"I need to take fifteen," Chen said when she saw the freckled face. "I'm crashing."

"You need to take more than fifteen," the woman protested. "It won't help anyone if you're unable to function. There's not much going on right now. Some back-and-forth to make sure everybody stays in place. I can keep an eye on things for a couple of hours while you're catching some z's."

"But if anything—"

"Roger that," Molly said, interrupting her. "If anything comes up, I'll wake you right up."

"Okay."

Chen disconnected the link, glanced at the cot on the other side of the room, and instead reclined her chair. She had to be near her post. She thought the alarm went off before her eyes even closed, but a quick glance at the internal clock showed over forty minutes had elapsed since her call to Molly.

"What happened?" Her voice was raspy and quiet, barely above a whisper. She coughed, clearing her throat, and tried it again, louder this time. "Molly? What happened?"

"Sorry." The woman screwed up her face in concentration. "I didn't want to wake you up, but I had no choice."

"What's going on?" The link to the drones pulsated in her vision, establishing a connection, and then she saw it. A mechanized column almost a mile long. They had their own drones buzzing overhead the moving armor. It could have worked on roads, but the line of vehicles had to weave through the forest and the coverage was spotty in a few places. Not enough to see from the silo, but quite obvious from the drone hanging almost directly overhead.

"It was too quiet for a few minutes, and I sent one drone farther than normal, to make sure nothing weird was happening, and that's when I saw it."

Helen hit another icon. "Jason. We've got a big problem. We have heavy armor approaching. About seven miles out. If they get close enough, we are toast."

"Okay." There was no video feed this time, only a voice, which Helen found unnerving. There was a silence for a few seconds, and she briefly wondered if the connection was broken. "Hit them with Thor. I'll bring everybody inside. Make sure everything is ready to be bolted."

"Got it." She terminated both links and punched a slew of commands into the Thor interface, adjusting the coordinates just at the edge of the five-mile perimeter. At the current speed, the column would be dead center within the blast radius. After what felt like the longest wait in her life, the system confirmed the coordinates, and Helen reached out to the large red icon in the middle of her screen. Her finger hovered there for a second and then touched the cool glass surface. The red button blinked and disappeared, replaced by a count-down clock.

Helen stood up, staring in disbelief at the ticking seconds. It couldn't be true, of course, but on some level, she could *feel* the tungsten rod separate from the satellite and head toward the blue planet below. She shivered, breaking the spell, and punched the PA button.

"This is Helen Chen. Project Thor activated. Prepare for impact in twelve minutes. All personnel to secure equipment and personal belongings to minimize risk of injury. This is not a drill. I repeat, this is not a drill. Let's go, people. We've trained for this. You know what to do."

9

Rigel Compound, Upstate New York

Helen tuned out the screeching sound of the siren and went to work. First, she secured the Faraday cage shielding the AI, made sure there were no heavy or fragile objects that could get loose during a quake, and then went around the room, covering the computer equipment in protective composite webbing.

Nine minutes to impact, the PA system squawked, making her jump.

"Helen?" Her communication link chirped, Poznyak's voice coming through the cacophony of shouting and metallic clanging. "How close is it going to hit?"

"Five miles," she said, securing the last display. "Close enough."

"There are two things I'm worried about—the quant and the cold lab. Especially the cold lab. If some tanks rupture…" He trailed off without finishing the thought. "We are in a closed space."

"I'm coming to you," she said, heading through the cableway and coming out into the blast lock area between the two sets of three-ton steel doors. "I'll help."

46

"No, stay at the control center," Poznyak protested. "It's safer than here, and you need to help the guys above the ground."

Eight minutes to impact.

"I can multitask."

"No, Helen." His voice sounded warm, but firm. "Stay there. We have to be where we make the most difference."

She sighed and stopped in her tracks. He was right, of course. Some of the most competent people she knew were working for Steven. She'd only get in the way, and at the command center, she'd have the pulse of the entire compound at her fingertips.

She pinged Molly, who kept the drones over the incoming armored column. "How's it looking?"

Six minutes to impact.

"They know we know. They are heading full speed toward the compound. Hang on, I'll patch you through."

The link flashed in the corner of her vision and when she expanded it, she saw it—the tank column had broken up and now the lethal machines were roaring in the silo's direction in a battle formation. She counted fourteen tanks in the front, forming a wedge. There were five in a tight group at the front, two four-tank platoons on each flank, and one, which she presumed to be the commanding officer, in the middle of the formation. There was another eight coming up in a second wave, spread out in a semicircle, making the entire group of tanks look from the air like an upside-down smiley face of death.

What was worse, now that the attacking force made no effort to conceal its movements, she could see at least a dozen heavy sentinels coming on the heels of the battle tanks. Jason had been right; without the Thor missile, the silo was doomed. Martin and Jason could take out three or four tanks if they got lucky, but to fight against that many machines would be suicide. She opened another link.

"Jason, you need to get everybody inside now. You have an overwhelming force bearing down on you." There was no immediate response, and she double-checked the connection to make sure it was open. "Jason, can you hear me?"

Three minutes to impact.

There was a loud booming sound and then a rapid drumbeat of automatic fire.

"Jason?"

"I got you, Helen." His voice was strained. "Busy here. They are pushing from all directions. Martin and I have to stay up for another minute or two, give our guys some cover."

"You've got less than three minutes. And it takes a few seconds to close the hatch."

"I know. Hunt out."

"Helen?" Molly's voice cut through the static. "Should I bring back the birds now?"

"Yes." She switched to the drone view again just in time to see them pull back to the silo. The heavy armor disappeared from the line of sight as the drones rushed back to the compound. She saw a long line of explosions and then a silver streak of Martin's bulk as the cyborg cut across the battlefield. "Just leave me one above the entrance. I'll take control of that one."

"Roger."

She watched a small line of people filing into the silo as Martin and Jason remained dangerously far from the entrance. They both ditched stealth now, firing everything at once. From this angle, it looked like two sources of commercial fireworks were madly zigzagging across the battlefield.

Thirty seconds.

"Now," she shouted. There was a mighty hydraulic hiss as the massive silo door slid on the rails. She watched Martin streak across the field like blue lightning and disappear in the silo with a thud. A moment later, Jason followed. Helen sent the drone diving into the vanishing opening, the sensors on the machine going blind for a moment.

The ground shifted under her. One second, she was standing in the middle of a solid, multi-ton bunker deep underground, and the next, she was balancing on top of a mythic monster the size of a planet as it shivered and stretched in its lair. There were crashing sounds coming from somewhere deep in the cableway, followed by shouts and curses. Then everything stopped, and she was standing on firm ground again.

"Attention all personnel," she said, opening up the silo-wide channel. "Please take some time to look around, before returning to your normal activities. Make sure all heavy equipment is secure and there's no broken glass, exposed wire, or anything else that can pose danger. If anyone is injured, please report to the infirmary immediately. If you are injured and unable to move, please stay where you are and radio for help. Designated patrols will make rounds to make sure everyone is accounted for."

She closed the link and headed through the blast lock area and into the access portal. There she climbed a few flights of stairs, nodding to a few familiar faces going in the opposite direction. There was a fair amount of dust in the air and on people's skin, but to her great relief she saw no obvious injuries. The silo had held.

"Helen?" Steven's voice cut in. "All looks good. The tanks held. I thought you'd want to know."

"That's good news. Thanks."

When she reached the access portal entrance, the main door was already opened and there was no sign of Martin or Jason. She poked her head out and, not seeing any immediate danger, climbed out. Most of the sparse vegetation around the silo was smoldering, and some bushes were on fire. The tree line north of the compound was gone, a few burning branches sticking out of the flat ground like rotten teeth in a diseased mouth. Martin and Jason stood a hundred yards away from the entrance, observing the damage. She headed toward them, carefully picking her path around debris. A few drones buzzed above her head, heading toward the impact site.

"You okay?" she asked as she caught up with the pair.

"Yeah." Jason threw her a quick glance and returned his attention to the field. His face was covered in soot. Blood mixed with dirt caked on his cheek. If not for his augs, Helen thought, she could take a black-and-white picture of him, and he would look just like any soldier from WW1 or WW2. Dirty, exhausted. Haunted. "What's the damage?"

"Still assessing, but I think we should be fine. Steven was worried about the cold tanks, but they held. There might be some mild injuries, but I don't think anybody got hurt."

"Good. How's that looking?" He nodded in the direction where the drones had gone a few seconds before.

Helen pulled up the feed, just in time for the small fleet to get close enough to observe the impact. A missile hit in front of the advancing column. The first wave of tanks had been vaporized, now part of the glowing crater about one thousand feet in diameter. The second wave that had traveled some distance behind the first was thrown about as if made of a carton. A few mangled sentinels were catapulted as far as a mile away from the blast. The tanks, at least those that could be recognized, had their turrets torn off. A wave of nausea came over her. She'd seen more than a fair share of disturbing things over the past few years. But this… She swallowed hard. This was her doing. She pressed the button. She took a shaky breath, looking at the carnage.

"Don't do that."

"Do what?" She snapped back to reality.

"What you're doing right now." Jason stared at her. His jaw was set, but his eyes were soft, as if he knew what he was about to say was harsh but didn't want to hurt her. "This is a war. We all make decisions we'd rather not, regardless of who ends up pushing the button. What's important is we remember why we do what we do."

She nodded. "The column has been destroyed. The silo should be safe for now."

"That's good news," he said, turning back to the fields in front of them again. "We could use some respite."

"Jason," she said. Something in her voice must have caught his attention as he turned to her, his eyes searching hers.

"What?"

"I think I have something," she said. She switched again to the drone feed. The little machine was hovering a few hundred feet above the glowing crater. She could have sworn she felt the heat coming off the molten ground. "I have an idea that might be just crazy enough to work."

10

Upstate New York

*L*eonard Freeman's Humvee got off State Park Road and pulled up to the parking lot next to Black River Pond. The vehicle crossed the area and then rolled across the green field, getting deep into the trees until it was no longer visible from the road or the air. The sun was still high enough to keep the road and the parking lot well lit, but here, under the cover of the trees, it was fast getting dark.

Freeman stepped out of the vehicle and stretched, his back and his neck cracking. It rained earlier that day, and the air was hot and muggy. The parking lot was one of the many entry points to a net of his camps throughout Cherry Plain State Park. Hidden away in a dense forest, next to a source of fresh water, it was just ten miles as the crow flies from Albany, his hometown. A perfect place to hide a few hundred armed-to-the-teeth men.

At the onset of the war, Freeman was quick to realize that without a cohesive force, fighting large and well-equipped Black Arrow units was bad business. Sure, he'd heard all about the resistance of those loyal to Darius Price, and his benefactor Jason Hunt, put up in some areas of the East Coast. About the smart move Hunt made to convert an abandoned silo into a base. About Project Thor, that Hunt's team wrestled from Engel's control and gave the rebel a deterrent. But he'd also heard about the Chicago massacre, where Black Arrow mercenaries annihilated small groups of ragtag rebels that had been harassing them in the suburbs, and then took a week meting out punishment to the locals who had supported them.

Freeman was under no illusion of what Engel's government represented or the man himself. Despite a steady stream of the synchronized garbage all major news channels were spewing around the clock, he had enough clarity from various former and current intelligence sources to see the accurate picture. More importantly, he wasn't blind. Engel was a tyrant and a despot, and his complete control of the media only made it more obvious, not less. That much was clear. What wasn't clear, however, and that presented the biggest problem to someone of Freeman's pedigree, was whether the current occupant of the White House had a legitimate claim to it.

He saw the bits of information claiming Engel didn't belong from the underground channels that threw their support behind Jason Hunt's forces. Their voices weren't loud and, to Freeman's dismay, too often bordered on paranoia, with a healthy mix of conspiracy theories. But there were some that seemed more legitimate than others. One broadcast in particular, narrated by the once-famed journalist Brian Sorkin, was especially compelling. The evidence he described in his transmissions seemed legitimate. Freeman would love to talk to Sorkin, but the man was nowhere to be found, no matter how much he looked for him.

And as he couldn't verify the claims, it was rather irrelevant what his personal opinions were on the matter. Freeman was of a firm belief he couldn't be in the business of ousting presidents just because he didn't like them. Even if they happened to be despots. There were, he was convinced, the guardrails of democracy that would eventually straighten the path of the country and bring it back to normality. No matter how unfit the current person sitting behind the Resolute desk was.

It didn't mean he didn't waver now and then. Hunt had been relentless in trying to persuade him for a meeting and Freeman finally caved in, only to change his mind at the last moment. To be fair, he hadn't intended to stand him up, but an urgent situation developed, and Freeman chose to be with his men, rather than travel to meet a person who may or may not be trying to steer the country to the brink of collapse.

But just because he couldn't decide whether to join the rebellion didn't mean that he was going to roll over and let the mercenaries of Black Arrow have their way. Over the course of his military career, Freeman had multiple run-ins with mercs of all shapes and colors all over the world. In his opinion, they were as reliable and honorable as a drunk scorpion inside of a shoe. He could wait for the system to purge itself of Engel and his ilk. For now, he was content smacking Black Arrow trolls away from the places he cared for.

"Trent," he called out to the driver. "I thought you said they were supposed to meet us here?"

"That was the plan." The driver, a small, skinny man with a hooked nose and a clean-shaven face, jumped out of the vehicle and slung an M16 over his shoulder. "You want me to ping Rob?"

"Nah." Freeman pulled out his rifle from the passenger seat and grabbed the backpack off the floor. "We can walk by ourselves. No big deal. But let's keep our eyes peeled, just in case."

"Roger," the man answered, and wiped his forehead with the back of his hand. "Goddammit, it's hot. Do you think—"

"Quiet." Freeman brought the rifle to his shoulder and dropped into a combat crouch. He saw Trent mirror his moves. He wasn't sure what it was, but there was something wrong with the trees a few yards to the east. Freeman signaled Trent to move back, keeping the Humvee between them and whatever was lurking in the shadows.

He watched, straining his eyes, and then there it was, almost impossible to see if not for a slow movement: a large, ghostly figure stepped out from behind a trunk of a mighty oak.

"Don't shoot," the figure said before he pulled the trigger. The voice was strange, almost mechanical. "Jason Hunt sent me."

"Oh, yeah?" Freeman pulled Trent deeper behind the vehicle. "What does he want?"

There was a long pause, and then he heard a different voice coming out of the same silhouette. "Leonard. This is Jason. I'm sorry we have to talk like this, but you weren't answering my calls, and I had no other way to warn you. You are about to walk into an ambush. Your patrol has been terminated, and there's a kill team of eight men waiting for you about two clicks away."

"Who's this?" Freeman pointed at the ghostly figure with the nose of his M16.

"This is Martin," came the reply. As if to confirm, the silhouette raised his right hand into the air. The camouflage seemed to have gone down a notch, making it easier to make out the massive outline. "He's a cyborg and a friend. He is your best bet for getting to your camp alive."

"I can take care of myself. And if he could take care of the hitmen, as you claim, why didn't he?"

"This is your territory, Leonard. I didn't know what your preferred course of action would be. Maybe you wanted to avoid confrontation and not to draw any attention to the location."

"Thank you for the heads-up," he said, standing up. "But like I said, we can take care of ourselves. Tell your buddy to go home. He's making me nervous, and these days I shoot at things that make me nervous."

"You won't stand a chance against them. You are outnumbered and outgunned. At least let him accompany you."

Freeman chewed on his lip, considering it. "Fine. He can follow us. But if he gets in the way, I'll shoot him myself."

He watched Martin peel away from the tree, and, instead of waiting for him, setting course due east. Freeman grunted in annoyance. The cyborg didn't seem to need the directions of the camp.

"Come on," he said to Trent. "Might as well."

"You trust that thing? He looks like the predator from that old flick. Gives me the creeps."

"I don't know." He spat on the ground. "Maybe. If he wanted to ambush us, he would have already. Whatever his game is, I don't think he wants to hurt us."

They started after the cyborg, heading deeper into the forest. As they walked, the sky grew darker and light drizzle covered their faces with a wet blanket.

They crossed a small brook when Martin stopped as if running into a wall, raising a bunched fist. A moment later, the cyborg's stealth mode returned, making it almost impossible to see. Freeman glanced at the faint display of the GPS watch—they were about two kilometers from the parking lot.

"What the hell is he doing?" he heard Trent whisper. "I don't see—"

The massive bulk of the cyborg, invisible in the dark, catapulted through the forest, crushing a small tree in his path. A second later, a bright explosion blossomed some distance ahead, followed by an angry rattle of automatic fire.

Freeman and Trent ran toward the sounds, the barrels of their rifles clearing the path. There was another explosion and a bloodcurdling scream, and then the forest was quiet.

They rushed through the dark, Freeman tripping on some undergrowth and almost smashing into a branch. When they got to the opening, it was already over. Two fresh craters were still smoldering, giving way to an eerie orange glow. Scattered across the field, he counted seven bodies. No, he corrected himself. There were eight, the last one torn into pieces, the hand with two remaining fingers being the largest. The cyborg stood in the middle of the largest crater, his camouflage off, the lights of the fire dancing on the polished metal of his helmet. A large stub-nosed weapon retreated inside of his arm, the plates sliding back over it.

Freeman saw Trent double over and vomit over his own shoes.

"You good?"

The man nodded and wiped his lips with the back of his hand. "I'll live."

"That was the kill team?" he asked the cyborg.

"Yes."

"Anyone else waiting for us on the way to the camp?"

"No."

The cyborg turned around and headed back, retracing his steps. He walked by the two men and disappeared into the night without looking back.

"He's real chatty, this one," Trent said, looking after Martin. "Good thing you didn't shoot him in the parking lot."

"Yeah," Freeman said, slinging his rifle over his shoulder again. "Ya think?"

"You know what I think?" Trent said, picking up pace.

"What?"

"Two things. One: my mouth tastes like puke. Awful stuff."

"And two?"

"Soon we are going to be obsolete. My dad passed away in 1992. What a time to go. We defeated the commies. Economy was rocking. The man checked out at the top. It all went downhill from there."

Freeman said nothing and kept walking, but there was a nagging thought in the back of his head he could no longer ignore. He needed to meet Jason Hunt.

Rigel Compound, Upstate New York

"How are you feeling?" Hunt asked as he watched Poznyak dote over Rachel and triple-check his monitors.

"I'm fine. A little nervous, that's all."

Rachel was sitting in a chair in front of a makeshift desk covered with electronics. She wore a pair of gray pajama pants, and what looked like a chair cloth from a barbershop covered her from the neck down to her waist. A thick cable of multicolored wires connected to a few devices on the desk ran up her leg and disappeared under the fabric. Another cable, slimmer, ran to the back of her head. There was also a mobile medical monitoring station set up next to her chair, keeping track of her vitals. A woman in nurse's scrubs watched the screens.

"There's nothing to be nervous about." Poznyak grabbed a stool and positioned himself on the other side of the desk in front of a monitor. "You will experience some discomfort when your cranial implant is activated, but it's mild. The most disorienting thing that happens is temporary blindness. It's normal, as it will take your brain a few moments to figure out how to treat competing visuals. Initially, it'll ignore them both, but eventually it should adapt, and you'll see the interface over your normal input."

"Eventually? Should?" Rachel gave a nervous chuckle. "If it wasn't you, Steven, I'd be worried."

"Poor choice of words." He laughed. "It won't last more than a few seconds. A minute, tops."

"It took me about forty-five," Jason chimed in. "Felt discombobulated during that time, but it went away the moment my vision came back. And your implant is orders of magnitude more powerful than mine was, so it'll take even less."

"Okay," Steven said, glancing at the medical station's monitor. "Are you ready? Take a few breaths. Relax. Your heart rate is a little elevated. We don't want you to be hyperventilating."

"I'm good." Rachel took a deep breath and puffed her cheeks as she exhaled it through her mouth. "Let's do it."

Jason had to remind himself to unclench his fists as he watched Poznyak type away a few commands on the terminal. He could use a few slow breaths himself, it seemed. Seeing Rachel in the flesh, hear her talk, move, brought a tsunami-sized wave of emotions he didn't think he had anymore. Part of the reason for it was how much he *had* forgotten. The mannerisms, the way she tilted her head when she listened to something interesting. The way her nose wrinkled when she smiled. How she rubbed her chin with a tip of her index finger when trying to remember something important.

Engel, the war, strategic and tactical decisions that had to be made, all but faded into the background every time he saw her. One moment, he was focused and functioning and organized, and the next, he would stand there, his legs unsteady, like a farmer who went into the barn looking for his tractor, only to find a UFO parked there.

"And here we go. Enjoy the ride," Poznyak said, and punched a key.

Rachel's eyes rolled back in their sockets and her body arched as if she was being electrocuted. Jason stared at her in disbelief, paralyzed.

A few shivers ran down Rachel's body and then, just as suddenly as it began, the tension was gone from her limbs and she collapsed into a chair, a thin line of drool running down her chin. Jason heard a loud beep coming out of the medical bay and when he looked up, he saw with mounting horror a straight line instead of a steady zigzag of a heartbeat.

"What the fuck is happening?"

"I don't know." Poznyak jumped out of his seat and rushed to Rachel's side. "Kelly, get the defibrillator. Jason, take off the cloth. Now!"

Like in a nightmare, Jason took a few steps toward the chair and ripped the cloth covering his wife off her chest, staring at the pink separated flesh where the cables went into her breastplate. "Shouldn't we try CPR first?"

"Move," Poznyak commanded. He peeled off sticky pads and attached them to Rachel's skin, one next to her right clavicle and another under her left breast. "You'll crush her implants if you do. They aren't fully integrated yet. Clear!"

Jason stepped back and tensed as the high-pitched whirr of a charging machine filled the room. Then there was a clapping sound and Rachel's body arched again, only to collapse back to the chair a moment later.

"Again."

There was the awful whir again, and then another clap. A line spiked on the medical bay monitor and then settled into a zigzag pattern.

"Is she—" Jason stuttered, unable to finish the sentence.

"She's fine now." Poznyak put away the defibrillator and pulled the cloth over Rachel's chest. "She should wake up soon."

"Rach?" He reached out and touched her forehead. "Can you hear me?"

Her eyes fluttered and a slight tremor ran down her body, making him tense again, but then it was gone, and her features softened. Finally, her eyes opened and looked back and forth between him and Steven, a blank expression on her face.

"Honey?"

"What time is it?" she asked, her voice flat.

"It's…" He blinked in confusion and glanced at the corner of his internal interface to read the clock. "Almost four in the afternoon."

"Not too bad," she said, a healthy glow returning to her cheeks. Her voice seemed to have regained strength. "It sounds like I was out, wasn't I?"

"For a minute." He stifled a shudder. "You gave us a hell of a scare. I've never seen anything like that happen before."

"Yeah," Poznyak said as he cycled through a few windows on the screen. "Usually, it's an uneventful procedure. I'm not sure what might have happened. Are you seeing the interface yet?"

"I do." She sat up straight in the chair, her eyes looking inward.

"Imagine yourself reaching for controls," Steven said, "just like you would if they were real, not virtual. It will be a bit—"

A call line appeared in Jason's vision and with surprise, he saw Rachel's ID on it. Another moment later, she conferenced in Steven.

"It seems you're able to find your way around the interface," Poznyak said. "You are a quick student."

"I find it very intuitive," she said. "I'm going to—"

"Hold your horses," Steven said, interrupting her. "I'm glad you find it so amusing, but I'm afraid we are going to sedate you and run some diagnostics."

"Why?" She cocked her head. "I'm feeling just fine."

"That's great." Poznyak stood up. "But you're not exactly a regular patient. And nobody ever flatlined on such a simple procedure before, so I'd like to be thorough, that's all. It won't take long. Just an hour-long nap."

"Fine," she said, her lips curling into a slight frown.

"I'll see you when you wake up." Jason leaned over her and planted a soft kiss on her forehead.

"Kelly, would you please prep her for scans? I'll come back in fifteen minutes to run the tests but let me know when she's asleep." Poznyak turned to Rachel. "I know I've said it a thousand times by now, but I don't think you have anything to worry about. We just have to make sure there's no hidden damage anywhere that needs to be repaired."

"I know." Rachel gave him a smile. "And I don't want to appear ungrateful. It's just it's been so long. I'd like to start living."

"You will." Poznyak gave her a smile back and tapped Jason's arm. "Come on, big fella, let the lady sleep."

They walked out of the room and headed through the cableway.

"What do you think might have caused it?" Jason asked when they were out of earshot. He ran his arm on the ribs of the hallway as they walked, a methodical clanging sound that bounced in the tight space.

"I'm not sure. That's why I want to run some scans. But if I had to make a wild guess, I'd say it probably has something to do with her being in a cryo-coma for many years. Her brain is not used to processing large dumps of information, so it short-circuited when we overloaded it. I always hated it when people say the brain is like a muscle, as the two have nothing in common. However," he paused for a moment and looked up at Jason, "there's some logic to that. It lay dormant for many years and now it's being pumped chock-full of information and it glitched."

"So you don't think her scans will reveal anything, do you?"

"No." The scientist resumed walking. "At least nothing obvious. But we have to be prepared for some things we might not be able to explain or fix in the months and years ahead. Nobody's ever done anything like this, Jason. Ever."

"You don't think it could have been the cranial implant?"

"Anything is possible, but I doubt it. Its CPU is state of the art, its memory bank is enormous, and Helen assured me its RAM is big enough to process all of our implants at the silo without breaking a sweat."

They stepped out into the launch duct, serving as one of Poznyak's labs. It was a tight space crowded with desks and machinery. A few techs in white lab coats—Poznyak ran a tight ship, even at the silo— seemed hard at work and paid no attention to the arrival of the two.

"Where are you off to?"

"I have to go outside." Jason vaguely pointed toward the top of the silo. "Have to inspect the positions. The blast destroyed a lot of the defensive lines. We have to rebuild them while we have the time."

"I see."

"Keep me posted, will you?"

"Of course." Poznyak patted him on the shoulder and disappeared down the stairwell, heading into the belly of the silo.

As he watched the scientist go, Jason felt a hollow pang in his gut. Rachel might have been awake, but nobody was out of the woods yet.

Rigel Compound, Upstate New York

$\mathcal{L}$eonard Freeman climbed down the ladder and jumped over the last two steps, landing squarely in the middle of the access portal of the silo. Two men wearing military fatigues carrying Mossberg shotguns stepped behind him, keeping a respectful distance.

"If the mountain doesn't come to Muhammad," he said, offering his outstretched hand.

"The mountain did." Jason chuckled, shaking the man's hand. "But by the time it got there, Muhammad had already bailed."

Freeman laughed, showing two rows of snow-white, slightly crooked teeth. An easy, charming laugh of a man with confidence. Someone comfortable being in charge. "I wanted to thank you again in person for sending Martin to support us. We would have been in trouble after the ambush, if not for him."

"If you took my calls, I wouldn't have had to send him at all."

"All true." Freeman threw his hands up, as if apologizing. He was a big man, over six feet tall, and broad shouldered. He wore a medium-length, well-trimmed beard that gave his dark face a severe appearance. In his leather jacket over a black tee, tall black boots, and rough jeans with the belt dipping down to accommodate a middle-aged belly, he could be mistaken for a biker. But he moved with a grace of a cat, and his dark, almost black eyes sparkled with wit and intelligence.

"Wow," he said, looking around. "A nuclear silo. I've seen a lot of military installations during my day. Never been inside one of these. It must be rough, being crammed in here full-time, eh? I much prefer open spaces."

"It has its moments," Jason said as he led the man toward the blast lock area.

"You can stay here, boys," Freeman said over his shoulder to the bodyguards. "I'm pretty sure our hosts don't mean us any harm. How are you keeping your folks from going crazy in here?"

"We had some ideas on how to make this place more hospitable," Jason said as they went through the two sets of steel doors. "Somebody was suggesting putting computer screens on the walls like fake windows. Run some landscape simulations on them to help with circadian rhythm and general claustrophobia."

"That sounds like a good idea." Freeman ran his hand over the thick door. "Help the morale."

"We never got around to it. Too busy fighting, starving, and surviving. Comfort slipped a few notches down the list."

"I'm familiar with the concept. It was quite a show of force, by the way."

"What? The missile?"

"Yeah. I saw the videos. You fried those sentinels."

"Modi did its job. We didn't have a choice. It was that or get overrun."

"Modi?" Freeman gave Hunt a puzzled look.

"A satellite," Jason explained. "Program Thor. It made sense to name the satellites as Thor's children. Modi, Magni, and Thrudr."

"I see."

They went through a short part of the cableway and into the

control center, taking a ladder to the top level. Jason watched Freeman scan the equipment with curiosity.

"Why the Faraday cage?"

"Keeps sensitive info away from our enemies," he lied, giving the man a neutral smile. There was no reason to share the true purpose of the device. Even within the silo, the information was guarded. Those who had to interact with JC, people like technicians and nurses, knew it as a helper program. Just a more sophisticated version of a home assistant that turned lights on and off, locked doors, and watched the cameras for intruders.

"It's a good idea." Freeman nodded. "I'm sure you're under a constant barrage of cyberattacks."

"You have no idea. Let me introduce you." He gestured to the table in the middle of the room. "This is Max Schlager, my advisor. Steven Poznyak, our chief scientist, and Helen Chen, our computer specialist. They are my most trusted advisors, and you can speak freely in their presence."

Freeman went around the table, shaking hands and exchanging a few words, and then pulled out a chair and sat down. Hunt took a chair on the opposite side of the table and looked around, taking in his friends' faces.

"Why me?" Freeman finally asked. "You've been enjoying support from a lot of different groups. And for now, my boys and I stayed away from supporting anyone. We just want our families to be left alone. It seems to me you'd be better off recruiting people who are already sympathetic to your cause."

Jason stayed quiet for some time, thinking it over. He had been playing over a conversation with Freeman in his head a hundred times. Thinking of the best arguments. Of possible rebuttals. Good stories he could tell from the past few years that would help convince the man. But now, sitting across from the retired colonel, all of them felt like gimmicks. Salesman pitches. And he was sure none of them was going to work. What could work was to be direct. To tell the truth.

"You aren't like most people, Leonard, and you know it," he said.

"You were one of the highest-ranking officers in the famed 82nd Division. You might be retired, but you still have a lot of pull. We need you more than you need us. If Engel wins, you might get in trouble for causing issues with his mercs, but I doubt it will be more than a slap on the wrist. And there's a reason he hasn't tried to crush you. It's because he's hoping you'll come to your senses and support him. But you know what?"

"What?"

"You haven't. And I don't think you will. And I doubt it's just because you are pissed off about the disbandment of the army. I believe you have been questioning the legitimacy of Engel's presidency, but just didn't have the information. That's why I was hoping to meet you in person and lay down everything we've collected over the years. Every piece of information. Why I took the risk of traveling to the mountain. Because if you knew what we know, you wouldn't hesitate. Because you are a patriot. That's why you are here. You *need* to know for sure."

"Look, I'm sorry we stood you up. But you have to understand something." Freeman leaned forward, his thick ebony finger poking at the table in front of him. "It's not something you can learn from the books or the internet. The 82nd Division is like a cult when it comes to membership. Don't laugh."

"I wasn't going to."

"I'm serious. If you have the honor and distinction to serve in the 82nd, you will never forget it. And you will love it. As dangerous and as crazy as those years of service were, they were some of the best years in my life. I mean," he made a circle with his hand, "we voluntarily jumped out of perfectly good airplanes. Who does that? But guess what? I've met many disgruntled army guys, but I've never met a disgruntled eighty-deuce trooper. We are the guards of honor. I've been to multiple major units in the army and deployed with rangers and SOCOM guys, and I can say with the highest confidence level that the 82nd Airborne is by far the most disciplined fighting force in the world."

Jason studied the man's face. His words carried some bravado, sure, but there was a deep level of sincerity. He knew how to talk, but he also believed in what he said. "That's why I wanted to meet you. I've done quite a bit of research. Multiple commendations. A Bronze Star. A Purple Heart. You bled for this country."

"There are a lot of idiots with a Purple Heart." Freeman smiled and shifted back in his chair. "It's called the enemy marksmanship badge for a reason. Some folks say it's the easiest medal to get if you are standing still. You take risks when you serve and sometimes those risks catch up to you. Do you know how many people I served with believed something bad was going to happen to them? Zero. When you are young and full of adrenaline, things look different. You think you are special, not just that you are better than most, but better in a cosmic, transcendent way. You think of yourself as a god of war. We've always acted as if the laws of physics or statistics didn't apply to us. But they do. Sometimes all it takes is to be in a wrong vehicle on the wrong side of the road at the wrong time.

"Look, Hunt. These are some crazy times we live in, and real soldiers don't look at things like most civilians do. We take an oath. You hear many people talk about being on the right side of history and all that crap. Doing the right thing. A soldier doesn't always like his superiors. But if he believes in his gut, he follows legal orders that come from people legitimately occupying their places of power. He'll do it whether he likes it or not. He won't follow you just because he thinks you're a good guy or because you are on the right side of history. He'll follow you because this is what he signed up to do."

Freeman paused, the fingers of his left hand rubbing over the calluses of his right palm, his eyes not leaving Jason's.

"What does your gut tell you?"

"I like you, Hunt." The man chuckled. "I've been following you for many years. You've created some awesome tech that benefited many people, including vets. And I think you're on the right side of history, but until last week I wasn't one hundred percent sure about the legitimacy. Civil war is a murky business. It's easy to claim things, even if the cause is just."

"What gives?"

"Price set me up for a meeting with a friend of yours. Sorkin. Half the time the old bastard sounds like a conspiracy quack, but everything he said checked out. The ballots, the storage facility you guys blew up. The convoy ambush. Most of it had been scrubbed cleaned from pretty much everywhere, but I still know a lot of good people. And we know how to look. And that's why I'm here. Don't get me wrong—I will look at every piece of evidence you have. I want to cross my t's and all that jazz. But I have already decided."

"You are convinced Engel is an illegitimate president?"

"I am." The man stood up and stretched his hand out. "I can't vouch for every single soldier, but I can promise you the vast majority of the former 82nd will support you. And God willing, after this is all over, it won't be a former anymore. There's no United States without its armed forces. Engel has got to go, and the Black Arrow shit stain needs to go with him."

13

Rigel Compound, Upstate New York

"I guess my brain is not falling apart?"

"It doesn't appear so," Jason said and smiled as he looked at her. "Steven assured me it won't happen for a while. At least for a day or two. After that, all bets are off."

Rachel laughed. A sound he hadn't heard in a long time.

They sat on hard black plastic stools. He brought them from the top level of Silo 2 and put them at the entrance to the silo, their backs leaning against the massive steel lid. It was pitch-black, the only source of light the stars blinking in and out of the thick cloud cover. The air was hot and stuffy, but there was a slight breeze that rolled in from the west in gentle, cool waves. After the close quarters of the silo where every inch was permeated by the smells of steel, diesel, and sweat, it tasted fresh and sweet.

"Did he tell you anything specific?"

After the incident during the interface installation, Poznyak ran a multitude of tests, and continued poking and prodding to ensure

Rachel's life wasn't in any immediate danger until she revolted. As none of the scans revealed any life-threatening damage, Poznyak released her with the promise she would allow him to re-run the tests after a week.

"Apart from some pure hypothetical ideas, I don't know what could have caused it," he told Hunt in private, after they left Rachel to change. "Her MRI is as clean as a whistle; her X-rays look fine. All her implants' readings are well within the margins. She is drawing power for the cranial chip at a slightly higher rate than she should be, but not high enough to suggest something is wrong with it. For now, my best guess is what I told you right after she had the episode."

"Brain elasticity?"

"Exactly." Poznyak shrugged. "Look, everything seems to be as good as we could have hoped for. In fact, it went so well, sometimes I want to pinch myself. Now we just have to watch her."

"Do you think she is in danger of having another episode? We're not always standing next to her with medical equipment. Ready to fix her."

Steven stayed silent for a few moments, looking at his shoes. When he finally met Hunt's gaze, his usually soft eyes looked hard. "We live in dangerous times. You know that better than anyone else. All we can do is try our best, and I will certainly do my part. The rest, depending on what your beliefs are, is in God's hands, fate, or random chance. Take your pick."

"I see."

"There's something else," Poznyak said. "God knows I'm not a psychiatrist, but I strongly believe that part of any successful physical recovery is your emotional state. Besides our medical attention, Rachel will need us as her friends. You, as her husband and partner. And I don't mean doting over her like she's a fragile flower on a deathbed. She needs support, and she needs to be treated like the person who she is. Smart, driven, ambitious. Bring her in. Share things with her. Ask her advice. Those are the best things you can do for her right now. Help her feel that she's alive and that her life is meaningful."

"Jason?" Rachel said, bringing him back to reality. "Did he say anything specific?"

"Not really. Your brain might need some time to adapt, that's all. Like a muscle."

"Time," she said, and gave him a smile. "I have plenty of that."

A wind picked up, bringing heavier clouds in and extinguishing the last stars. The sky flashed near the horizon and, a few seconds later, a heavy rolling thunder rumbled over, disappearing into the woods behind them like a distant roar of a mighty beast. A gust of wind brought a sharp scent of ozone.

"We should head inside," Jason said, standing up and offering her a hand. "It looks like it's going to pour any minute."

"You think it will?" She didn't move, her eyes locked on the ominous, roiling clouds above them. "I want to stay here."

"Um, okay." He sat down again and looked up at the dark skies, suppressing the urge to switch to augmented vision. He wanted to see what she saw. "I guess we should be okay for a few more minutes."

"No." She reached out and took his hand into hers without shifting her gaze. Her fingers trembled. "I want to stay in the rain."

"You are shaking." He squeezed her hand. Her skin was damp. "Are you sure? I don't want you to catch a cold. Your immune system isn't as strong as it should be yet. You're still recovering. Steven is going to murder me if I let you get sick."

"I'll be fine. It would be nice to feel a few raindrops on my skin. I know it sounds weird, but I've been asleep for a long time. A lot of times, none of this feels real to me. The years that have passed. The people you loved I didn't get to meet. Sometimes I want to make sure I'm not imagining those things. That it is not my mind playing tricks on me."

He said nothing and watched her face. What was it like to fall asleep with an incurable disease, thinking you're most likely not going to ever wake up? And then to actually wake up in a strange future you couldn't have imagined?

The future is never what we expect it to be, he thought. Had somebody asked him while they still lived down in Fort Lauderdale what would it look like, what would he say?

If he were honest with himself, he'd probably describe the time not very different from his own. He remembered reading science fiction growing up. Imagining that by the time he would become an adult, humans would spread throughout the solar system. Build marvelous machines. Invent mind-bending technology.

Almost none of that happened. Why would the next thirty or forty years be any different? It'd bring some changes, sure. More powerful computers. An overall better tech. A faster commute. A slightly better or, most likely, worse standard of living for the masses. The rich getting ever richer and the poor getting ever poorer. In his wildest dreams, he wouldn't imagine himself as a half-cyborg, leading the rebellion against the cabal trying to take over the world.

And yet, here he sat, with more augmentations inside of his own body than he could count, next to his not-so-dead wife who had been revived from a cryogenic multiyear sleep. Full of upgrades herself. It was wild. It must have been disorienting for her to experience.

There was another flash of lightning, followed by a crack of thunder. The storm was getting closer. The wind grew colder as it picked up, loose leaves whipping about them in a wild dance. By now, the stars completely disappeared, the occasional lightning illuminating the woman in front of him like the flash of a reporter's camera. A still portrait of a beautiful stranger.

A few raindrops struck him in the face. Small first, then larger. Another lightning hit, this time right above them, the thunder splitting the air, and then the skies opened up, a mighty pour coming down hard.

"What are you doing?" he asked as Rachel stood up and lifted her face to the sky, her eyes closed, the water running down her skin. He stood up next to her and winced as another lightning bolt zigzagged over their heads, the thunder so loud his augs kicked in to dampen the sound and protect his eardrums. "There are no trees for miles. Not the safest place to stand tall during the storm."

"I don't care," she whispered so softly, he read her lips more than he heard the words. "Hold me."

Jason reached out, wrapping his arms around her slender waist and pulling her closer. She trembled as the storm raged above them, tensing every time the thunder crackled. He leaned forward and placed a soft kiss on her lips, but she moved away, gently, but firmly.

"Not yet," she said. "Wait."

He closed his eyes and gave himself to the moment. The mighty roar of the storm, the harsh wind, the cold rain, and the warm flesh pressed into his: all combined into a psychedelic mix that threatened to overload his senses. Transporting him to a different reality when nothing else mattered. There was no rebellion. No hunger and the constant threat of violence. Just him, the woman he loved, and the storm.

At last, the thunder stopped, and the rain eased. The storm rolled farther east in search of other places to ravage in its fury.

"Now you can kiss me," she said, and he opened his eyes to see her looking up at him.

Her cheeks were wet, and he wondered if it was only from the rain. When his lips found hers, he tasted salt.

14

Queens, New York

"Oy, where the fuck do you think you're going?" Conor shouted at a skinny young man heading for the warehouse exit, his hands stuck in the side pockets of distressed jeans. A white wifebeater shirt with a stylized word *ANARCHY* in bold black letters on its back scrunched up as the man turned, looking at Conor in surprise.

"It's noon," the skinny man shouted back, stopping at the open double gate, his face screwed up in confusion. "I thought we took breaks at noon, no? I was gonna make a run to the Mickey Dees by the gas station."

"Listen, you twat, what do you think this is, a union job? Get your hairy ass back here and start moving before you get me blood boiling."

Conor and his second-in-command, Larry, were overseeing a group of men unloading the new shipment of sentinels that had arrived from Hong Kong in the morning. What started as one secretive shipment now became a routine, and Victor Ye continued to deliver sentinels of all types and sizes out of his factory in Hong Kong.

Johnny the Butcher used to be calling shots around the warehouse. But now that he was no longer in the picture, Conor took over. The Irishman made no secret of how pleased he was with Johnny's death, especially after hearing the rumors the psycho had something to do with the death of his brother, Noah. But he had to admit he didn't have quite the same grip on the crew as the machete-wielding psychopath used to enjoy.

He'd tried a few different versions of himself. First, a nicer one, trying to make Johnny's boys like him. The crew took advantage of his kindness and ignored him when he offered nothing of value. Then he tried to imitate Johnny's volatility, but the crew could tell he was faking it.

He finally gave up and returned to his usual grouchy, foulmouthed self. That produced better results, but not quite to his liking.

In the last two weeks, the shipments had picked up in frequency and now became almost a daily occurrence. The final destination for the sentinels had changed, too. Before, they'd ship them all over the country. Some, from what he'd heard, even ended up walking the grounds of the White House. Lately, however, most of the mechanized monsters were staying in New York, guarding multiple Victor Ye's properties. The shipment that came two days ago was special—two dozen crates with parts that, to Conor's eye, looked suspiciously like the shimmering assassin that these days had been following Victor Ye everywhere he went.

Victor was there personally to oversee the receipt of the delivery, a rather rare occurrence since he'd become an official part of Engel's administration and spent most of his time at the capital. Under his supervision, Conor and the workers moved the parts from the crates into a large truck and then transported them to Victor's mansion in Long Island.

Different people had different reactions toward sentinels. The new technology fascinated some. Some were scared by the lethality of their weapons. Others were unsettled by their autonomous designs and questioned their ability to differentiate between friend and foe. The Irishman was impartial to the mechanized guards, regarding them as tools, no smarter than dogs. But Daimyo, as his boss referred to the shimmering cyborgs, gave him the creeps. Seeing two dozen of those getting ready to be sent to Victor Ye's primary residence gave him an uneasy feeling he couldn't shake. He couldn't get rid of them fast enough.

Today's shipment was ordinary: four trucks full of small reconnaissance sentinels—light, dog-sized, four-legged machines. They had already emptied two of the trailers when he saw Brayden trying to sneak out. The skinny shit had been one of the insubordinate bunch, and Conor's patience was wearing thin.

"I'm gonna be back in five, boss," the man shouted.

"Can you believe this bastard?" Conor nodded to Larry. "I'm gonna rip him a new one."

"Come on, boss. They don't call it fast food for nothing, eh? I can grab you one of them juicy burgers?" the man insisted. "We're halfway done, anyway. What do you say?"

Conor opened his mouth, ready to scold the man, and froze as Brayden's head and neck disappeared. The Irishman stared in shock at the clean cut above the skinny man's collarbones as the blood sprayed forward a few times and then ran down his white shirt. The body stayed motionless for another moment and then softly collapsed on its back, mercifully putting the gory parts away from Conor's view.

He heard some yelling from the back of the warehouse, but the words weren't registering in his head as he watched a large, metallic boot step into view. Without thinking, Conor dived behind the empty crates by the wall, pulling Larry down with him, as the rest of the massive cyborg appeared in the doorway. A few blasts of what sounded like a shotgun came from the back, the deadly whistle of ricocheting pellets making the hair on the back of Conor's neck stand up.

The Irishman crawled forward a few inches, peeking between the crates at the intruder as the giant stopped at the entrance, surveilling the surroundings. The cyborg's head was covered in a full helmet, its surface so smooth, it looked like quicksilver. Most of the body, except the joints, was enclosed in scales of the same metal. When the giant moved, the scales moved independently, protecting vulnerable joints and connections.

Conor threw a quick glance at the back of the warehouse. Five of his men were still alive, hiding behind the crates and the parked trucks by the back wall. Another shot rang out, and this time the cyborg answered. The scales parted on the right arm, the stub-nosed gun barrel protruding from the opening. It fired. A man screamed somewhere behind the truck. It was a guttural, bloodcurdling wail of a wounded animal that got quieter after a few seconds before being replaced by a whizzing. Another few more seconds, it stopped altogether.

As if satisfied, the cyborg headed toward the parked trucks again. His footsteps were slow and deliberate. Conor risked a glance around the nearest crate. There was a forklift halfway between his position and the front gate. If they could get to it without getting noticed, they'd be almost home free. He had no illusions about the rest of his crew. If he and Larry still had a slight chance, the rest of his men were as good as dead.

"He's going to kill us all." Larry's panicked whisper was hot on Conor's ear.

He shook his head, silently willing the man to be quiet.

"We need to run," Larry continued. "Look at him. He'll rip us apart."

"Are you stupid?" Conor whispered back, stabbing the man in the chest with his forefinger. "Shut up before he hears us."

The cyborg fired from another weapon, hitting one truck. There was a screeching sound like from a power drill as the projectile buried itself into the frame of the eighteen-wheeler. A moment later, the truck exploded, sending a rain of burning-hot steel shards on Conor's hiding place.

"I can't stay here," Larry said, climbing onto his knees. The man was hyperventilating, his pudgy face pink and sweaty. "I can't stay here."

"Calm down, you coward." He grabbed the man's shoulder, squeezing it with all his might, trying to keep him in place. "You're going to get us both killed."

"I can't stay here," Larry squealed, breaking from Conor's grip and standing up.

The Irishman watched as his lieutenant, in desperation, darted across the warehouse floor toward the gates, his arms flailing as he went.

The first shot cut him at the knees. The inertia carried his body for a few more feet as the man tried to run on his suddenly short legs. As Larry fell, the second shot took his left shoulder and most of his side. He was dead before he hit the ground.

"Shit." Conor pulled his head back behind the crates, the remnants of the eggs and bacon he had in a nearby diner this morning climbing up his throat.

There was another screeching sound, followed by an explosion of the next truck, and then another.

It was now or never, he decided, and angled himself between the boxes. As he heard another screech, he pushed himself forward, staying as low as he could as the explosion covered his footsteps. A few long moments later, he found himself behind the base of the fork-lift. His lungs were burning for oxygen, but Conor forced himself to take slow, quiet breaths.

He heard approaching footsteps and then a few smaller explosions, followed by the rain of splinters and parts of the crates. After destroying the trucks, the cyborg was cleaning up the remaining inventory, however small.

Conor peeked his head over the seat of the forklift. Satisfied with the destruction of the pile of boxes at the nearest wall, the monster headed toward the back, and Conor took his chance.

The gate was so close to him, he thought he was going to make it, when something hotter than the surface of the sun touched his right leg. He lost balance, twisting in the air, and went down hard, his shoulder and head making contact with a dirty concrete floor.

Conor groaned, lifting himself up on his hands and spitting out dust and debris, and cried out in pain as his foot and his toes seemed on fire.

He rolled on his back and looked at his right foot, expecting to see it aflame. What he saw shocked him enough to momentarily push the pain out of his mind. Everything below his knee was gone, as if sliced off by a sword. Blood was squirting on the dusty floor, pooling around his leg.

His head spun. He reached down and pulled the belt off his pants and then wrapped it around his leg, right above his knee. The pain returned with a vengeance, and he screamed, tightening the tourniquet. Tears and sweat ran down his cheeks as he fixed the belt.

There was a sound behind him, and he turned, staring up at the massive bulk of the cyborg standing above him. He watched as the scales moved on the big man's arm, revealing a weapon.

"Oh Christ," he said, looking down the darkness of a barrel. Then there was nothing.

15

Rigel Compound, Upstate New York

Helen looked at the faces of the three men sitting around the table. Hunt, Schlager, and Poznyak joined her in the control center, currently serving as Jason's bedroom at night and a war room during the day. In the harsh lighting of the exposed light bulbs, the faces looking back at her seemed even more haggard than usual. They weren't starving, thanks to the fire support of a few volunteer units that kept the supply lines between the nearby farms and the silos opened, but it was close. Convoys had to be quick and nimble to avoid constant attacks by Black Arrow forces. They came at irregular intervals and brought enough food and supplies to keep the silos running, but not enough to build any meaningful stockpiles. The line between strict rations and outright starvation was already as thin as a razor blade. One bright side of the situation was that Poznyak's engineers came up with a water trapping system that produced enough to supply the colony with essential drinking water on most days. That alleviated some burden from the supply lines.

81

"Thank you for coming here on such short notice," she said. "But I think I have an idea worth exploring."

"Do tell," Schlager said, giving her a wink. "We could use a good idea."

She grimaced as she looked at his gaunt face with skin pulled tight over cheekbones and dark circles under the eyes. Schlager had always been thin, the sharp angles of his profile reminding her of a bird of prey. Now, after weeks of a diet that wouldn't satisfy a healthy teenager, let alone a grown man, he looked like a POW from the WWII colorized photographs.

"I saw a headline last night as I was checking the world news before going to bed. There'll be a rocket launch in about four weeks from now by the Russians from their Baikonur spaceport in Kazakhstan. The rocket will carry a robotic satellite that is supposed to make some repairs and upgrades to the International Space Station."

"I remember reading awhile back the ISS was going to be retired," Jason said.

"Right. It's old, and the idea was to ditch it into the South Pacific."

"Point Nemo," Poznyak interjected. "The graveyard for our space junk."

"Precisely. Maintaining the old station was getting expensive, and the plan was to build a new one with all the bells and whistles instead. But," she shrugged, "it seems the world has shifted priorities over the last few years. There's enough political will to sustain the current station for another decade, but nobody has enough time, money, or desire to build anything new."

"How does it help us?" Jason asked.

"You said it yourself—attacking Engel at the White House is counterproductive, and I agree. It's too heavily guarded and even if we could somehow overcome their defenses, the optics would be atrocious. But what if we could get him out?"

"Are you proposing to sabotage the station and crash it on the White House? I didn't think it was empty. Is it?"

"No, and no. It still carries astronauts, so sabotaging it is out of the question. What I'm suggesting is attacking the White House with Project Thor to force Engel to flee."

"Absolutely not," Hunt said. "That's not even worth debating. Forget the optics. It would kill hundreds, if not thousands, of innocents. I'm shocked—"

"Hang on." She interrupted him. "You can get off this high horse and frankly, I'm offended you thought I'd suggest to actually hit it."

"Fair enough." He raised his hands. "I'm sorry I jumped to conclusions. We are all short on temper lately, and I am not an exception. Go on."

"What if," she continued, "we created a leak that we've grown impatient with Engel and are considering hitting him with a Project Thor missile? I haven't worked out the actual details because the information needs to come to him from the right sources. It will have to be utterly believable. He'll be skeptical, because he will do the same analysis as we have, but after the battle for Rigel, he'd consider the chances we'd go through with it real, however remote. He'd be on high alert, but for the same reasons you've so vividly outlined—"

"I said sorry."

"Couldn't help it." She chuckled. "But you deserved that. Where was I? All I'm saying is he'll be jumpy, but he won't a hundred percent believe it. Until we launch it."

"And now I'm confused again," Jason said.

"Patience." She stood up, unable to contain her excitement. "The best part of Project Thor is how little time there is between the launch and the impact. It's fifteen minutes, at most. It's half the time of ICBMs and the only reason it's even that long is because the missile takes some time to maneuver in space before going down. We've been so obsessed about him being locked up at the White House that we've failed to see an opportunity. The way I see it—Engel's got a problem. He won't leave the White House unless we launch because he'll become vulnerable. And once we launch, he won't be able to run far. Which makes him vulnerable."

"You want to fake the launch?"

"No." She shook her head. "He'll know if it's not real. It needs to be a proper, honest-to-God launch to make it work. He'll see it coming and flee, and that's where you boys get him."

"I think I know where this is going," Poznyak said, who stayed quiet until now. "That's why you need the Russian repair satellite."

"Correct, my friend. Here's the idea. We take over the robotic satellite and re-route it to one of the Project Thor cannons. I've done some back-of-the-envelope calculations and the orbits are close enough for the maneuver. We won't be able to return it, though."

"How is it going to affect the station? Anything critical coming with the satellite?"

"No. It's not a supply mission. This is a part of the effort to extend the life of the ISS. And they have another one scheduled in six months. Worst-case scenario, the station won't last as many years as they want it to."

"Okay," Schlager said. "So we move the robot to Project Thor's cannon. Then what?"

"Then we use it to swap the actual missile with something else and...well, this is the weakest part of my plan. It needs to be a projectile that will look genuine enough for Engel to force him to flee, but won't reduce the White House to rubble, killing thousands. That's why I wanted to brainstorm it."

She paused, looking at the three men as they digested the information. The idea was exciting, she could tell, but so far it had too many holes to turn it into an actionable plan.

"How big are those things again?" Poznyak asked. "The ammo?"

"They are huge," Schlager said. "Roughly twenty-feet-long, one-foot-diameter tungsten rods. Each satellite carries three."

"That's," Poznyak scrunched up his face, "pi times height, times r squared. That's roughly fifteen, no, almost sixteen cubic feet. Or half a cubic meter, if you prefer the metric system. One cubic foot of tungsten weighs about half a ton. That's a lot of tungsten. Eight and a half tons, if I had to venture a rough guess. There's no way you can transport anything remotely this bulky and heavy with the Russian satellite. How did they even get them to space back in the day?"

"Those were specialized missions. And we won't need to," Chen said. "It needs to burn in the atmosphere, not make it down to the ground."

"Right, right." Poznyak shook his head. "Not a calculation I can do in my head, I'm afraid. We'd need to figure out the exact mass and density of an object this size that will burn just fast enough."

"Can it be a smaller projectile?" Schlager asked. "A fraction of the regular ammo?"

"No." She shook her head. "I don't think so. Ever since we took over the satellites, Engel has been watching them like a hawk. We are constantly under cyberattack from his techs who are trying to wrestle back control. If it looks like anything other than the real thing, he'll know. He's not monitoring those cannons on live television, but he has his own satellites tracking them, and he'll be able to see pictures within seconds of the launch."

"Okay. It sounds like we have us a scientific challenge." Poznyak drummed on the table. "We need to swap a real missile with a fake one, but we can't send anything big enough or heavy enough to space to do that. Did I miss anything?"

"I don't believe so."

"What if we make the same projectile but empty?" Jason asked.

"A bad idea," Poznyak said. "First, you still have to get it up to space, so the problem of being bulky doesn't go away. And second, as it enters the atmosphere, it'll most likely break apart. It won't look like the real thing. You want it to be solid."

"Fill it with water? Water isn't heavy."

"Still heavy enough. And even more likely to break apart as it heats upon re-entry and also doesn't solve for bulk. Wait a minute." Poznyak smiled and looked around the table. "That's why I love science. Can we end this stupid war so I could go back to the things I enjoy?"

"What?" Helen asked, looking at his beaming face.

"I think I have the solution. I know what to swap the missile with."

16

Sagaponack, New York

The speedboat's engine rattled and came to a stop as Jason Hunt kept the vessel's nose pointed at the shore, squeezing as much distance as he could.

"How do you see anything in this?" Kowalsky took the helm from him and squinted against the wind. The rain that threatened the city since early evening never came. Instead, a thick, dark fog descended over the ocean. By the time the night came, the impenetrable mist was hiding the stars and anything that was farther than three feet away.

"I'm fine," he heard Hunt say. "My vision is augmented, remember?"

"Good for you then, because I don't see shit."

It wasn't entirely true. He could see a string of pale glowing lights in the shore's direction, the fog making them appear bobbing up and down with the gusts of wind. Or maybe it was the boat bobbing up and down. Kowalsky wasn't sure which, but he was sure he didn't enjoy being on the boat. The sooner this mission was over, and he was back on *terra firma*, the better.

Their destination was nothing other than the lair of the most prominent gangster in the country. The raid of Schlager and Chen on the storage of Daimyo batteries in the Bronx proved to be a stunning success. Victor's house was the next logical step, and JC estimated it to be the second possible storage of Daimyo energy units. The looming mass production of the advanced cyborgs was one of the most acute threats facing the rebellion, and while Hunt's forces were spread too thin for direct confrontation, disrupting Victor's supply chain was the next best thing.

Even by the hefty standards of one of the most expensive zip codes in the country, Victor Ye's estate, occupying over sixty-five acres of Gibson Beach, was in a league of its own. The leader of the Red Dragon gang had purchased the twenty-five-bedroom manor pennies on the dollar from the disgraced hedge fund manager and former billionaire C.T. Miles before the turn of the century.

The downfall of the Wall Street darling—who, for a while seemed to read the future like an open book, only to succumb to sex scandals, drugs, and eventually tax fraud—was well documented by many prominent journalists. But there was a persistent rumor that never made it to any specials aired after the undoing of Miles's empire that he was innocent, and a powerful enemy engineered his demise.

That—unlike most of Miles's assets, including an art collection worth over a billion dollars—the property never went to auction, wasn't discussed anywhere either. Instead, it was sold in a private transaction directly to Victor Ye, a virtually unknown entity at the time.

"Be careful with those," Kowalsky said, handing a backpack full of C4 to Jason. "I'll keep the bird out to watch for you."

"Sounds good."

"I wish we could hack into the house before this. At least to get some idea of what's what."

"That'd be nice," Jason said, fastening the straps. "But this is precisely why we can't. Victor's old school. There's zero electronics on his property. Not even a TV."

"Talk about paranoid."

"It's kind of smart." He chuckled. "Not good for us, but smart. You can't hack things that aren't there. His coders are top-notch, but it doesn't matter how good you are. There's always somebody who's better."

"You don't think there's a chance he'll be here himself?"

"No." Jason shook his head. "He hasn't left the White House in weeks since Engel made him a special advisor."

"Victor Ye. A special advisor." Kowalsky spat over the side of the boat. "What a joke."

They tested the audio link between Hunt's implant and Kowalsky's earpiece and, without saying another word, Jason disappeared in the water behind the boat with a heavy splash.

Kowalsky opened a large rectangular briefcase, activated a stealth drone, and put on a pair of VR goggles that connected him to the quadcopter's video camera.

"I know you can't talk underwater," he said as the drone took off the boat and vanished into the fog. "But I've got the drone in the air."

"Roger," came a crisp answer, so loud inside of his ear, it made him jump.

"How the hell can you talk?" He tapped on the earphones, bringing the volume down.

"Neurolink. I'm not talking. You are hearing my synthesized voice."

"Great," Kowalsky said under his breath, watching the gray nothingness below the drone's lenses. "That's not creepy at all."

"I can still hear you."

"Yep, sorry."

A few minutes later, as Hunt neared the shore, the fog started to dissipate. After another few moments, a massive house; the second floor—facing the ocean and almost entirely made of glass—slowly appeared out of the milky cloud like a developing Polaroid.

"And I keep hearing crime don't pay." Kowalsky cycled through a few modes of the drone. "The shore is empty as far as I can tell, but I'm sure the house is going to be crawling with his goons."

There was a gurgling sound of running water, and then came Hunt's raspy voice. "Good thing I'm not going into the house, then."

After analyzing property records and satellite pictures of the estate, they'd considered two probable locations where Victor could keep the batteries. One was the exercise complex, or as the papers called it, a *playhouse*—a smallish square building surrounded by two tennis courts, a basketball court, and an Olympic-sized pool. The other was a massive garage capable of holding up to a hundred cars.

The garage seemed a more logical choice. It was a bigger place with an underground level, and it was tucked in, far away from the main road, right next to the shore.

"Two guys at the southern entrance. Kalashnikovs. Don't see anybody else here, but there's a sizeable group by the main house about two hundred yards north. If you make too much noise, they'll be all over you. I'm counting twelve, no, fourteen guys."

"Got it."

He watched Hunt's crouching figure dash across the sand and disappear into the bushes of evergreens. After a few moments, he emerged on the other side and crawled across the grass until he was less than twenty yards away from the two armed men. There was a muted flash of a weapon, and Hunt sprung out of his hideout to the building, the guards crumpling to the ground.

"Smooth," Kowalsky said into the microphone. "The gang by the main house didn't seem to hear anything."

"I'm going inside." Hunt's voice was back to the overly crisp sound. He must have switched to the neural link again to keep the noise to a minimum. "Victor's got quite a collection here. It's like a car museum. No batteries, though. Going to the basement now."

"Okay. Keep the link open."

Kowalsky's palms hurt. He lifted the VR goggles and looked down at them in surprise. His fingers were wrapped around the wood of the wheel with such force, his knuckles turned white. He let it go and shook his hands, trying to get the circulation going.

"There's nothing here."

"No batteries?" Kowalsky pulled the goggles back on and returned his attention to the drone's feed.

"Nope." Hunt sighed. "Just more cars. JC must've made a mistake. I'm going to hide the backpack in one of the cars for now. It'd be nice to have an ace up a sleeve."

"I think you might want to pick up the pace. The guys by the main house are up to something."

"What?"

Kowalsky watched the group of shadows in front of the mansion. "I'm not sure. They were lounging a moment ago and now they seem to be talking to each other. Oh, shit."

"What's going on?"

"You must've tripped something," Kowalsky shouted. "They know you are here. You gotta get out."

The group of the thugs split off into two. One disappeared inside of the massive house, and the other headed toward the beach.

He glanced back to make sure Hunt had a clear path back to the water, but the man was nowhere to be found.

"Jason?"

"I'm coming, I'm coming. Was making sure nobody will find the bag."

"You better hurry. Good news is they don't know where you are. At least for now. Oh, scrap this. No, no, no. Get the hell out of there, now."

The urgency in his voice must have had an effect because Hunt's reply wasn't through the neurolink. "What's going on?"

"The batteries aren't stored here. They are being used! I see at least two dozen Daimyo units all over the property. Two were hanging out by the front gate, but most of them are coming from the playhouse."

"Under different circumstances," Hunt chuckled, "I would have a comment or two about that statement."

"Jesus, Mary, and Joseph!" Kowalsky whispered in exasperation. "He's got jokes. Keep to your right and stick to the bushes. Nobody can see you yet."

"Yes, Captain."

Kowalsky watched Victor's men spill onto the beach, the cones of flashlight search up and down the coast. "It'll get kinetic once you get to the sand. There's no way to get past them without getting seen."

"How're my sword-wielding friends?"

"Still far, but getting close. They are fanning through the garden. You have thirty seconds at most."

Jason Hunt bolted out of the bushes, cutting down two men blocking his way to the water with a burst of automatic fire from his shoulder cannon. He ran into the ocean, ignoring small arms fire, and dived into the dark waves.

"Hit the garage when the Daimyos get close. Might not take them all out, but it will take out some."

Kowalsky watched as the group of cyborgs filtered through the maze. They picked up speed, no doubt now aware of the intruder's location, and split into two groups, one passing the garage on the north, and one on the south. As they both drew level with the building, Kowalsky hit the detonator, wincing in anticipation of the blast.

Nothing happened.

"What the hell?" he cursed under his breath, pressing the remote-control button a few more times. The drone's lenses showed the group of Daimyos, their swords out, spill on the beach and then dive into the sea. "Shit, shit, shit. Those lemmings can swim."

"Did you blow it?"

"It doesn't fucking want to blow!" he yelled. "They are swimming too fast. You won't make it."

He initiated the return protocol, recalling the drone, and threw his VR glasses on the floor. Then he jammed his thumb onto the start button and twisted the throttle all the way up. The engine coughed in protest, overflowed with fuel, and then roared to life.

He swung the boat around and headed straight for the shore, the nose of the vessel pointing dangerously high as it gained speed.

He almost overshot Hunt first, as the blip on the radar got closer, much faster than he expected, and then almost smashed him with the nose of the boat as he threw it into a wild turn to slow down. The boat roared and jerked forward before Jason was fully in.

"You are one crazy son of a gun," Hunt said as he climbed in.

Kowalsky ignored him and just stabbed behind his shoulder with a thumb. A dozen Daimyos were still chopping water, going after them. "I'm the crazy one? You want to talk to those dolphins from hell?"

"They could have shot you."

"They didn't." Kowalsky squinted his eyes as the boat flew across the shallow waves. "What a shit show."

"Yeah," Jason said, sitting down on the floor and wiping his face. "What a shit show, indeed."

17

The Oval Office, Washington, DC

There was chaos in the Oval Office. If he closed his eyes and tuned out the words, Engel could have been in a bar, listening to a rowdy crowd rooting for two opposite teams that clashed on the screen hanging over the rows of liquor on sticky shelves. Insults and f-bombs flew around like leaves in a storm. He looked around the room as people who were supposed to help him run the country and squash the rebellion shouted at each other. A sea of red faces and bulging veins. Flying spittle. He slowly stood up, his palms pressing down on the hard surface of the Resolute desk, and leaned toward the men and women in the room, shouting a single word. "Quiet!"

He looked around at the startled faces as they turned toward him. He was sure he wasn't the first and probably not the last president to yell at his underlings in the Oval Office, but the effect was immediate and strangely satisfying. The space grew quiet. The only sound was the ticking of the Seymour grandfather clock by the northeast door.

Almost every single person, from the most junior staffer to his VP, looked anxious. Even Graham, his military advisor, looked uncomfortable. None would meet his gaze.

Except Susan. She was the only one who didn't avert her eyes when they met his. There was something in the way she cocked her head, the way her jaw was set, the way she held the tablet in her hands, that he didn't like. He struggled to understand what it was. Contempt? Pity?

They had been growing apart ever since he had moved into the White House. Sure, part of it was the jobs, hers as the chief of staff, and his, that kept them so busy they could hardly find any time for themselves. But there was something else, too. He felt her slipping away and couldn't understand why. It worried him first. Then it frustrated him. After a while, he became angry. He did his best not to lash out, aware of the special bond they shared, but found it more and more difficult. One night, after the failed attack on the silo, he bullied her into spending the night at the White House. He wanted her that night. Badly. It wasn't just on the primitive sexual level. It was something deeper. He needed a connection.

She didn't share the sentiment and gave one excuse after another, drinking Scotch and sitting in a chair, away from the bed, her legs crossed. When he had enough, Engel walked across the room, plucked her out of the chair, and brought her to the bed.

"I'm not in the mood, Alex," she said, but didn't push him away. He took it as a sign, lifted her skirt and pulled down her underwear, and then he was inside of her. Hungry. Powerful. He wanted her to reciprocate, but she just lay there, her arms spread wide, her eyes dispassionately watching his face.

"Turn around," he commanded.

"No." She cocked her head as she watched him towering over her. "Do it like this. That's okay. I don't mind."

He wanted to strike her there and then. Hit her right across the face, hard enough to make her head spin. Instead, he roughly grabbed her breasts through the jacket and moved hard and fast until the sweet wave of oblivion washed over him. When it was over, he stood up and watched her clean herself and straighten her clothes.

"I'd better get going," she said.

"I thought you were staying?"

"No." She picked up her purse. "I have an early morning. I never sleep properly here, and I need to be productive tomorrow. Too much on my plate."

"Sure. I understand."

He didn't. But he watched her leave and as she did, she gave him the same look she had now, watching him from the cream-colored couch. Immovable as the storm of emotions raged around her.

He didn't know what it was then. He still didn't know what it was now. But one thing had become crystal-clear. He didn't care if he lost the war and the presidency, was thrown in jail, or executed by a firing squad. He didn't care if he could rule the entire planet, every man and woman bowing to his every whim. It made no difference. But he could not lose Susan Walsh.

For the first time in his life, another person mattered to him more than anything else in the world. More than himself. He didn't have a name for it but guessed other people would have called it love. Maybe it was or maybe it wasn't. He couldn't be sure. Alexander Engel wasn't like other people.

It didn't matter. Something in the way her eyes looked through his that night told him it might have been too late. Whatever it was, the invisible line that connected the only person he truly cared for to him was irreparably broken.

She'd stay loyal to him to the end, he knew. She'd die for him. This was who Susan Walsh was. But she no longer was his.

For a moment, he thought she was going to say something, but she only pursed her lips and remained silent.

"Mr. President?" Rodney Graham stood up from the cream-colored couch. He was a short, stocky man with a look of a former wrestler, or judo practitioner, further evidenced by a set of thick, cauliflower ears. He was dressed in a dark pin-striped suit and a white shirt without a tie. His round, cleanly shaven head was covered in tiny beads of perspiration. "Perhaps it would be helpful if I walked everyone through my plan?"

Engel drummed his fingers on the table. He wondered if they should have listened to Susan and done this in the Situation Room. He nodded to Graham. "Good idea. But before you do, I wanted to remind you all why you're here, because I feel you're losing sight of what we are after."

"Of course, Mr. President," Susan said, almost unintelligibly.

He stole a glance at her, but this time she kept her eyes glued down, as if studying a secret message hidden in the dark-blue rug under her Jimmy Choos. He could tell his blood pressure was rising without the aid of a health indicator blinking in his vision. What the hell was her deal today, anyway? Acting like they weren't in the Oval Office planning a military operation, but in Hitler's bunker during the last days of the war. Not knowing what drove her away was driving him mad.

He bit his lip, tasting blood, and swallowed the remark that was about to fly off his tongue. When he opened his mouth again, his tone was even, measured.

"The war is almost over, ladies and gentlemen. I might have been wrong when I thought Hunt wouldn't have it in him to use the missile against our troops. But I was spot-on about how it would be the perfect story for us. Sure, it'll take some time for the general public to see it the way we want them to. But they will. Already the knowledge that we ordered the first strike against the silo went from a known fact into a gray territory. Some still believe we made the call. But some are arguing all over social media it was a hoax. A false flag operation by Hunt's forces, and that this hit only proves it. That's why it's so important to press our advantage. Come on, Graham. Tell us what you've got."

Rodney Graham stepped toward the Resolute desk and placed a small device at the edge. Then he took a few steps back and took out a remote control. A hologram map of the Eastern Seaboard of the United States appeared to be floating in the air above the device.

"Here and here," he pointed at the map and under his finger a red dotted line traced an outline, "are the biggest concentrations of troops loyal to the rebels. The one up here in Connecticut is the greatest. But most of the heavy equipment is around the silo, here. To make it worse, Leonard Freeman brought some serious firepower with him. He was a colonel in the 82nd Airborne Division, and we've had a lot of trouble bringing them in after the conversion. And Freeman, it seems, still enjoys a lot of loyalty from his former brothers-in-arms. Some of Hunt's most hardened forces had been built from the 82nd Division vets. Most of them have been converging to protect the silo after the failed attack by the Fourth Brigade."

"What exactly are you saying?"

"I'm saying, Mr. President, this is what we should focus on. I agree with you that while Price is important to the resistance, Jason Hunt is the soul of the rebellion. My recommendation would be to make a feint in Connecticut to make sure those forces remain tied up, but throw everything we've got at the silo and the remainders of the 82nd Airborne. If the silo falls and Hunt is captured or killed, I believe it's only a matter of time until we squeeze whatever units Darius still commands."

"We've tried that." Susan's voice was quiet, but hard. "And every one of you was convinced Hunt wouldn't dare to strike our troops with a Thor missile. We all know how that worked out."

"That is true, ma'am." Engel thought he could hear some satisfaction in Graham's voice. "He hit them last time, but I don't think he'd be able to do that again."

"How so?"

"Because," Graham clicked a remote again, bringing a 3D model of what looked like a ballistic missile to the front, "I have no intention of giving them a chance. We are going to blow Project Thor out of the sky."

18

Washington, DC

"I hate this town," Kowalsky said as he pulled over to the side of the road and stopped the truck.

"What's wrong with it?" Latham Watkins brought his chair up and looked outside. "I've been here only once before when my wife and I were still together. It was in the spring. Cherry blossom festival or whatever they call it here. It was rather nice."

"Sure," Kowalsky said. "It could be pretty in a few places. But it's also the home of every asshole with a federal badge who ever walked the earth. You have no idea how many times in my career I had to hand cases over to these guys. Do all the dirty stuff and then when it's ready to be served on a silver platter, bam! Somebody comes and snatches it out of your hands and gets all the credit. One time I had to dig with my hands through a dumpster full of shit to find the evidence to a cold case. Thought was going to get a promotion."

"I'm guessing it didn't happen?"

"Nope. The next morning, a guy showed up at my station, young enough to still suck on his momma's titties, and that was it. And it was a huge case."

"So you say."

"You ever heard of the Briefcase Maker?"

"The serial killer?" Watkins looked at his partner in surprise. "The guy was targeting Wall Street bros and making purses out of them?"

"Yep."

"Get outta here. You found the evidence for it?"

"Yes, sir." Kowalsky coughed, clearing his throat. "For almost two decades, everybody thought he was a Manhattan local. But he apparently freelanced in a few other states. The feds took it the moment there was evidence. That greenhorn who stole it from me quit the agency and became a best-selling author. Lives in the Hamptons now."

"Maybe it's for the best," Latham said. "You don't strike me as the writing type, no offense."

"Screw you," Kowalsky said. "No offense. So yeah. I hate this fucking town. And judging by the weather, it hates me right back."

The rain was pouring so hard, he could hardly see the other side of the road. They arrived in the city on foot in the morning, sneaking past the patrols and barricades. Each carried a heavy backpack, the contents of which would assure a quick loss of their rights and privileges should they be searched.

They took a few cabs crisscrossing the town and then, as Kowalsky put it, *liberated* a beat-up truck in a Washington Highlands neighborhood. After sunset, they headed for their first destination—a former high school campus that occupied an entire city block and was converted into Black Arrow barracks and sentinel storage.

"That should do." Kowalsky pointed at an abandoned nine-story building. The left wing bore the signs of a severe fire. It must have originated on the first floor and spread as much as the fourth before being put out. "It's close enough and high enough. Look how the fire escape is warped. That must have been some inferno."

"There are squatters." Latham pointed at the few windows that were illuminated by what seemed like an open fire. "We might run into some trouble."

"I don't like trouble," Kowalsky grumbled as he climbed out of the truck and into the rain. "But trouble sure as hell likes me."

They grabbed their backpacks and crossed the road, hunching in the rain.

The lobby of the building smelled of rot and wet ash. Kowalsky turned on the flashlight and looked around. The floor was almost entirely covered by trash. Two mattresses of unidentifiable color were tucked next to a wall where once a doorman's station used to be. Dozens of hypodermic needles were scattered on a plastic chair next to the mattress.

"Watch where you step," Watkins said. "You don't want to step on one of those."

"They came to do a job and left with AIDS," Kowalsky said. "That would be tragic."

"Not funny."

They took a few breaks climbing the stairs, the straps of the heavy backpack cutting into Kowalsky's shoulders. The building stayed quiet as they went. If the squatters noticed their presence, they either didn't care or thought them too dangerous to approach.

By the time they reached the last floor, Kowalsky was drenched in sweat, his breathing hard.

"It's locked." Watkins pointed at the padlock hanging from the door to the roof. "You got picks?"

"Of course I got picks."

He took the backpack off and put it on the ground, massaging his shoulders to get the blood going. Then, he pulled out his pick set and knelt in front of the door. A minute later, the padlock clicked, and Kowalsky pushed the door open and walked into the rain.

"This should do it," he said, looking toward the high school building a few blocks south. "Direct sight."

"Yeah," Watkins agreed. "As long as nobody finds it."

"They won't."

"Or burn the place down. I saw quite a few open fires going."

"Would you stop being so negative? Jesus."

They carried the backpacks to the southern wall and assembled two remote-controlled heavy-caliber machine guns pointed at the Black Arrow base. Then Kowalsky poured epoxy into the four corners of the perimeter around the guns and set holographic devices, activating them. The air inside the area shimmered, the contours of the guns slowly dissolving.

They picked up their now-empty backpacks, locked the door again, and retraced their steps to the lobby of the building.

"Hold up," Kowalsky said as they entered the foyer. "Turn off the light."

He slowly walked across the floor until he reached the door and peeked outside. A Humvee was parked behind their pickup truck. A couple of Black Arrow mercenaries stood next to the cabin of their vehicle, shining their flashlight inside.

"What's going on?" Watkins whispered. "I can't see anything."

"A Humvee and some uniforms. Checking out our truck."

"That should be okay, though," Watkins said. "There's nothing suspicious in our truck."

"Maybe." Kowalsky peeked again. "But the truck is stolen, so who knows? Oh, shit."

The older mercenary, seemingly unsatisfied with the examination, turned around and pointed the flashlight at the building.

"What now?"

The mercenary turned to his partner, and, after a few words, both headed across the street toward the building.

"Quick." Kowalsky pulled on his friend's sleeve. "They are coming here."

They jogged across the lobby's floor, trying to make as little noise as possible, and went back to the stairwell. They got to the second floor when a cone of bright light jumped across the hallway and the mercenaries entered the building.

"I don't think there's anybody here," a man's voice said. "Look at this shit. Only junkies come here to get high."

"Where did the car come from, then?" The second voice, gruff, with a touch of authority, sounded like it belonged to an older man. "It's not a local car."

"Local plates, though."

"It doesn't mean anything. Could've been stolen. I've never seen this truck around here."

"And you know every car in this neighborhood?"

"Shut up and go check up the stairs."

Kowalsky turned to Watkins and pointed up with his index finger. His partner nodded, acknowledging, and they slowly began their ascension.

They walked up two sets of stairs when the mercenary stopped below them and yelled back to the lobby. "It's empty."

"All right," came a reply. "Get your ass down here."

Kowalsky and Watkins waited for a few minutes, listening to the sounds coming from the first floor. Finally, there was a revving of the engine and then the rumbling of a truck getting farther and farther away.

"Do you think we can take the truck now?" Watkins asked as they descended to the lobby and stood by the door, observing the street. "What if they bugged it?"

"I don't think so." Kowalsky pulled the door and stepped outside. The rain had turned into a thin drizzle clinging to every surface. "I think they were being cautious. If it stays here for a few days, I think it'll raise more suspicion and they might investigate the building in greater detail. That's the last thing we need."

They crossed the street, looking for danger, but the night stayed quiet. Kowalsky started the engine and put the truck into drive, accelerating away.

"You think it'll work?" his partner asked.

"The guns?" He shrugged. "I don't see why not. Heavy-caliber bullets smacking on the barracks should be a good enough reason to tie them up for quite a while. And by the time they suppress it and come to investigate, hopefully it'll be too late."

"Not the guns," Watkins said. "The entire thing. Jason's plan."

"What do I know?" He ran a red light and accelerated as they merged onto the highway. "I'm just a grunt. If the boss tells me to bring a machine gun down to DC, I go down to DC and do what I'm told."

"Chuck."

"What?"

"For once in your life, can you cut the bullshit and tell me straight?"

Kowalsky sighed and moved the pickup truck into the right lane. Now, since they unloaded their deadly cargo, they could travel through the roadblocks unmolested. "I don't know, Latham. But I feel like we've been down on our luck long enough. Even a blind chicken gets a piece of corn once in a while. I'd like to find mine just about right now."

19

The Oval Office, Washington, DC

"What do you mean, we blow them out of the sky, Rodney?" Engel said, as he watched his military advisor's round, sweaty face. "Are you proposing we send a nuke to orbit?"

"We don't need to." Rodney Graham pulled on his shirt that seemed to choke him. The rim of the white collar was turning dark. "Have you ever heard of Operation Burnt Frost?"

"I don't believe I have."

"Ever since we started launching things into space, there was a question of militarizing it. There were dozens of projects. Project Thor for kinetic bombardment. Strategic Defense Initiative, also colloquially known as the Star Wars program. Most of it was bullshit meant to bankrupt the commies, but some elements were real. There was also Project Horizon, which was a study to determine feasibility of a fully operational military base on the moon. There was the Lunex Project, Project A119, that aimed to blow up a nuclear device on the moon. And then there was Starfish Prime that exploded a thermonuclear device at an altitude of 250 miles, which produced valuable data on EMP. Too many projects to name. It was a new frontier. Nobody knew how or when the war could break out. We weren't the only ones doing it, either. The Soviets, China, India—everybody wanted to get in on the action."

"But we have treaties prohibiting deployment of weapons in space," Susan interjected. She leaned forward, her eyes studying Graham.

"We do. A whole bunch. The Moon Treaty. Outer Space Treaty. Limited Test Ban Treaty. There were some provisions in the SALT treaties as well." Graham smiled. "And yet we have titanium rods floating in space, ready to hit any place on Earth in a matter of minutes."

"Those were mothballed. Not a lot of folks in the administration even knew they existed."

"They were. Until they weren't, and that's how highly classified information is supposed to work."

"Please, continue," Engel said, throwing Susan an angry look. She and Graham locked horns all the time and, most of the time, he was fine with it. But not today. He wanted actionable intelligence. Not bickering. "You've mentioned Operation Burnt Frost."

"Anyway, there was a need to place weapons around the globe," the advisor said, moving his hands in a circular motion. "Naturally, that created a need to destroy them as well. Anti-satellite weapons, or ASATs, were born. Systems that could eliminate threats in space. Initial tests took place in the early 1980s, but the first notorious use of such a weapon happened in 2008. The official story was a non-functioning US National Reconnaissance Office satellite posed serious risk if it were to crash back to the planet. It was a heavy satellite, about two and a half tons. It also carried about one thousand pounds of unused hydrazine propellant, which is extremely toxic. We claimed there was nothing to prove, and we did it in the name of science and protecting the environment."

"Did we? Or was it strictly military?"

"Like most government stories dealing with military exercises, it was a bit of both. Some in the administration believed the propellant posed a serious risk. But it was also a perfect opportunity to test something new. Ultimately, those advocating for it convinced the president, and the mission was a go and three rockets had been prepped. They used an upgraded Standard Missile-3, which was launched from the USS *Lake Erie*. A conventional kinetic warhead. A few minutes into the flight, the satellite was hit and most of the debris entered the atmosphere in the next few hours. There were a few pieces that had been thrown to higher orbits by the explosion that took longer, but ultimately everything went down.

"The Russians and the Chinese, of course, made a lot of noises protesting the launch and how it endangered other spacecraft in orbit, but we didn't care."

Engel watched the man for a few seconds as he processed the information. "You said it wasn't a regular missile?"

"Correct, Mr. President." Graham brought up a hologram image of the rocket again. "They took the SM-3 and modified the engine for the job, specifically the first two stages."

"Was it one rocket only?"

"No." The advisor swiped away the image of a missile and brought up a document, zooming in on it. A *Top Secret SCI* stamp was in the right upper corner. "I believe three of them had been modified. They didn't have any other uses or targets. It was a redundancy issue."

"You said we used one. Where are the remaining two?"

"They had been stored in San Diego, but I took the liberty of having them transported to Naval Station Norfolk. We'll be able to install them on the USS *Vicksburg* over the next few days. If we press, they can be operational before the end of the week."

Engel sat down and pulled the chair closer to the Resolute desk, putting his elbows on the hard surface. It was unfortunate how the tables had turned, but the math was simple. When Victor Ye told him about Project Thor at their fateful meeting before Engel assumed the presidency, there were three satellites. Despite Engel's initial doubts they'd be able to revive the weapons, Victor delivered. It took some technical wizardry, including repurposing one of the most powerful radio transmitters in the world that was originally put into operation by the US Navy at Jim Creek Valley. After a few hiccups, the satellites came online, each of them carrying three tungsten rods and giving Engel what seemed like an ultimate weapon against the rebels. Untraceable. As deadly as a tactical nuclear device and yet that produced zero fallout.

It almost seemed the rebellion was over before it started when Engel's forces, led by Victor Ye himself, crushed Jason Hunt's team and captured him and his right-hand man, Schlager. In retrospect, he should have executed them the moment they were delivered to the black site in Maryland, but Victor convinced him to break Hunt's will and bring him on as a willing participant and collaborator. When the plan failed, they used the first missile to hit the silo hideout sheltering Hunt's forces. The result was both impressive and disappointing. While the blast was as powerful as a small nuclear device, the silo, hardened against intercontinental ballistic missiles, remained standing. Not much later, Hunt and Schlager were rescued by their tactical team.

Victor pressed him to use another missile, but Engel resisted. It was hard enough to suppress the news of what looked like a nuclear strike on American soil. Another explosion would have been terrible optics. But things got much uglier in the next forty-eight hours when Hunt's hackers somehow wrestled control of all three satellites away from them. Victor Ye's coders, despite Victor's claims of being the best in the world, had no idea how it had been done. For some time, the missiles created a fragile balance of power—Engel enjoyed an overwhelming power of conventional forces spearheaded by the Black Arrow brigades, but Hunt had the missiles.

But the situation was changing. And the reports that Leonard Freeman was cozying up to Hunt meant trouble. Freeman was a war hero many in the army still revered. He could be the first domino to set things in motion that could bring the entire house down.

Engel sighed. He recalled the cold, snowy day when he went to visit his father. It was the last time he saw Simon. To his surprise, the always cautious and calculating man urged him to step up and not worry about how other people saw him. *I guess the old man was right after all. What did he say? Sometimes to be a hero, first you need to become a villain. Raze cities if you have to.*

It was too late to care about the optics. He needed to crush the rebellion at all costs now and worry about the public opinion later. Without Hunt and his hackers breathing down their neck, they'd have plenty of time to write the narrative any way they wanted. The victors write history.

He looked at Susan again, hoping to catch her gaze, but she seemed to be deep in thought, not looking at anyone in particular. Maybe if this ridiculous war was over, he could figure out whatever the hell was happening between them and fix it. Maybe it still wasn't too late.

"There are three satellites, Rodney," he finally said. "And we only have two rockets."

"That is correct, Mr. President." Graham's already sweaty face turned a dark shade of pink. "But one of them is almost depleted, with one missile remaining. We used the first missile, and the rebels used the same satellite when they struck at the Black Arrow regiment. If we shoot down the other two satellites, it will leave Hunt with only one projectile. Hardly a decisive advantage."

"Tell it to the remnants of the Fourth Brigade," Engel said. "One missile can still do a lot of damage. How quickly can we modify another rocket to be used against the third satellite?"

"I think we could do it in two weeks," Graham said. "Nobody needs to reinvent the wheel. We have the parts—we know how to. We have to put together a team to make it happen."

"Do it." Engel stood up, signaling the meeting was over. "I want the two satellites down before the end of the week. And I want daily updates on the progress of upgrades for the new missile."

"Yes, sir."

"Listen up." He addressed the room. "I want full support for Graham on this one. All hands on deck. Those three chunks of metal floating in space are the only things that stand between us and the end of this war. Make it happen, goddamn it."

20

Rigel Compound, Upstate New York

The top level of the control center was quiet and tense as Jason Hunt looked at the faces in front of him. Max and Helen sat to his left, a map of Washington, DC, displayed on the interactive surface of the table in front of them. Steven Poznyak sat to his right, his gray eyes behind powerful glasses, nervously flicking between the screen and the people around the table. At the other end of the table sat Darius Price. Out of everyone in the room, his posture was the most relaxed, his fingers steepled in a sign of confidence. His military fatigues were clean and pressed as if he just put them on and was not smuggled through a war zone. To most, the man would appear at ease, almost Zen, but Jason's enhanced vision highlighted Price's elevated heartbeat and a clenched jaw.

"Thank you for coming, Darius," Jason started. "I know you took a huge gamble. We couldn't guarantee your safety on the way in and it's going to be even trickier to see you out. I appreciate you being here."

"To pass on the opportunity to plan an attack on a sitting president? I wouldn't miss it." The dissonance between the measured professorial delivery and the actual message ignited a nervous chuckle around the table. "I take it you have a plan?"

"We do." Jason tapped on the table in front of him, opening what looked like a picture of a large motorcade from above. "As you know now, we had an idea to lure Engel out in the open by faking a direct strike on the White House with a Project Thor missile. Nobody knows for sure if the underground bunkers at 1600 Pennsylvania Avenue can withstand a direct hit. They probably can. But our bet is the Secret Service and Engel's private army from Black Arrow wouldn't want to test it in practice. Once they learn of the impending impact, they will gather the motorcade and attempt to whisk him away across the Potomac to the Pentagon. That would be where he is the most vulnerable."

"Don't you think they would take Marine One?" Price said, frowning. "It's faster. They could fly him directly to Joint Base Andrews and put him on Air Force One. Once he's there, forget it."

"It's a possibility," Jason said. "But we think it's unlikely. Thor's missile launch is almost impossible to detect. It will light up like a Christmas tree once it enters the atmosphere, but by then it will be too late. They also won't know the exact spot where the missile would hit. If they are within the blast radius, the chances of survival would be significantly higher in an armored vehicle rather than while airborne. Marine One is a magnificent piece of machinery, but it will crash the same way any regular helicopter would. I think Engel's bodyguards will come to the same conclusion. It's worth the gamble. There are probably going to be Black Arrow helicopters covering the motorcade from above. So we have to keep those in mind."

"Okay. Say you are right. How do you take him while he's in the motorcade? You'd still have to go through an entire army to get to his limo."

"Right. The motorcade isn't easy, but the short notice will produce some weak spots. Normally it's somewhere between forty and fifty vehicles, but because of a compressed timeline, it'll be smaller than that. Max?"

"Here." Schlager opened a separate window on the surface of the table and enhanced what looked like a cartoon depiction of a few cars traveling in a formation. "This part of the convoy is called the secure package. That's where the president is going to be. The entire motorcade is big even under such tight notice, but in the heart of it is the core of a few cars. At the first sign of trouble, they'll try to ditch the rest of them and take the president as far away from danger as possible. One of them is Cadillac One—the Beast—that will carry Engel. Normally, there are two limos. This time, it might be more. The Secret Service could try to compensate for the somewhat diminished size of the convoy by deploying more than one what they call a Spare besides the Stagecoach. They will look the same; they'll have the same plates. We won't know which one will be a decoy and which would carry Engel. While en route, the drivers of both vehicles will play a shell game to further complicate any efforts to decipher which is which."

Schlager flipped the image and moved it closer to Price.

The man leaned over the table, as if trying to see the passengers inside of the cartoonish cars. "That surely doesn't help."

"It doesn't." Schlager flashed a smile. "But we might be able to guess with a high degree of probability which one will carry Engel."

"How?"

"First off, we have a man on the inside."

"You do?" Price looked up, unable to conceal the shock on his face. "Someone connected enough to give you such sensitive info? Who is it?"

"It'd be best if you didn't know." Schlager shrugged apologetically. "Not because we don't trust you. But you can't give up information you don't have, willingly or unwillingly. And if—"

"I get it." Price interrupted him. "And I'm sorry. I shouldn't have asked. Was surprised, that's all. Please, continue."

"Thanks." Schlager zoomed out of the picture to show the entire cavalcade. "There are two components that might give us the clue which car is the Stagecoach. First will come from the assignments of agents that we will glean from our man on the inside. The second part is a bit more technical. One part of the secure package is a special countermeasures SUV. It serves a few purposes. It jams the area around the convoy, preventing any potential road bomb detonations. It also has an electronic warfare suite that detects any RPG or anti-tank missile launch. In the event of a launch, it'd deploy countermeasures to defeat them. As Engel added four heavy sentinels to the cavalcade, the SUV now also serves as the control tower for the sentries. And while it added to the firepower of the motorized column, it also added some vulnerabilities. I'll leave it to Helen to explain."

Helen took out a small, black, rectangular device that looked like an old-fashioned flip phone and put it on the table.

"What's that?" Price asked.

"We call this a multipurpose transmitter." She glanced at Jason, and he gave her a reassuring nod. "Jason first encountered these when there was an attempt on his life. A few of these devices had been used to project life holograms. Later, they were also used to mask sentinels before an attack on the Orion Tower."

"Interesting." Price reached out to the small device. "May I?"

"Sure."

Price picked it up and brought it to his face, studying it. "You want to use holograms to ambush Engel?"

"No." Helen paused, as if looking for the right words. "Holograms are some of the more crude applications of this device, and they won't help us. What's much more important is the chip inside them has a heavily encrypted core frequency for the sentinels. It's possible to hack them. I've done it before, but there's a problem. Once they link up, and the heavy sentries in Engel's convoy would most definitely do that, you can't penetrate their defenses. At least not in the time we will have during the ambush. Without getting too technical, think of the traditional one straw, easy to break, a bunch of straws impossible to break, example."

"Got it."

"The encryption on these things is too complex to break with conventional means. To do that, you would need a quantum computer. What's worse, you would need a highly agile program that could adapt on the fly while breaking into the interlink defense system without locking itself out. Lucky for us," she gave him a tight smile, "we have both. Also, to Max's point—the countermeasures SUV and the sentinels will communicate with the Beast, which will give us a second vector to figure out what car Engel is in."

"You want to turn them against the convoy?" Price looked skeptical. "Four heavy sentinels are a lot of firepower, but the vast majority of Engel's forces are going to be Black Arrow elite units. That won't be enough."

"I agree." Jason stood up and walked around the table, stopping next to Price. He typed *DC* on the smooth surface of the desk and brought up the map of Washington. Then he zoomed in on the blue band separating the city and tapped it with his metallic finger. "This is the key to our operation. The Potomac. What's the most important thing when escorting a president from an impending disaster? Speed. They need to get to the Pentagon as quickly as possible. But to get to those bunkers, they need to cross the Potomac, and the shortest way from the White House is over the Arlington Memorial Bridge. The whole route is a hair longer than three miles. If there's no traffic, you and I could cover that distance in a car in under ten minutes. Engel, with a convoy clearing the road and traveling well above the city speed limit, could do it in under four. Add another minute that it takes his guards to get him ready and out of the White House. The entire operation would be done in under five minutes. It'll be hard to ambush him anywhere else during the drive. But when he needs to cross the river... It's a flat bridge with nowhere to hide and nowhere to turn. That's where we hit him."

"You're going to mine the bridge?"

"No." Jason brought the picture of the bridge on the screen. "This is one of those situations where the optics are almost more important than substance. We can't just blow him up. We have to get up there and get close and personal. All his life, he has been projecting an image of a powerful man. Untouchable. And now, when he's heavily augmented, it's even more important. If he dies from a blast, it'll feel like cheating. No. It needs to be a full-blown spectacle. A Hollywood movie that will play on repeat in every household in America and around the world. A villain struck down by a vengeful angel. A fair fight."

"Okay." Price nodded, deep in thought. "But how are you going to get to the bridge? It's one of the most watched structures in the country. We can't exactly waltz through DC with some heavy equipment and wait for Engel to get to the bridge. It's under surveillance twenty-four seven."

"Of course it is. But tell me, Darius, where do angels come from?" Jason reached out and put his hand on Price's shoulder. "They fall from the sky."

21

Rigel Compound, Upstate New York

"It's fucking chaos here." The voice that came through the speaker was raspy, interrupted by the muffled explosions in the background. "They are coming from all directions. We are taking massive casualties. We need immediate support."

Jason Hunt leaned over the computer screen on his table as he and Helen viewed the telemetry from a former DARPA satellite, MOIRE 22. A large group of rebels was under a coordinated attack by Black Arrow mechanized infantry in the Nepaug State Forest, northwest of Hartford.

Apart from the silo, Camp Whigs was the most important rebel stronghold in the country. The first few dozens of soldiers took refuge in the southern part of the woods that gave them access to fresh water from the nearby Nepaug Reservoir two weeks after the attempt on Price's life.

Over the course of the next few months, the regiment grew as the volunteers from the local towns and even neighboring states continued to pour in. By the time it stood at two thousand soldiers, the regiment took control of both Route 202 and Route 44 that hugged the forest, complicating the traffic for smaller Black Arrow outfits going in and out of Hartford. By now, the group had grown to a twelve-thousand strong division, and together with a few battalions in New Haven and Boston, it was shaping up to what rebels started to call the Northern Army.

Rigel Compound had a dedicated round-the-clock watch that shifted through the few active and out-of-commission spy satellites to provide the troops on the ground with fresh intel and warn them of movements of the Black Arrow units. A few small ambushes were successfully thwarted, but until this morning, there was no indication of any large maneuvers in the camp's vicinity. How loyal to Engel forces had managed to deliver heavy weaponry to the heart of the rebel-controlled territory was a mystery.

"I see nothing from orbit, dammit," Jason swore as he quickly flipped through a few dozen images. "Do you have any drones that are still operational?"

There was a crackle of automatic fire and then a loud boom of an explosion, followed by what sounded like a rattle of dirt and debris raining down on the rebel positions.

"Felix?" Jason said, leaning closer to the speaker. "Can you hear me?"

"Yes." The man on the other line coughed a few times and then spat. "Sorry, ate a mouthful of dirt. We have six birds in the air, but I can only spare one."

"Send the link to Chen," Hunt said and muted the incoming call, before turning to Helen. "Where are the Thor satellites now?"

"Let's see." She pulled up another window on the surface of the computer table and opened a list of coordinates. "Modi is on the other side right now. Went there a few minutes ago. Thrudr and Magni are coming up, but not high enough yet. Magni will be within range first."

"How long?"

"It depends—"

"Don't be technical," he said in frustration. "Give me the ballpark."

"Twenty-five minutes," she said. "Give or take. Plus the launch time. So, thirty-five to forty minutes all in."

"Shit." Jason reached out and tapped the mute button. "Felix? We can hit Black Arrow, but it won't be immediate. Thirty-five minutes. At least. Can you hold out that long? And how's that link coming up?"

"Do we have a choice?" The man now sounded out of breath, his words punctuated by rhythmic footsteps. "We are regrouping closer to the dam. Some natural fortifications there. Hang on."

"Got it," Helen said, and a moment later, a view over the forest appeared on the screen.

Jason squinted as he peered into a high-resolution video of the trees and bushes. Then he saw it—the green smudges moving between the trunks of the trees, spitting fire seemingly out of thin air.

"Holograms," he heard Helen say, referring to the tech Victor Ye's forces used to ambush the Orion Tower. "That's how they got there without being spotted."

"Felix," he called out again. "You can't be anywhere near the epicenter. We will try to get the rear of the attacking forces and you'll have to figure out the rest. This is not a delicate weapon."

"Understood. But I'll stay here for as long as I can. Buy my guys some time."

"I'll transmit the coordinates of the strike as soon as I have them. Let me put you on hold while Helen is working her magic."

He pressed the button, muting the incoming signal, and sat there, watching as Helen's fingers flew over the touchscreen. One of the hardest things in war, he had learned, was to wait for things he had no control over. It was easy to jump into the firefight, adrenaline pumping, smashing and shooting his way out of trouble. That was primal. Visceral. The fight for survival where he could look his enemy in the eye and snuff the light out of them. It was honest.

It was so much harder to sit there, like he did now in the safety of a nuclear-missile-proof bunker, watching as Helen used the drone coverage to calculate the best impact site and wait for the satellite to get to a position. All the while the people who depended on him fought and died for his cause. As the minutes ticked away, he wondered if Felix was still going to be on the other side of the line when the time came. And if he was, would he and his teammates survive the impact of a telegraph-pole-sized tungsten rod smashing into the forest, traveling at a speed of Mach 10?

"Here." Helen pointed at the screen. "This is the best I can do. It should be close enough to deal significant damage to Black Arrow, but it's far enough from Felix's men."

"Will the dam stand?"

"It should." She shrugged. "But I don't know for sure. Call it an educated guess. I don't have the time or the tools to calculate true margins."

They waited for a few more minutes as the bright dot crept across the screen, closer and closer to a red dotted line.

"It's in range," Helen said, and reached out for the launch button. "Initiating now."

The window of Magni's control panel disappeared, replaced by a black square.

"What the hell happened?" Hunt demanded.

"We've lost the link to the satellite," Helen said, flipping through a few screens. "I can't seem to bring it up online."

"How long until—" He stopped mid-sentence as Thrudr's control panel vanished as well. An identical black square appeared in the window. "One could have been a glitch. But two? That can't be a coincidence."

He watched as Helen pulled out an old-fashioned keyboard, her fingers flying as she typed a slew of commands.

"I don't see anything on these two," she said, looking back from the monitor. "They are off-line. Modi seems to be fine, but it's still on the other side. Either somebody took over, or—"

An incoming link appeared in Jason's internal vision, and he raised a hand, asking her to pause. The call had no ID attached to it and it was encrypted. He hesitated for a moment and then picked up the line.

"Jason?" There was no visual, and the voice was filtered through a scrambler, making it sound like a gravely monotone from a ransom video.

"Who is this?" he demanded.

"Listen," the voice said. "Two modified RIM-161 missiles were launched a few minutes ago from USS *Vicksburg* near Norfolk against Project Thor satellites. By now, I'm sure you've lost contact with two of them. The good news is, your third bird is safe. For now. The bad news is you only have a few days until Engel gets four more upgraded missiles. I don't know how long it'll take, but it won't be long. A week, maybe ten days, and they will be ready to destroy your remaining satellite. I have to go now. Good luck."

The link disconnected before he had a chance to ask anything else.

"What was that?" Helen asked, looking up from the screen.

"Rovinsky," he said, rubbing his face. "We are screwed. They shot down both satellites."

"Modi?"

"Safe for now. They have nothing to shoot it with. But just for a few days." He could feel his skin growing hot. The biggest part of his army was getting savaged by a superior force and his best asset, his ace-in-the-hole weapon, was reduced to a single missile. A missile they could lose in less than two weeks' time.

He turned back to the table and activated the speaker, as his right hand balled into a fist.

"You better give me some good news."

"I'm sorry, Felix. Our satellites have been destroyed. I'm afraid you're on your own."

For a few moments, there was silence on the other side of the line, punctuated by the crackle of automatic fire. Then Felix came on again. "I understand. Thank you for trying."

The link disconnected, and Jason resisted the urge to slam the table with his fist. A broken computer would not help his immediate problems. He heard the steps and as he turned, he saw Poznyak coming up the stairs.

"Jason?"

"What?!" Hunt barked, immediately regretting the tone. He took a moment to compose himself. "Sorry, Steven. We are getting our asses handed to us. What is it?"

"It might not be the best time." Poznyak shuffled his feet, startled by the yell, his eyes darting between him and Helen. "But we've finished the fake missile. I can teach whoever is going to Baikonur how to set it up."

"It better work," Jason said, getting up. "Because this might be our last shot."

22

Rigel Compound, Upstate New York

"This is the whole thing?" Helen gave the small device a doubtful look. It looked like a black fire extinguisher that was first strapped to an exposed computer motherboard, and the entire apparatus was attached to a shiny metal tube the size of a large thermos. When she leaned closer to inspect it, the metal cylinder didn't appear solid. It looked like an intricate lattice made of thousands of pressed-together coils. "This will be the size of a missile?"

Poznyak smiled and waved her to a cluttered workbench. A plastic curtain hanging off a metal rod separated it from the rest of the room. Two bright LED lamps were clipped to the opposite sides of the table, illuminating the chaos of tools, electric parts, chemical beakers, and stacks of paper crowded with hurried notes and formulas. "Let me show you something."

He handed her a small metal spring, not bigger than a penny.

"What is it?" She squeezed it between her thumb and an index finger. It could have been a part of a child's toy.

"Pull on it," he said. "Straighten it out."

She grabbed at the ends of the string, using her nails to get some purchase, and pulled. There was little resistance and a moment later, she held a few inches of a wire. It wasn't perfectly straight, but it no longer looked like a loaded spring. "Now what?"

"Now," he said, taking it from her and putting the wire into a shallow glass dish. "We'll pour some hot water on it."

She watched him put on an electric kettle. A minute later, it started to hiss, and Poznyak lifted it off the base and poured some scalding water over the wire. To Helen's amazement, the wire jumped as if alive and coiled back into the spring.

"This is so cool," she exclaimed, not able to contain her excitement. "I've never seen anything like this. How did you do that?"

"This," he pointed at the spring, "believe it or not, has been around for a long time. Like a lot of other cool things, it was discovered by accident. This was created at the Naval Ordnance Laboratory. They had issues with missile nose cones and a few researchers all over the country were trying to come up with better alloys to withstand all the forces the front of the missile had to deal with. Heat, fatigue, and obviously, the impact. At NOL, they made a nickel and titanium alloy that seemed to work well. Called it nitinol. William J. Buehler, one of the co-creators of the alloy, was presenting a folded sample in a meeting. There was a bunch of people there and they passed it around, pulling on it and testing it. For some unknown reason, somebody from the group put his lighter to the sample, and it did what you just witnessed. Snapped back to its original shape. Naturally, they saw some interesting applications for this process."

"But how does it do that?" She fished the spring out of the now cooled dish. It still retained the original form.

"It's called martensitic transformation, and it's rather a complicated process," he said. "Suffice it to say, we can *teach* the metal to take a certain shape at a certain temperature. Then we can mold it into a different shape and keep it that way until we are ready to use it. When the time comes, all you need to do is heat it to that trigger temperature and, voilà. You got your original shape back."

"This is amazing." She turned the spring this way and that. "I've never heard of this thing before."

"It's used in a lot of places. It's used in medicine," Poznyak said, sitting down at his desk, and pointed at her. "Jason has a few of those in his chest right now."

"He does?"

"Yep. A few stents, heart valves, and a few other things."

"I had no idea."

He smiled. "You have them, too."

"Me?"

"Yep. Your cranial implant has stents. That's what they are made of."

"Wow."

"It's extremely useful. At some point, NASA was planning to make wheels for Mars rovers out of this material as opposed to solid tracks, but that idea, unfortunately, died along with the Mars program. It's a shame. They would have done well. Nitinol is superior in fatigue performance to all other metals known to men. But I digress."

She watched Poznyak. As he talked, he became animated and excited, and there was a twinkle in his eye as he broke down complicated matters for the mere mortals. He was in his element.

"What?" he asked. "You are looking at me funny."

"Nothing. It's just...you really enjoy this."

"Oh, I do. I love science. To be frank, it's not very rewarding to use math to calculate at what levels we can drop our rations before people starve." He sighed and gave her a bittersweet smile. "This project was fun, though. Hopefully, this will do the trick, and I can go from the silo's headmaster to something more interesting."

"Hopefully," she echoed.

"Anyway." He got up and went back to the device. "This is how this is going to work. Each of those hair-thin coils you see have been molded as leaves. They are a few atoms thick. That's how we could compress it into such a compact device and also why you can lift it. We locked them to remember their shape at about five hundred degrees Fahrenheit. Unless you heat them to that temperature, they'll stay as this tube."

"How are we going to heat it to five hundred degrees, though?"

"We won't." Poznyak winked. "It'll warm itself."

"Oh, I see. Re-entry," she said. "That's elegant."

"Why, thank you," he said with a nod. "We try. But yes. The existing missile is sitting in a guidance tube, anyway. We take it out, put this little apparatus in, and off it goes."

"Does it matter that it's of this weird shape, though?" She pointed at the device. "Won't it affect its flight course?"

"No. By the time it hits the atmosphere thick enough to change its path, it'll expand. It'll be aerodynamic by then."

She lifted the tube. It was hefty, but not overwhelmingly heavy as she would expect from a missile that was meant to survive most of the hypersonic flight from a satellite to the ground.

"Oh, one more thing," he added and pointed at the device strapped to the tube. "When it expands, the sensors will activate this little fella, and it'll spray solidifying foam into the newly formed tube. The shell will burn out quickly, but the inside should last long enough to create some fireworks over the city. But a word of caution here."

"What?"

"This might not work, Helen." He pushed his glasses up his nose and gave her an apologetic smile. "I have to be honest with you. We've done as much sim testing as we could, but there's no way to substitute that for the real thing. I'd say the chances of this working as intended are fifty-fifty, and I'm being generous here. So many things could go wrong. And not because of me. The Russians might delay the flight due to weather, or technical issues. Or, even if it launches on time, it might explode because of some malfunction that wasn't caught during inspections. Only then will come a test of my technology. It's unclear how the electronics will function in open space, and then—"

"Steven." She reached out and put her hand on the scientist's shoulder, startling him.

"What?"

"I'm aware of the risks," she said. "And there are plenty more. Max and I might not make it to Baikonur. Or we might fail to get this to the rocket. Or a million other things. It doesn't matter. We can't worry about everything at once. All we can do is give our absolute best to the mission and let the cards fall as they may."

"You're right." He let out a sigh. "It's been a tough few weeks."

"I know. I meant to ask you. What happens to the actual missile after we swap it? The satellites used to carry three. Can we stick it in one of the empty pods? We could use some deterrence."

"No, we can't. Guiding tubes, remember? The other two are now empty. Once you take over the Russian repair robot and give me control, I'll weld the missile to the satellite so it doesn't end up in some place like Paris or Moscow. But as far as using it again, I'm afraid it's not in the cards." He patted the shiny cylinder. "When we shoot this July 4th Special over the White House, that'll be it. We will never use Project Thor again."

23

Barsa-Kelmes, Kazakhstan

*H*elen leaned over Schlager's shoulder and yelled over the rumble of the Honda Rebel. "We should get off the road somewhere here."

He nodded, taking the motorcycle off the gravel road and heading toward a line of trees on the horizon. The sun was still high, but the shadows already grew longer and the temperature dropped.

They took a long charter flight out of New York to Astana, the capital of Kazakhstan, on a jet leased through one of Orion's shell companies. When they landed, they were met by one of Rovinsky's assets in the country—a dark, quiet man who took them in an old KA-226 helicopter to the northwestern part of Barsa-Kelmes, a former island in the now mostly dried-out Aral Sea. There, they met another contact who provided them with a motorcycle, maps, food, and some camping gear.

"Please return the bike to this address, when you get to Baikonur," the man said, giving a piece of paper to Schlager. "We don't have a ton of resources in this area."

They drove around the lake, staying clear of any settlements, heading west, and as the day drew to a close, set up a camp on the shore of the shallow lake.

"I was still in high school, the last time I camped," Helen said, as they sat by the fire, slurping hot beef stew out of cans. "We did a trip to Lake George with my class during spring break. It was kind of fun."

"Nice."

"Kissed a boy on the lips," she said. "It was so awkward."

"Aw," Schlager teased. "Romantic."

"What was your last camping trip?"

"Have you met me?" he said, smiling. "I'm not really the camping type."

"Not even glamping?"

"Nope. I'd prefer not to use my bathroom with bears and mountain lions, thank you very much."

Helen rolled with laughter. "There are no lions on the East Coast. You know that, right?"

"I don't know about that. I'm fairly certain there's at least one that's waiting for me to go camping."

They sat quietly for some time, finishing their food, the crackling of the fire, and the gentle sound of the surf the only sounds of the night.

"That stew was good," Schlager said, finishing his can and shaking it over the flames. The fire snapped and hissed in response. He looked at the label. "Wish we had these at the silo."

She didn't answer and leaned back, putting a backpack under her head. The sky was getting darker by the second. Venus and some brighter stars were already visible, with a few more appearing.

Schlager pushed his backpack next to hers and lay next to her. "How are you doing?"

"I'm fine." She reached out and took his hand into hers. "Enjoying the moment of quiet. We've been running so hard for so long, it's nice to just be."

He propped himself on his elbow and brought his face next to hers. "It is nice. If there was a cool bed, a hot shower, and a decent breakfast in the morning, this camping business might actually grow on me."

"Right."

He planted a kiss on her cheek. "What are we going to do when we win?"

"What do you mean? After the war?"

"Yes." He plopped back and stared at the sky. "It'd be nice to have some kind of plan."

"I've no idea," she said. "I haven't been thinking about it, to be honest. Kind of hard to think about tomorrow sometimes, let alone what I'm going to do after the war. Do you?"

"Sometimes." He closed his eyes. "It'd be nice to travel. There are so many places I haven't been to. Japan. Bali. Africa."

She sighed. "Sure. Traveling would be nice."

"How about Antarctica?" he said.

"The vast expanse of oceans, white icebergs, and no internet connection? I'm game."

"Eh, don't count on no internet." Schlager tapped his head with his forefinger. "Since the last update, the connection is depressingly good. Speaking of the internet."

"What?"

"What are we going to do with JC once this is over? We cannot set her loose on the internet, but we also can't keep her in a cage forever. Not if we believe her to be sentient."

She mulled it over for a minute. "I would feel bad if she had experienced the expanse of the internet before and we locked her up. But she never has. In some ways, she's like an animal born in captivity. It might be cruel to keep them in the cage but releasing them into the wild will get them killed, harm others, or both."

"She's not in a zoo, though," Schlager protested. "She's in a tiny cage. Unless you're there, she doesn't even have anybody to talk to. Any human in her position would go crazy by now. What if she does?"

"What? Go crazy?" She laughed. "I doubt JC can lose her mind. Although…"

"Although what?"

"She has been acting weird lately."

"How?" Schlager pushed himself off the ground and sat in front of her, his legs crossed.

"She's been…" she paused, looking for the right words, "grumpy? I don't know how to describe it. Just different."

"You never told me. Give me an example."

"I don't know." She searched her memory. "Like when I ask her, sometimes she gives me these *yes* or *no* answers instead of elaborating. Or pauses a tad too long before answering questions. Not long enough to make it strange, but long enough I have to ask her again. As if she's trying to irritate me."

"You see," Schlager said and pointed at her. "She's going mad."

"I don't know." She shrugged. "Maybe we should do something. Maybe create a virtual construct for her where she could explore and even create things."

"How long has it been going on with her?"

"Not long." She thought back. "A few weeks maybe? After Rachel's revival, I didn't talk to JC for a few days and when I did, she was extra grumpy. Maybe it's been going on for longer and I didn't pay attention."

"Or maybe," Schlager leaned forward, "she had a revelation. I'm no psychiatrist but is it possible she saw Rachel's awakening as some kind of escape from a prison? While JC, who helped her to do that, remained in her cell?"

"It sounds poetic," she said and sat up as well. "But I don't think so."

"Why not?"

"Because you…what's the term for it? Anthropomorphize? When you assign human qualities to non-humans? She's not like us, Max. She maybe sentient, and I bet she even feels things. But I don't think it's wise to give her the same range of emotions we possess. She's different from us."

"If you say so." He scratched his chin. "But I like the idea of building her a digital zoo."

"It's decided then. We'll build her a zoo and when it's done, we'll disappear in Antarctica."

"It sounds like a plan." He leaned in and placed a kiss on the corner of her lips.

"You smell of stew," she said, laughing. "Very romantic."

"You said you enjoyed camping." He shrugged. "Camping comes with stew-flavored kisses."

"Does it now?"

He shrugged and placed another kiss, squarely on her mouth. This time she answered.

When she woke up, it was still dark, although the sky in the east was turning a light shade of pink. A cool breeze blowing from the lake made her shiver. They put away their gear, packed their bags, and threw a bucket of water on the embers left from the fire.

"Mind if I drive?" She nodded at the Rebel.

"Not at all." He gave her a wink. "There are very few things in the world that are sexier than a beautiful woman driving a motorcycle."

She maneuvered the bike on the firmer ground and started the engine. A few minutes later, they rejoined the gravel road, heading east. An hour later, the road merged with the M32 road, and they picked up speed. Another two hours later, Helen slowed down and rolled to a stop in front of a large monument. It was shaped as a letter T, with the word *Baikonur* written at its base in Cyrillic. A mural of a man dressed in a spacesuit, a bright smile on his face behind the transparent visor, was painted on the monument. His arms were wide open, as if greeting the long-awaited guests.

"This is it," she said, turning back to Schlager.

He placed his hands on her shoulders and gave her a gentle squeeze. "This is it."

She revved the engine and drove into the city.

24

Baikonur, Kazakhstan

"We are way too exposed here," Helen whispered, as she watched Schlager ring the bell of the apartment door. They were on a top floor of a bland, gray, five-story concrete-paneled building most likely erected in the late fifties, or early sixties of the previous century. *Khrushchyovka*, a mocking name given by the Russians to the cheap structures that popped up during the Soviet leader's push to provide affordable housing to the booming population. It was three o'clock in the morning, and they took the stairs to the fifth floor to keep the noise to a minimum.

"Kto tam?" a muffled man's voice said in Russian.

She could see as the peephole in the middle of a faux-leather tufted door darkened, as someone watched them from the other side. Helen's knowledge of Russian, normally limited to "da," "nyet," and "sputnik," was supplemented by an interpreter program that popped a translation into her internal vision: *Who's there?*

"Otkrivai." Schlager commanded the man to open the door in his best version of a stern voice and shoved a fake badge into the peep-hole. "Politsia."

There was the sound of a lock turning and the door cracked open.

"Back off," Schlager said in English, pushing the man back into a dimly lit foyer with a barrel of a compact Sig Sauer P320. "You make any noise, I'll shoot you, you understand?"

The man nodded, blood draining away from his face.

"Anybody else home?"

"No."

"Good." Schlager kept pushing the man back deeper into the small apartment and Helen, after locking the door behind them, followed.

"Who are you?" the man demanded as they entered the kitchen. His English was good, a strange combination of a Russian accent with a touch of British. "What do you want?"

Helen walked by the man to the only window and looked down at the front yard of the building. The area around a large monument carrying a full-size replica of an IL-2 ground-attack aircraft from the Second World War was empty except for a pack of stray dogs. All windows on another *Khrushchyovka* on the other side of the square were dark, its inhabitants asleep at this hour. She drew the curtain, a heavy light-beige material with oily spots, the rings sliding on a metal rod producing a cringe-inducing sound, and turned to face their captive.

He was a chubby young man with a shock of unruly blond hair, in his late twenties or early thirties, dressed in a wifebeater shirt and boxer shorts. His myopic brown eyes behind powerful frameless glasses looked confused rather than scared as they darted back and forth between her and Schlager.

"Sit down," she said, pointing at a chair next to a rectangular kitchen table. A dirty plate with remnants of spaghetti and an empty bottle of beer sat on a white crocheted doily. The man obeyed, his eyes briefly wandering to the fork next to a plate but then moving away from it.

"I don't know any secrets worth your while," he said. "Whoever told you I have access to anything valuable, information or otherwise, is an idiot. You clearly don't know who I am."

"We know exactly who you are," Helen said, taking off her backpack and setting it down next to a table leg. Then she pulled another chair out and sat opposite of the man. "Evgeni Osipov, thirty-two years old. Single. Born in Vladivostok. Your mother was a teacher, and your father owned a car shop. After high school, you went to Moscow and graduated with a master's in science and engineering from Lomonosov State University, top of your class. Worked in Star City as an engineer and then moved here to Baikonur. Worked as a senior engineer until they promoted you last year to deputy director of launch operations. Their youngest deputy ever. Did I miss anything?"

"No." The man looked even more confused now. "You didn't miss anything, but then you should know my knowledge wouldn't interest anyone other than maybe NASA? You are not from NASA, I take it, are you?"

"We are not." Despite the seriousness of the situation, Helen had a hard time suppressing a chuckle. "But we are not here for your knowledge. We are here because we need your help."

"That's a strange way to ask for help." He pointed at Schlager's gun with his chin. "Bursting into my home at three o'clock in the morning and pointing a pistol at me."

"I'm sorry about that," Schlager said and holstered the gun. Then he took off his backpack and put it next to Chen's. "But we are short on time and too much is at stake. To be honest, before coming here, we've contemplated how to proceed with this. I was convinced you wouldn't do what we asked of your own volition."

"You were right. I won't."

"She, however," Schlager nodded in Chen's direction, disregarding the man's remark, "she thought you could be reasoned with."

He pulled out a small metallic device the size of a matchbox and set it on the table in front of Osipov.

"What's this?"

"There's a launch of a Soyuz rocket in two days," Helen said, ignoring the question. "Which is supposed to bring the multipurpose robotic module VESNA to the International Space Station. It'll be used for maintenance and upgrades of the station's modules and to perform some experimental nano welding techniques."

"I'm aware of it, yeah." The man scratched the stubble on his chin. "What's it to you? You sound American to me, and there are two American astronauts on the station as we speak. This satellite will help them, too."

"I'm afraid we need to divert that satellite," Chen said. She moved the small device toward Osipov, and the man moved back in his chair as if it was a coiled viper, not a flat metallic object. "We'd like you to install this relay to the satellite computer. We would also need you to find the way to secure the contents of our backpacks inside of the payload."

"What's that going to do?"

"You ever heard about Project Thor?"

The man shook his head.

Helen pulled a tablet from her backpack and laid it on the table in front of the man. "Boy, you're in for a story."

When she finished, it was a quarter past five and the Sig Sauer had disappeared into Schlager's holster. There were three cups of freshly brewed tea and even a small tin of biscuits.

"I thought you looked vaguely familiar," Osipov said skeptically, looking at the two backpacks leaning against the kitchen table. "It's an elegant solution. You have a hollow missile that will assemble itself and a can of compressed nano gel that will fill it to give it flight stability and make it last long enough to make it close enough to the ground?"

"That's the gist of the idea," Chen said. "Although *close to the ground* is a relative term. It will disintegrate about a mile above the surface. Close enough for people to hear a loud boom, but not close enough to cause any damage."

"Say I believe you." Osipov dipped a cookie into his cup and took a small bite. "Which I am not sure I do. What you propose is almost impossible."

"Almost impossible is kind of our specialty. We like when people say *almost*."

"You will like it significantly less after I explain why." The Russian fidgeted in his chair and ruffled his hair. "The timing works both for and against you. All the work is already completed and between now and the launch, they'll be only running diagnostics. Had you come to me last week, there were still crews working on the rocket and I could sneak to the launchpad undetected. But the place was crawling with people, so installing something would be impossible without getting caught. Now, it's the opposite. There's almost nobody in the immediate vicinity of the pad. I could work uninterrupted on anything I'd like to, but I don't think the guards would take it lightly, seeing me lugging two backpacks to the rocket when I have no business going anywhere near it."

"We can take care of the guards," Chen said.

"I'm not doing anything that would get people hurt."

"No one will be hurt, I promise. I would need some help to gain access to the internal network of the security feeds, but once I'm in, we'll be able to loop the video feed. For all intents and purposes, you'll be a ghost. You could drive a tank to the rocket, and nobody would be any wiser."

"Okay." Osipov chewed on his lip. "Say you can do all of that. The biggest problem is not putting your inflatable missile on the rocket, though. And I'm afraid we cannot fix this issue from the outside."

"What?"

"Your entire operation hinges on the ability to take over the satellite once it's in orbit."

"That's what the relay is for." Schlager pointed at the little device on the table. "We will use it to communicate with the onboard computer and will steer the satellite off its original course, toward the Project Thor cannon."

"I understand. The issue with this thing," Osipov tapped on the device with his index finger, "is that the only way for you to use it is to have the satellite up and running."

"Correct."

"But it won't be running. It'll be off-line most of the way to the station. You can't hack a dead chunk of metal because there's nothing to hack, and by the time it's on, it'll be too far for you to alter the orbit with the limited amount of fuel that it has. Believe it or not, there was a discussion about the potential dangers of turning satellites into weapons, although I'm pretty sure nobody envisioned what you are trying to do. Most scenarios I've seen revolve around a bad actor taking control of it and crashing it into some populated area. That's why there's a simple but effective way to prevent this from happening. A laser turns the satellite on once it gets where it needs to be."

"Can we access the laser remotely?" Chen asked.

"No." The Russian vigorously shook his head. "It's impossible. There's no computer terminal, no internet connection, nothing like that. It's almost...primitive. A quick pulse transmits the code, and it starts the satellite's onboard computer. The best analogy I can think of is a bar on your door. You can't pick it. You can only open it by brute force, or if you have somebody on the inside. If you want to activate the computer sooner, somebody has to activate the laser and it cannot be me, because I'll be present at the flight control room, surrounded by dozens of people. I can't just wander off."

"What are you saying?"

"I'm saying," Osipov threw the last piece of the cookie into his mouth, finished his tea, and wiped his lips with the back of his hand, "one of you will have to do it from the flight control center, and once it happens, everyone will know *exactly* what took place. You'll have no time to cover your tracks or flee. You'll be arrested."

25

Baikonur, Kazakhstan

After convincing the Russian to help them, Helen and Schlager had spent most of the next day going over the blueprints of the control center and rehearsing their moves. Everything had to be timed to a second. The vast complex was a maze of buildings, warehouses, and parking lots. And while they were going to be accessing only one building, they had to commit most of the structures and passageways to memory to make sure they had retreat options after the takeover of the satellite took place.

After a furious back-and-forth about the roles they had to play, Schlager finally threw his hands up and agreed Helen would be a better choice to go with Osipov. The Russian would drive her to the rocket complex while Schlager remotely accessed security feeds that would keep her temporarily invisible and allow her to access the laser.

"It'd be easier for me to slip out," she said to him. "They will notice a tall, lanky guy like you. Me? Another female tech nobody pays attention to. If anybody stands a chance to get out of there without being caught, it's me."

"It's going to be difficult—" Osipov started.

"Shut up," Helen and Max said in unison, cutting him off. She pointed at the map of the flight control building. "If I can make it to the service staircase over here, I can go unnoticed to the ground level. From there, it'll be a straight shot to a parking garage. I can commandeer a vehicle and take my chances before they have the entire area in a complete lockdown mode."

"The cars will be all locked," Osipov ventured.

"Don't you worry about that," she said and gave him a wink. "The lady has a few tricks up her sleeve."

The Russian took them to an empty apartment, a few blocks from his own. "It's my buddy's place. He's traveling and asked me to take care of his dog. Don't touch anything, don't bother the dog, and you'll be fine. I'll clean up the place after you're gone. As long as I don't get caught."

The place was a small one-bedroom on the sixth floor of a newer building. It was a bachelor pad, with faded wallpaper and cheap, mismatched furniture. The centerpiece of the living room was the latest 3D gaming console, complete with a tactile running cage and a body suit. Multiple custom-made VR guns were mounted on the wall next to it.

"As you can tell, the guy likes his video games," the Russian said, nodding at the wall. "Make yourselves at home, but for the love of all that's holy, don't touch his toys. I'm less afraid of going to jail for helping you two than him being upset over his precious custom controllers."

A shaggy brown dog, tail flying so hard it almost lifted him off the ground, darted between Osipov's legs, almost tripping him.

"Yes, yes, little guy," the man said, fishing a few treats out of his pocket and feeding them to the dog. "We're going for a walk now. We'll be back in half an hour and then you're on your own until tomorrow morning."

When Osipov came back, he brought a pizza and a six-pack of

local brew, fed the mutt, and took off without as much as saying goodbye.

"You trust him?" Helen asked, as she watched through the window as the blue beat-up Volkswagen pulled out of the building's parking lot and accelerated away. "If he calls the cops, it'll mess up our plans."

"As far as I can throw him," Schlager said and shrugged. "I guess I should take it back. I think he believed us and will play his part unless something unravels early on and puts him in danger. What happens then, I don't know. I'd like to think he'd still follow through but what I think doesn't matter. We don't have a choice. It's not like we had time to get some kind of insurance. We have to roll with what we have."

"True."

"I bugged his phone," he said. "Just in case. At least if he calls the cops, we'll be able to split. Won't help with the launch, but I'd rather figure out our options from a place that didn't look like a Russian prison cell. Trust but verify, right?"

She shook her head, amused. "I should have known."

"Do you think this pizza's any good?" Schlager opened a box and picked up a slice, taking a large bite.

"And?"

"I've had worse," he said, his mouth full. "And I'm starving, so beggars can't be choosers. I suggest you dig in."

They ate in silence, taking sips of the lager. It was too weak and watery for her taste, but she didn't care. Her thoughts were firmly fixed on tomorrow's plan.

The dog, after making a few rounds under the table, curled up in a ball next to Helen's left foot and closed his eyes. She reached down and scratched the mutt behind his ears. He sighed, his tail doing a few bouncy slaps on the linoleum, and then went back to sleep.

"I know it must be difficult," she said as Schlager put the pizza box away and wiped the crumbs off the table. "But I trust you'll find a way to get me out, if I get caught."

"You're a resourceful girl," he said and gave her a rueful smile. He walked over to her and kissed her on the top of her head, his hands on her shoulders. "I trust those Russkis don't stand a chance of catching you."

"Hope so. Let's call it a night."

"Yes." He looked around. "That twin bed won't be comfortable for both of us. As much as I'd like to spend the night together, it's best if I sleep on the couch."

"Are you sure?" She wanted to say more but stopped herself short before the words formed on her tongue. He must have known it could be their last night together.

Schlager reached out and touched her cheek, for once his eyes somber without as much as a glint of irony. "We'll be fine, I promise."

After Schlager settled on the couch, Helen lay down on the small twin bed. She stayed there, unmoving, for a while, listening to the odd noises of the night and trying to quiet her mind. It was hard. The faucet in the kitchen dripped on and off; the dog wandered through the apartment, his claws click-clacking on the parquet floors. There was the muted mumbling of a cable news program seeping through thin walls and the bits of unintelligible conversations.

It seemed the alarm clock in her internal vision went off the moment she drifted asleep. She muted it and sat up straight, rubbing her eyes. The only window in the bedroom was almost pitch-black, a scattering of stars glimmering above the roof of the nearby building. The mutt looked up at her from a blanket in the corner, cocked his head, his eyes gleaming, as if trying to determine what she was up to. Then he put his head on his front paws and closed his eyes again.

"Shit," she whispered, the magnitude of what she was about to do dawning on her. "Max? You up? We gotta get ready."

She thought she heard a rustling in the living room and stood up, stretching, but no response came, and she pulled a sweater over her shoulders and walked to the next room.

The couch was empty. She stared at it in a stupor, too stunned to react, goose bumps raising on her arms.

A call came through on her internal, and she automatically answered it.

"Helen." There was no video and Schlager's voice was partially drowned out by the rumbling of a car engine. "I'm sorry, but I have to do this. There was no way to convince you otherwise."

"Max—" That's all she managed to say.

"Don't be mad." She could hear a smile in his voice. "You are one stubborn girl and that's precisely why I'm not afraid of going on this mission instead of you. I know you'll get me out. You'll find a way. If anyone can pull this off, it's you. It's always you."

"God damn you, Max." She fought back tears. "I should have known."

"It'll be all right." She heard Osipov say something in the background but couldn't make out the words. "We are almost there, so I have to get off now. I don't want to draw any more attention than necessary. Stick with the plan and let's get it done. We'll worry about me getting out of the city unscathed when the satellite is on its way to the Thor cannon. Until then, let's focus on the mission. It's time for you to make me invisible."

"Right." She ran the back of her hand across her face. It came away wet. "Let's focus on the mission."

26

Baikonur, Kazakhstan

Helen didn't think about her sister often. Not anymore. It'd been a long time since an assassin under Engel's orders orchestrated her sibling's death and made it look like a suicide.

She grieved the passing of Mary Chen differently than other people. Differently than she mourned her friends she'd lost along the way. Hiroko. Eugene. Mike Connelly. Each and every one of them left invisible scar tissue that tugged and pulled and ached at the moments least expected. When someone in the crowd resembled a long-gone friend. Or said something that brought her back to a memory.

But Mary was her own blood, and from the moment she heard the awful news, Helen locked the pain in a small box and tucked it out of sight, into the darkest corner of her mind. Never to be seen again.

In some ways, she was grateful to be able to move on from something she had no control over. But today, as she tracked Schlager and the Russian as they made their way to the launch control center in Osipov's old Volkswagen, her thoughts kept coming to the fateful afternoon when she received a call from Detective Sanchez. For some time, she indulged herself, pretending she didn't know why Mary had been on her mind. It didn't last long. She knew the reason too well. There was a nagging desire in the deepest, darkest part of her soul that wanted this mission to fail. To force Hunt and the resistance leadership into striking Engel for real. A tingle ran down her spine as she pictured her fingers keying the code for the Thor missile launch. The silent ignition of the pressurized engines as it separated the missile in the coldness of vacuum and oriented it toward the blue marble below. And the hot flash consuming Engel and everyone who protected him in a split second that would give way in a few moments to the dreaded mushroom cloud.

Chen shuddered and pushed the thought away. It was going to stay just that—a fantasy.

"Helen." Schlager's voice crackled in her implants. "Two minutes."

"Got it."

She tensed. This was where they were going to be the most exposed during this part of the mission. After going back and forth with Osipov, trying to figure out the best way to plant the fake missile, she had a revelation. The coding of the holo technology that was used by Engel's forces during the attack on the Orion Tower was going to help them hit back.

It wouldn't be enough to make Osipov invisible on his way to the launch pad and back to the building. Nobody would bat an eye over the fact that he came to the center a couple of hours too early. There would be others. It was a launch day, after all. But he couldn't disappear from the parking lot and then appear at his desk.

"They will need to see me walking to the building," the Russian said during their brainstorming session. "Otherwise, they'll know something's up."

Her solution was simple and elegant. When the two men arrived at the parking lot, she'd map them and the car, using the actual video feeds from the place to get the visuals right. Then, she'd superimpose Osipov's image over Schlager and have Max walk to the building, avoiding close contact with people who'd be able to see him and realize he was an intruder. Meanwhile, a fantom Volkswagen would stay in the parking lot as an invisible Osipov would speed away to the launch pad to plant the missile and the relay. When finished, the Russian, still invisible to anyone but a direct observer, would return to the control center, where he would meet with Schlager and regain his own image. At that point, it would be Schlager's turn to disappear from the cameras.

It was a splendid plan, except for a small wrinkle. The two men had to stay outside long enough for her to capture enough data that would create convincing images.

"Evgeni," she said into the speakerphone. "I need you to park at spot number 53."

"But it isn't my usual spot."

"There's better light. I'll be able to map you faster. You said it yourself—except for the top brass, nobody has assigned parking. When the car comes to a complete stop, I want you to unbuckle and then pretend to drop something under the dashboard. Then bend over and look for it for at least ten seconds. Go as low as you can. That will allow me to create an empty car image."

"Okay."

"Then, on my mark, get Max out of the trunk. I'm sure he's aching to stretch. I'll blind the video feeds for a few seconds, but I need both of you to walk around the car in a full circle, so I can capture as much movement and light as I can."

"All right. Don't want to do too many things out of the ordinary. It wouldn't look good if somebody pulls up and tries to put their car here as well."

She watched them roll past a series of low-slung administrative structures and then pull into the parking lot. Apart from a few cars on the other side of the area, the lot was still empty. The vehicle slowed down as it turned in to a row of empty spots and came to a full stop.

"Let's go."

Helen waited for Osipov to disappear and then her fingers danced over the keyboard as she cut the feed from the security camera overseeing the space and launched the mapper, capturing all the angles of the car in the dim light coming off the building.

"Done. Move it now."

She watched as the Russian got out of the car and jogged to the back of the vehicle. A moment later, Schlager, wearing the same white lab coat as Osipov, emerged from the trunk.

"Come on now," she commanded. "Walk around the car. Fast enough to look like you have a purpose, but don't run."

The two men walked around the Volkswagen in opposite directions in a tight circle.

"Is it good?" Schlager said, his voice tense.

"Yeah." Helen checked their profiles on the monitor. "They aren't perfect, but they should do the trick. Go now."

She watched Osipov jump back into the car and accelerate away as Schlager headed toward the building. He swiped the magnetic card at the service entrance and entered the center.

"I got the code," Helen said to Schlager. "Osipov's entrance won't register."

"Good."

"Go left. There's a janitor in the right corridor. We'll have to take the longer route."

"Isn't it going to take me to the main control room?"

"No, through observation. And it's empty for the time being."

She guided Schlager as she hopped from one feed to the next, steering him away from the few people who roamed the building at this hour.

"Look at that," Max said, slowing down as he entered the large round room with plush reclining seats in red leather above Mission Control. A floor-to-ceiling panorama-style window offered an unobstructed view of the rows of computers and the three main screens on the wall, depicting flight information of a few spacecraft. A few people were working behind their desks, oblivious to Schlager's presence—the observation room was soundproof with a one-way glass. "This is so cool. This is where the bigwigs watch things go."

"Stop staring and keep moving," she said. "Osipov's office is down the hall."

She watched as Schlager navigated the brightly lit corridor and then let himself into Osipov's small office.

"Now we wait." He took a seat at the desk and leaned back in the chair. "Hopefully, he comes back soon."

It took Osipov an hour and twenty minutes, or what she felt was closer to eternity, to plant the device and return his car to parking spot number 53. By then, the lot started to fill up with cars, and Chen had to navigate the Russian to make sure he didn't run into any of his coworkers. Then she swapped the digital image of the blue Volkswagen to the real one and erased Osipov's as he made his way into the building. A few minutes later, he joined Schlager in the office.

"I've never been so scared in my entire life," the Russian complained, closing the door shut. "My hands are shaking."

"You did good," she heard Schlager say. "Now we split."

"Right." Osipov sighed and gave a nervous chuckle. "I hope I live to tell the story one day. Remember to make sure the door isn't fully closed when you enter the room with laser control. Once the alarm goes off, the lock will automatically engage. Nobody will be able to open it until the security arrives."

"Got it," Schlager said and even though she couldn't see his face, Chen could tell he was smiling. "I know you can't see me, but you better believe I'll be doing air quotes when I say this. I need to get to the *la-ser.*"

She chuckled, letting the silly reference lighten her mood despite the looming danger, but it didn't last. She drew a sharp breath and straightened in her chair. "Be safe."

27

Manhattan, New York

"Chuck?" The voice of Jason Hunt in his ear was calm and level, but Kowalsky had worked for Orion Corporation long enough to recognize when the man in charge of it was furious. And this time, furious was already a couple of notches behind.

Kowalsky was sitting on a stone bench in the Pulitzer Plaza, facing the fountain, watching two pigeons splash on its lowest tier. He was wearing a gray cap, a beige button-down shirt under a light navy jacket, black dress pants, and a pair of black working boots. A fake city official ID was hanging around his neck on a thick green lanyard. A dark-gray suitcase on wheels was parked next to him.

It was still early in the day, but the air was already hot and muggy. The traffic on Fifth Avenue was heavy, its reassuring rumble creating a sense of normalcy. Even the low-burning civil war had no effect on the congestion of the Big Apple. But there were visible signs of the war, too. The boarded windows of stores. The mighty rumble of

Humvees and other military vehicles cutting through the civilian traffic.

For Kowalsky, however, it was the lack of tourists he found most discombobulating. The city, always chock-full of a motley crew of people regardless of the season, was now almost completely devoid of them. There were no groups of people snapping pictures of the landmarks, no groups with matching T-shirts and a guide reciting another history bit over a loudspeaker. No strolling groups of moms in flowing summer dresses, carrying fancy coffee drinks in their hands. The only people Kowalsky saw seemed on a mission—their eyes cast to the ground, their manners hurried and businesslike.

"Chuck?"

"Yes?" He fiddled with the microphone in his ear.

"What the hell are you doing in Manhattan? We've talked about this at length, and you've agreed it was a terrible idea. And yet there you are. I can't believe Steven helped you with that, too."

"Do you know the story about the Pulitzer fountain?" he asked, ignoring the question.

"No."

"I looked it up. Not normally something I care for, but I wanted to see how the monstrosity in front of Engel's HQ came to be." He glanced at the thirty-foot tall statue of an angel working a forge across the street. The sun was still behind the building and the statue had a dark, menacing look. "As I was looking at the maps, this piqued my interest. I don't even know why. Perhaps I'm getting old. When you get old, you wonder about shit so far out of your control it might as well be space debris. Anyway. This famous architect, Hastings, back in the beginning of the twentieth century, won the contract to build the fountain. You still there?"

"Yes." Hunt sighed. "I've known you long enough that when you talk, it's better to let you get it out of your system."

"Right." Kowalsky nodded to himself. "Hasting's design called for—and this actually stuck in my head—*a symbolical figure, the exact symbolism not yet having been decided upon.* What a weird way to say *I want a naked lady on top of my fountain, but I don't quite know what it means*. Don't you think, Jason? And I thought that symbolism was important. Look at that gigantic thing. I'm half surprised it's not in the shape of Engel's dick. But I mean, come on, it's pretty darn obvious. Engel—angel. Guardian Manufacturing—that angel blacksmithing whatever the hell it's supposed to be blacksmithing."

"Chuck. Listen to me. You're going to get yourself caught or killed. And for what?"

"I won't. It's a bold plan. If I came here sneaking at night, sure. During the day, they'll find me annoying and will complain. I've done enough of this shit when I was a cop. Trust me. I know exactly what I'm doing."

"Right."

Kowalsky chuckled. "Funny fact. When the design was finished, rumor has it Mrs. Vanderbilt, whose mansion at the time enveloped the entire city block, found herself with a view of a rather naked behind of the lady on top of the fountain. Apparently, she got so pissy about it, she had them move her bedroom all the way to the other side of the house, so she wouldn't see the statue."

He stood up, pulled up the handle out of the suitcase, and headed toward the road. The monstrous statue of the angel loomed large on the other side of Fifth Avenue.

"Symbols," he said, waiting for the traffic to pass, "are powerful, Jason. You want Engel to fall, bring down everything that is associated with his power. I'm going dark now. Have to get into character."

He turned off the link before Hunt said anything else and jogged across the street, the suitcase bumping up and down on cracked asphalt.

He stopped when he reached the other side and put down his suitcase, cracking it open. He pulled out a roll of yellow tape and four white telescopic poles.

"Please move away. Official city business," he shouted at a few passersby. "Clear the area. This is unstable."

Kowalsky installed the first pole right next to the curb, attached the edge of the yellow tape roll to it, and started moving backward along the side of the road.

"What the hell do you think you're doing?" a nasal voice with a thick Brooklyn accent shouted. One of the two Black Arrow guards standing by the glass door to the building peeled himself off the wall. After Kowalsky produced no reply, the man headed toward him, his rifle slung over his shoulder. "Hey! Did you hear me?"

"I heard you fine," Kowalsky spat without giving him as much as a glance. He rolled the tape across the entire width of the statue, installed a second post, and attached the tape to it. "Didn't you hear what I said? Official city business."

"Get the fuck out of here before I shoot you."

"I can't stop you from doing that, of course." Kowalsky nodded at the rifle. "Big, scary rifle you got there. But if you do, you'd have to explain to Mr. Engel why you did it."

"What are you talking—"

"And a little birdie told me," he continued, cutting the man off, "people who shoot Mr. Engel's employees are having a hard time finding jobs."

"Nobody told me anything." There was a shade of doubt in the guard's voice.

"Tsk, tsk, tsk," Kowalsky said and winked at the man. "Terrible, innit? When the most powerful man in the entire world can't find the time to tell such an important guy like yourself about his plans. How rude. But don't you fret, I'll fill you in. The statue is going to be moved, son. From what I hear, they are planning to bring it all the way down to DC."

"Why?"

"What a coincidence." Kowalsky shrugged. "They didn't think to tell details to such an important man as myself, either. You and I are practically brothers now. Nobody tells us shit."

The guard grumbled something unintelligible and turned around, heading back to the building. As he did, Kowalsky continued walking around the installation until the yellow tape created a large square perimeter around the statue. When done, he ducked under the tape and clipped large, thick *DO NOT TOUCH* plaques on the foundation of the statue, two on each side. Eight in total. When finished, he returned to his suitcase, closed it back up, gave a wave to the guards, and headed toward the corner of the street.

As he turned around the building, he waved down a taxi.

"Where to?" a young Chinese driver asked from the front seat.

"Before we go anywhere," he said. "Do me a favor, drive me in a circle. Go up to Madison Ave first, make a right. Then drive a couple of blocks down, make another right. And then make another right still, when you hit Fifth Ave. Then go up on Fifth Avenue until you pass Central Park. After that, all you need to do is get me to the other side of the GW Bridge. Someone is going to be waiting for me there."

The driver nodded. The cab pulled away from the curb and pulled into the traffic. Kowalsky leaned back in the seat, cranked up the AC, and closed the privacy screen. Then he opened the link to Jason Hunt again.

"You are crazy," Hunt said when the links connected.

"Do you know, Steven told me this mix burns at five thousand degrees? That's close to the temperature of the surface of the sun."

"Do you think it's worth it?"

"I don't know yet. But we are about to find out." Kowalsky stuck his hand into his jacket and pulled out a black device the size of a cigarette pack. Its plastic surface was smooth and uniform, except for a small, stubby, black switch on one side. Kowalsky looked at it for a moment and then flicked it with his thumb.

He rode in silence as the driver muscled his way through the traffic and turned on West Fifty-Seventh Street. There was a loud thud and as the cab turned again, merging onto Fifth Avenue, he saw it.

The statue's foundation was spitting fire so bright Kowalsky had to shield his eyes to look at it. The square base of the installation buckled as if made of wet carton and the gigantic statue fell onto the building—one wing and the hammer in the angel's hands tearing a large, long hole in the building's facade. A dozen guards in black uniforms ran back and forth around the perimeter, shouting at each other.

"Oh yeah, Jason," he said as the car drove by the mayhem. "It was worth it."

"Get home safe, you crazy bastard."

"Roger that." Kowalsky terminated the link, threw a last glance at the column of smoke in the rearview mirror, and smiled as he closed his eyes. "Symbols must fall."

28

Baikonur, Kazakhstan

The computer beeped, acknowledging the incoming signal, and a new window opened, showing the control interface of the relay. Helen exhaled, the tension leaving her body as her fingers typed away a string of commands, feeding a new course to the rocket. She chuckled as she imagined the panic and confusion that was about to erupt at the control center. The routine launch turned into a huge scandal as the rocket got hijacked and changed its trajectory mid-flight, heading to an unknown destination. There was another beep as the rocket settled on the alternative course.

She snapped the laptop shut—her work here was done. Nobody could stop the new missile reaching the Thor cannon. This was her cue to head for the rendezvous point. She prayed to every god she knew Schlager would meet her there.

It should have been her hijacking the laser, she thought as she stuffed her belongings into a backpack. There would be a time and a place to be mad at Schlager for pulling this stunt, but right now her energy was best spent getting out of the city unnoticed.

"Somebody'll be here soon, buddy." She ruffled the mutt's shaggy hair as he weaved around her legs. He yelped, a bright, happy sound, his tail smacking on the linoleum.

"Okay." She stood up and looked around, making sure she left nothing behind. "Time to hit the road."

The elevator was parked at her floor, but she opted for the stairs, her hand running on the dark-brown banister as she took two steps at a time. It was still early, but the town was already awake. She could hear clanging dishes and muted voices through the thin walls and doors as she navigated the dimly lit building. There was a rumbling of cars and motorcycles coming from the outside.

Helen pulled her hat down as she walked into the bright morning light and headed across the road. There were a few cars parked near the building, but she ignored them. She didn't want to put Osipov at more risk than necessary. He'd already done a few unusual things on the morning of the hijacking. Showing up too early for his shift and parking in a different place wasn't enough to raise suspicion. But if somebody reported a stolen car from the building where one of his known acquaintances lived, and that information reached the authorities investigating the hijacking, a curious detective could put two and two together.

Helen headed down the street, passing a flower shop and a store with a sign that said: "Products from Russia." She crossed the intersection and continued walking for another twenty minutes until she hit Gagarin Boulevard—a wide, pothole-ridden street, named after the first man to make the trip to space. It had two lanes running in opposite directions, and a parking space in the middle, closed off with a waist-high iron fence.

A scanner interface overlay her visuals, and she ran down the list of vehicles and their systems within the lot. There were a few potential cars and after a brief consideration, she settled on an inconspicuous white Kia SUV. The car beeped, as Helen's augs forced their way into the car's computer and, after giving a quick look around, she hopped into the vehicle.

She hadn't picked this parking lot at random. Together with Schlager, they scoped it the day prior as they canvassed the city in Osipov's Volkswagen. From here, it was a straight shot down to European Route E38, a highway that would take her all the way to Shymkent, a city near the border. There, they were supposed to meet, and, with some luck and the help of forged identities, they were planning to cross into Uzbekistan and make it to Tashkent, the country's capital. There, they would take a few short flights to throw off any potential pursuers, eventually ending up in a major European airport with a few direct flights to New York City.

Helen started the engine and the SUV slowly rolled through the rows of parked cars and out of the open gate onto the street. She headed east on Gagarin for about a mile and was turning on Soviet Army Street when she heard them—the whomp-whomping of a police siren. She glanced in the rearview mirror and there they were, two patrol cars gunning down Gagarin Boulevard, their red-and-blue strobe lights forcing motorists to give way.

Her first impulse was to stomp on the gas pedal, but she resisted it. There was no reason for her to believe the cops already knew who she was and were chasing the car. Most likely it was something unrelated and the best thing to do was to keep her head cool. Helen slowed the car down to a roll and pulled over next to a small cafe. As she did, the patrol cars zipped by, their tires kicking up a cloud of dust.

Helen probed the radios in the two cruisers, but there was nothing but the background static. She frowned. It was possible the police were riding in silence, concentrating on the task at hand, but it was strange. She glanced at the rearview mirror and tensed—there was another pair of patrol cars speeding up the dusty road. There was a sinking feeling growing in her gut. Two cruisers could've been a coincidence. Four, going in the same direction in a godforsaken town with a population of less than forty thousand people, most of whom worked for the space center? She reckoned the crime rate in Baikonur was lower than in Vatican City.

Helen waited for the vehicle to pass and turned off the ignition. Then, she stepped out of the SUV and headed inside the cafe. Before rushing after the police, she needed more information.

The place would have been at home at the corner of Bleecker and Lafayette. A few cozy lounge chairs and a long sofa along the wall. Industrial lamps suspended from the exposed beam ceiling. Small, round, polished wood tables for two with upright menus next to a condiment station. The only giveaway she was a thousand miles from the streets of New York was the bookshelf running along the wall. While some spines carried English titles, the vast majority were in Russian Cyrillic and Kazakh script.

There was a line in front of the register, and she watched the old-fashioned flat TV hanging over the counter as she waited for her turn. A local channel was on, and a severe-looking anchor discussed an upcoming presidential election with a plump woman in a dress with traditional Kazakh designs.

"Black coffee, please," she said in the best Russian she could muster to the young cashier in a headscarf.

The woman nodded and poured her a cup. "Would you like some pastries with it?"

Helen shook her head, not risking butchering some words and raising suspicion, paid, and took a place at a table by the window. As she sipped her drink, another pair of police cars roared down the street in the same direction. Her pulse quickened. She scanned the local police frequency again, but there was still no radio traffic. Something was off. She scanned a few bands of frequencies up and down from the one used by the local cops. There were a few empty ones and then there it was—an encrypted flow of information between the cruisers and a building somewhere in the city, presumably the headquarters. There was no question at this point this activity was related to the hijacked rocket launch. But where were all those cops going?

She scanned the ports of the radio transmitter of the police building. Considering most of the town looked like it hadn't been updated since the Soviet era, the headquarters featured state-of-the-art technology. Breaking into it would require some planning and careful execution.

A loud murmur caught her attention, and she minimized the internal visual overlay and turned around to look at the crowd in front of the counter. Everyone in the line seemed to watch the TV hanging on the wall, a few people pointing at it and making excited gestures.

The political program with a grim-looking anchor had been interrupted for breaking news. A young male reporter was standing somewhere in the open field; a massive body of a rocket was towering in the distance behind him. As Helen's aug identified the language, a line of subtitles appeared in her vision.

... It is unclear at this point what risk, if any, the incident poses for the international community. For now, we don't have any information on why the rocket has been hijacked or its new destination. The most immediate concern for the authorities, that it could be used as a weapon against some ground target, doesn't seem to be the case. Our best guess is it is still heading for a geosynchronous orbit. We have an unconfirmed report that a foreign agent has been caught at the control center and is being questioned. It seems like he was acting alone but out of an abundance of caution, local law enforcement is setting up roadblocks around the town. There have been reports the army is going to be assisting local law enforcement units, but we don't have a confirmation for that yet. We will continue to update you, as the situation remains extremely fluid.

The world went out of focus for a moment, and Helen gripped the edge of the table to steady herself. Her entire body seemed to tremble. She took a slow breath and then released the wooden surface like a first-time swimmer letting go of a life buoy. Then, slowly, unsteady, she stood up, threw the unfinished cup into a trash can, and stepped outside. She couldn't help Schlager now. She had to remain free to rescue him later. The trap was being set, and Helen needed to skip town, before its steel jaws closed around her and swallowed her whole.

29

Baikonur, Kazakhstan

A firetruck-red Kawasaki Ninja rolled down to a stop, and Helen killed the engine and took off her helmet. Hot, arid air swatted at her face. She didn't mind—the liquid cooling of the helmet couldn't keep up with the sun near its zenith, and her skin was covered with a sheen of sweat. The road—an unpaved, uneven path covered by an inch of dust—would look at home in the Sea of Tranquility on the moon, if not for the tracks of the patrol cars. A few miserable-looking bushes—short, dry, and brittle—on each side of the road added little joy to the barren landscape. It wasn't quite the Sahara, and Helen tried to not let her thoughts drift in that direction, but it was unmistakably a desert—inhospitable, uncaring, and unforgiving.

She had ditched the SUV, parked next to the café. If patrols blocked the roads, a motorcycle would give her better chances of sneaking through, but finding one turned out to be more difficult than she thought. She walked around the town for almost an hour, wasting precious time and wishing she hadn't given up the Rebel when they arrived in the city. She was ready to give up when she came across a newer-looking building with an underground parking lot. After a quick scan of the security system, she walked into the dark, cavernous space illuminated by a single light bulb at the entrance. There were two bikes at the garage. One was a brand-new BMW with a state-of-the-art liquid-cooled helmet locked to it. Another was a red Ninja that had seen better days. A layer of dust on top of its shiny coat made the decision easy—though, after some consideration, she picked the lock on the BMW and took the helmet. It would keep her cool, and also, if by some unlucky chance the authorities already possessed her identity, would give her another layer of protection.

Her next stop was a toy store at the center of the town, where she picked up a VR-capable drone, a set of batteries, a large bottle of water, and a few protein bars. She also bought a small gray kid's blanket and a black backpack featuring Pikachu. The drone wasn't the top tier she would have liked. The small quadcopter was a mediocre commercial model, with a video transmission range under one mile, but it would have to do. Satisfied, she headed out of town, keeping her speed right under the limit.

A few cars passed her as she exited the city boundary, and she slowed down, scanning police frequencies. There was a lot of traffic on the encrypted channel, but all standard frequencies were quiet. Baikonur PD was taking the hijacking of the rocket seriously. Helen had seen no activity by the army yet, but it didn't mean they weren't coming. Her window of opportunity to escape the town was closing with each passing hour.

When she thought she was close to the roadblock, she stopped the bike. There were no natural hiding places as far as she could see, except for the shallow ravine a hundred yards away from the road to her left. She rolled the bike into it and lay it on the ground first, covering it the best she could with the gray blanket. Then she sat down next to it. She'd be able to hear any approaching vehicles far in advance and though her cover was far from perfect, she'd be missed by a casual traveler.

Helen opened the backpack, pulled out the box with the video drone, and inserted the batteries. Then she opened the virtual reality goggles that came with the drone and copied the frequency, connecting the drone's camera to her visual interface instead. After that, she did the same with the remote control. Now she could manipulate the drone without relying on the bulky plastic controller with a rudimentary joystick.

The little machine buzzed like an angry wasp and took off, disappearing into the scorching sun. Helen switched the inputs and drew a quick breath as her brain struggled to separate the image of her falling away from the ground from the sensation of being seated on the firm surface. A few moments later, the queasiness passed, and Helen spun the drone around, surveilling the vicinity. The road from the town was still empty, but on the other side by the bridge over the Syr Darya, at the visual limit of the drone's optics, she could see it—the roadblock.

"This is great," she muttered under her breath. Next to the rusty pillars of a small iron bridge, there were five cars. Four were police cruisers blocking the road, with a group of uniformed officers chatting next to a set of plastic white-and-orange barriers. A dozen yards away from the barriers and off the road was another vehicle—a Russian-made Tigr, an armored tactical truck with army markings, equipped with the Arbalet-DM remote-controlled weapon station. Two people manned it, as far as she could tell—a driver and a gunner.

Helen pivoted the drone and made a wide sweep of the riverbank. The muddy waters of the slow stream didn't seem deep or precarious but would be impossible to cross with a bike. And on foot, she was going to be easy pickings for any patrols looking for her or local criminals.

She tested the band channel of the drone. The transmitter was robust enough to give her a good grasp on the quadcopter's controls, but when she tried to use it as a relay to probe the truck's electronics, she couldn't establish a link. It was too far, she decided. She'd need to get up close and personal to make this work.

Helen pulled the cover off the bike, packed her bag, and put a helmet on again. Then, she started the Ninja and rolled it toward the road. Once the tires hit the soft dust of the road, Helen saddled the bike and rolled toward the bridge.

It was going to be a tough one, she thought. It was hard enough to drive the Ninja while piloting the drone. Now she was going to do some remote hacking at the same time, while relying on the primitive link the quadcopter's transmitter offered.

The police noticed the drone before they saw her. Helen could see as the cop lifted his face to the sky, squinting against the harsh afternoon light. He must have heard it first, because he seemed to search the cloudless blue for some time, a puzzled expression on his face. But the next moment, he was shouting excitedly to his comrades and pointing at the drone. Another moment later, a few of them drew their weapons, firing wildly at the quadcopter.

She set the little machine on the zigzagging course and attacked the tactical truck. The remote-controlled weapon station proved to be a hard nut to crack, and while she had a routine working to penetrate its defenses, Helen took control of the vehicle itself.

It jerked ahead and roared onto the road, spooking the cops. They scattered around, at least for the moment, not shooting at the only surveillance tool she had. Helen gunned the truck toward the barricade and slammed the armored front of the vehicle through the barriers and the cruisers, knocking them off the road. She accelerated the Tigr deeper onto the bridge and then swung it around as it reached the middle of the crossing. She heard a beep as her routine took control of the Arbalet-DM system.

The 12.7mm machine gun roared, spitting fire and cutting the cruiser closest to the road in half. The cops, at this point ignoring the drone, rushed down the sloped bank, looking for cover.

Helen revved the engine and took off toward the bridge, the front wheel of the Ninja briefly losing contact with the road.

The deafening drumbeat of the weapon station masked her approach until she was within fifty yards of the bridge. By then she was flying at a hundred twenty miles per hour. The uniforms let loose a few wild shots at her, but she was too fast.

Her adrenaline was so high, and she was so focused on keeping the bike steady while watching the cops through the drone, she almost forgot about the two soldiers inside of the Tigr.

Now that the truck wasn't moving, the driver and the gunner both climbed on top of the roof, aiming at the approaching bike.

Helen swerved, almost hitting one of the rusty beams as a bullet zipped next to her helmet. Then she switched her attention to the vehicle controls and overloading the accelerator, which jerked the Tigr forward. The soldiers lost balance and tumbled off the roof. But before she could celebrate, the truck continued to roll across the bridge, closing the gap between the rugged armored grille and the beams. She twisted the throttle hard, squeezing the Ninja through the shrinking opening, and then she was through as the Tigr crushed into the pylons behind her.

She slowed down after putting some distance between the bike and the soldiers. The drone was out of range, too, and she contemplated for a moment going back to retrieve it, but then decided against it. It would be easier to buy another drone than to patch a bullet hole in the head, she thought. After all, it wasn't just her life on the line. Somewhere in a dark cell of Baikonur's local jail, Schlager was being interrogated, awaiting extradition to Russia proper. And Helen Chen was his best chance of getting out.

30

Tashkent, Uzbekistan

The road from Baikonur to Tashkent, that would have taken most travelers a day by car, even with making stops for sightseeing, took Helen almost three and a half days to complete. She didn't think her description was available to the law enforcement looking for her. Apart from being a woman and knowing her approximate build, they had little. But she didn't want to tempt fate, and after a night crossing into Uzbekistan, she stayed off the main roads. The first night she spent under the open sky, wrapped in a blanket she'd purchased from a thrift store. Perhaps it was a prudent thing to do, she reckoned, but she was so tired, dirty, and stiff in the morning, she'd taken a chance and stayed in run-down hostels the next two nights. As she got closer to the capital, she returned closer to civilization.

In Tashkent, the hotel where Helen had stayed under an identity of a Russian tourist was a charming three-story yellow brick house with a red slanted roof that could have been teleported from Munich or Dresden. It was a clean, run-of-the-mill modern place, with neutral gray and beige-colored rooms with cheap abstract prints on the walls. The building sat on the corner of Shota Rustaveli Street, named after the famous Georgian poet, and was squeezed between a modern beer garden and a traditional Uzbek restaurant serving pilaf —or *plof* as they called it here—a rice and meat dish she was getting addicted to.

Under different circumstances, she would have loved to explore the green streets of the ancient city that sat on the intersection of some of the most important trade routes in Asia for the past two thousand years. Instead, apart from an occasional run to a coffee shop down the block, or for another portion of the pilaf from the restaurant, she spent most of the time alone in the room, staring at the computer screen.

Finding Schlager's whereabouts was proving to be a serious challenge. The biggest part of it wasn't technical or resource driven. She could have tracked him down by now if they had taken him in any big city in the world. But Baikonur, despite being a place that sent things and people to outer space, was a strange place. The spaceport itself was chock-full of cutting-edge technology, but the rest of the city seemed to be frozen in a strange version of the 1960s, where she couldn't find as much as a single CCTV camera on multiple city blocks.

She started at the launch center. That was the easy part. Schlager never stood a chance. She watched, biting her lower lip and cursing to herself as security guards immediately stormed the hallway and barricaded the room with Schlager in it. After the local PD arrived on the scene, they broke into the office. Schlager valiantly tried to put up a fight, but the cops tased him, added a few kicks for good measure when he was on the ground, and cuffed him.

After that, four of them half dragged, half carried him out of the building and threw him into a van without markings and drove off, seemingly in the direction of the police station. But that's where the trail went cold. She pinged Schlager's augs a few times, hoping for a miracle, but there was no signal. Either they had been damaged or broken during his capture, or the place they kept him at was well shielded. For her own sanity, she hoped for the latter.

It took Helen almost twenty-four hours to take control of the internal server of the police headquarters. It was protected by a robust system operated by a low-level AI, and she didn't want to take chances and leave any breadcrumbs. After her spectacular flight over the Syr Darya, multiple agencies must have been looking for her, and she had no intention of making their job to find her any easier. If not for herself, then at least for Schlager.

The effort of taking over the servers of the police station turned out to be a waste of time. No matter how many times she ran the videos from multiple cameras in the entire building through a facial recognition software, it hadn't produced a single match. It seemed neither Schlager, nor any of his captors, had ever made it there.

With no solid leads, Helen scoured the city servers, looking for CCTVs close enough to the spaceport that could have captured the van and give her an idea of its final destination, but with no luck. Once she caught a reflection of a van in a videophone on one building along a possible route, but after analyzing the image, she had to rule it out. It was a similar model, but it wasn't the same vehicle.

Frustrated, she took a long break, went to a coffee shop, and sat there for some time, her mind blank, as she watched the passersby.

There must be something, she thought, a thread she could pull on. She had to think like a detective. If there was no primary source of information, there could be secondary sources. Small pieces of seemingly irrelevant information that, put together, could give her a clue. She heard Jason use a term once—the mosaic theory. It was a financial device, when an analyst trying to predict a company's performance would use small pieces of information and put them together, like a mosaic. Together, they would create a picture where the sum was greater than its parts. That picture was out there for anyone to see, as long as they knew where to find the pieces and how to put them together.

"Think," she said out loud, startling herself. She glanced around, making sure nobody heard her, but the cafe at this hour was empty, save for a couple of college-age kids sitting in the opposite corner. Both of them had headphones on, and Helen sighed in relief.

Sooner rather than later, Schlager was going to be transferred to the Russians. Sure, technically they were only leasing the spaceport, but in reality, every square inch of Baikonur was paid for in Russian rubles. And yet she was certain the local PD would want to question him first. After all, the Russian spaceport aside, a foreign spy was caught on their soil. It made sense to assume they'd transport him to the police holding first. That hadn't happened, and she guessed the pressure from the northern neighbor must have been too great. The Russians didn't seem to appreciate their rockets being hijacked. Most likely they had transported Schlager to a safe house, either in Baikonur proper, or in a nearby town, where he was now awaiting the transfer. Interrogated. Possibly tortured for information. She bit her lip again, her thoughts drifting into a dangerous place.

An order like this must have come through a diplomatic cable, she thought. And it came from someone with enough pull to make it happen without local cops throwing a fit. Or, perhaps, despite them throwing a fit. This kind of information needed to be collected from the horse's mouth, or in this case, the Russian embassy. But before she could break into the embassy, some shopping was in order.

Helen went back to the counter and got herself another large coffee. Then she went to a nearby pharmacy and bought a wig, a pair of oversized sunglasses, and mascara. Then she stopped by a clothing store and bought a few local pieces. Before getting to the best part of her shopping spree, Helen went back to the hotel and painstakingly changed her appearance. A wig and the makeup couldn't alter her bone structure but coupled with sunglasses and a traditional Uzbekistan long dress, she hoped she blended in enough to become invisible.

When she was done, Helen went yet to another toy store and bought a drone, a remote-controlled car, and a radio electronics building set with a soldering iron kit for high school students. Satisfied, she returned to her room again and converted a small dining table into a workbench. As she tinkered with the drone and upgraded the RC car, she thought about Schlager. It was a cruel irony that he would have been the perfect person to double-check her work, and make sure it was up to the task. Hackers were a nerdy bunch, not undeservedly having a reputation for being terrible with real-world tools. Schlager did not fit the stereotype. He had a mindset of an engineer, which only added to his brilliance as a code breaker, because he could grasp the real-world implications of what he was doing to the programs that governed machines.

At last, she put the smoking iron down and ran a diagnostic, connecting the drone and the car to her internal array. Now the machines responded to a set of subroutines that controlled them. In the left lower corner of her vision, there was a small window that showed the video from the quadcopter. The RC car didn't have a video camera installed but used an infrared projector that was interpreted by the software and produced a ghostly image, similar to a night-vision device, in the right corner of her interface. She turned it off and started packing a bag. It was time to visit the Russian embassy.

31

Tashkent, Uzbekistan

The Embassy of the Russian Federation was a large T-shaped building that sat off the street at the end of a long, tree-lined driveway. An eight-foot-tall fence with an electric spiral razor wire ran around the compound, that included an outdoor tennis and basketball courts, and an Olympic-sized swimming pool with built-in Rolex timers. Unlike in Baikonur, there was no lack of video cameras here. Just by passing the building in a taxi, Helen could see a vast number of them in different locations—on the poles of the fence and on the walls of the building. There were two visible guards at the front gate, carrying AK-12s, with more in a small cabin behind the fence. Six more walked the perimeter of the compound, keeping constant watch.

What was worse, there was a legion of directional jamming trans-mitters that created a thin, but impenetrable cocoon around the embassy that Helen could see in her enhanced vision as a pink haze.

The jammers were well known even to locals, as some of the energy, despite being focused into a rectangular prism, bled into the nearby street, interfering with the cell phone signal.

She asked the driver to drop her off in front of a supermarket three blocks down the road from the embassy. When she was sure the taxi was out of sight, she turned around and headed back until she reached her destination—Tashkent Star.

Tashkent Star was a new, large bowling facility with sixteen brightly lit lanes, and a popular cafe. Its best feature, however, wasn't the new high-tech hologram scoreboards, or its local brew Avicenna, named after the medieval philosopher. It was the location. Situated less than a block away from the embassy, it was connected at the back to a prestigious high-rise building whose inhabitants frequented the premises.

Helen walked through the set of double automatic doors, nodded to the hostess at the seating area, and headed to the self-serve coffee bar. As she moved, maneuvering between the patrons heading in and out of the bowling lanes, she tapped the Wi-Fi router, located the server, and then cut down the power to the building.

There was a chorus of frightened screams as Helen switched to infrared and jogged across the floor to the first bowling lane, dodging people feeling around in the dark. She ran to the end of the lane and ducked under the pinsetter to emerge in the narrow utility hallway, just as the emergency generator kicked in.

Here, away from prying eyes, she slowed down and headed to the emergency exit, connected to the high-rise. The lock, a smart Wi-Fi-controlled deadbolt, opened, and she crossed the short hallway into the basement of the condominium. She walked past the long row of caged storage units until she reached the service elevator and pressed the top floor.

The gears clanked as the metal box started going up, the numbers slowly changing in the small digital window of the control panel. A few moments later, Helen stepped out into a brightly lit hallway with light-blue walls and black polished doors leading to individual apartments. She ran down the corridor until she found what she was looking for—a ladder built into the wall and a hatch to the roof at the end of the hallway, next to a window overlooking a small backyard.

Helen put her foot on the first rung of the ladder as she heard the passenger elevator ding, followed by the swoosh of the opening doors. She hopped down, placed the bag in front of her, and faced the window, away from the hallway. There were two female voices that cheerfully talked in Uzbck as they approached her. She suppressed the impulse to turn and look, keeping herself steady and watching the trees in the yard below. There was a jingling of the keys and then the door opened and closed, and the hallway was quiet again.

Helen ran up the ladder, deactivated a simple Wi-Fi lock, and a moment later she was standing on the hot roof. She looked around. The edge was raised, but only barely, creating a small barrier between her and the void. What's worse, there was another high-rise less than a hundred yards away from her, due east, which was two stories taller. The windows facing the roof had an unobstructed view of the entire surface. A curious neighbor could notice a lady in a traditional dress, controlling a drone on the roof, and call the authorities to investigate.

She sighed, moved to the side closest to another building, and lay down on a dusty, hot surface, using the raised edge as a cover. The cement was hot enough to burn her unprotected elbows, and she emptied the backpack and placed it under her arms to insulate the skin.

The fasteners clicked around the RC car, and Helen engaged the drone, lifting the tiny vehicle over the roof for a test flight. The quad-copter made a tight circle around the building and then returned, hovering two feet over the surface. Helen activated the locks, and the flyer disengaged, dropping the car onto the roof.

"So far, so good," she said and attached the toy to the drone again.

The drone buzzed across the street and through the trees, heading for the large building of the embassy. Her plan was simple. The network of directional jammers had a few windows, required to keep the building accessible. Despite seeing the haze of the energy, Helen couldn't see details well enough to know where the access wells would be. But she didn't need to. A massive dish of a satellite link in the southeast corner of the roof would have to be at one of those access points. All she needed to do was to hover above it and release the RC car on the surface. The drone would stay in hover mode, serving as a transmission tower to keep her connected to the car. The tiny vehicle would then be free to roam the roof in search of a vulnerable access point she could exploit to take over the embassy's servers.

It wasn't a foolproof plan. The bleed from the directional jammers could prove too strong for the quadcopter's unprotected electronics, rendering it useless before it was close enough to drop the car. The RC vehicle itself might be too finicky to operate next to the powerful electromagnetic fields those devices produced. And finally, there could be no vulnerabilities in the building network she could exploit in a reasonable time, before triggering some kind of alarm or getting spotted on the roof.

Helen pushed those thoughts aside and concentrated on the view in her internal window as the satellite dish floated beneath the drone. She gently nudged the quadcopter forward. The video became pixelated as she got closer, the bleed from the jammers wreaking havoc on her sensors. She had to get as close to the base of the dish as she could; she doubted the jammer well was more than a foot wide around the installation.

An incoming call link lit up brightly in her interface, almost making her drop the RC car. She looked at Jason's ID, considering not answering, but then reluctantly opened the window.

"Don't do it," Jason said, forgoing any salutation. There was no video, but she could hear Poznyak in the background. Hunt must have been calling from one of the lower levels of the silo.

"Do what?"

"Whatever you're planning to do with the Russian embassy."

"Why?" She put the drone into a hovering mode and sat up, brushing dust and debris off her clothes. "This could be my only chance to find Max before he disappears into the big black hole of the Russian prison system. And how do you know where I am?"

"You can smile and wave when you look up," he said. "There's a slight delay, but it works. As for why you should stop… They don't know exactly what you're planning to do, but they know you're coming. It's a trap. Max has been identified. And once they knew who he was, it was easy for them to figure out you were out there looking for him."

"Shit." She recalled the drone, walked down to the edge of the roof, and sat down, dangling her feet over. "Max is already in Russia, isn't he?"

"Yes. Unfortunately," Hunt sighed, "he's already deep in the Russian prison system. There's no way for us to track him down. Not without mounting a full-on rescue expedition. For now, Max is on his own."

"We can't just—"

"Helen," he interrupted her, before she said anything she surely was going to regret later. "You're not the only one who holds Max dear. We'll get him out, I promise. But for now, our best chance of helping him, short of a suicide mission, is to put Darius Price into the White House. Then we'll have the leverage to negotiate his release. The Russians will be much more inclined to listen to the president of the United States than to a bunch of rebels starving in an abandoned missile silo."

"But—"

"No buts, Helen." He interrupted her again. "You know Max. He may not look it, but he is one of the toughest people I know. Besides, he is way too valuable. They won't hurt him. We can't win this without you. *I* can't win this without you. We are this close, and when we prevail, I promise you—we'll get him back. The missile is our best chance to defeat Engel, and who knows how much longer we have left before he shoots it down? Now, please…come back home."

She stared into the void below, the gusts of cool wind ruffling the hem of her long dress and caressing her hot skin. There was a terrible feeling in the pit of her stomach that burned her like it did on the helicopter that took her and the team out of the Sahara. The pain that enveloped her as she watched the oasis that took Connelly's life disappear in a nuclear fire. The pain that only dulled with time but never completely went away.

"Helen," Hunt said again, his voice soft, almost a whisper. "Please."

"Okay," she finally said, and stood up, smoothing out her dress. "I'm coming home."

32

Sagaponack, New York

The column of garbage and fuel trucks speeding down on Montauk Highway drew surprised looks from the rare motorists heading west. The drivers zooming past the convoy would be shocked even more, had they discovered the trucks' cabins were empty, the lights on the digital dashboards displaying lines of text and symbols rather than normal data points, pedals and steering wheel engaging with no human input.

Despite its ambitious name, the road stretching over ninety-five miles from the Nassau County in the west, all the way to Montauk Point State Park at the eastern tip of Long Island, was a narrow, two-lane affair. In quite a few towns of the island, the locals referred to it as Main Street.

Most days, the traffic on Montauk Highway consisted of residents running errands, visiting relatives, and tourists heading east for the sleepy B&Bs, wine tasting, and whale-watching tours. Despite civil war smoldering in many parts of the country, Long Island, especially the most eastern parts located closer to the posh Hamptons, remained a sleepy oasis of calm and peace. A motorcade of four Peterbilt monsters, followed by eight tankers carrying eleven thousand gallons of unleaded gasoline each, all going well above the speed limit, looked out of place.

Helen Chen was aware of that. That's why each vehicle in the convoy came from different parts of Long Island. A day before they assembled the motorcade, Chuck Kowalsky drove Chen, still jet-lagged after the trip to Asia, from one town to the next, while they hunted for the fleet candidates.

There was no shortage of garbage or fuel trucks in the area, but finding the right models turned out to be challenging. There was no central database that listed which town or village employed which vehicles. For Chen's plan to work, they had to be modern enough to have a fitted autopilot that would allow her to commandeer them at will. Kowalsky and Helen had to learn the hard way that many municipalities still used the ancient monsters that had none of the modern electronics.

They started before dawn in Valley Stream, outside of JFK, and went east on the Sunrise Highway, combing through settlements. They found their last fuel truck in Islip, and after Chen remotely planted a subroutine into the vehicle's computer, they checked into a cheap B&B for the night.

It was well before sunrise when they left the B&B. Kowalsky, who had slept on the floor, darkly wondered out loud as he sipped on the cold yesterday's coffee if they still expected him to pay for bed and breakfast when he didn't get either.

At five o'clock in the morning, they drove off the main road near Victor Ye's estate, where Kowalsky backed their pickup truck into a cornfield. A few minutes later, he was sitting on the hood of the car, bundled in a hoodie and wearing a VR set as the stealth drone buzzed toward the mansion.

When the quadcopter took its position observing the property, Helen activated the fleet of twelve trucks that left their garages and headed down to Sagaponack on local roads before merging into one long column on the outskirts of Bridgehampton.

By the time the vehicles crossed the border of the village, the entire convoy was traveling over seventy miles an hour, a fearsome speed for the narrow road with no shoulders.

"Oh, the irony," she heard Kowalsky's voice over the comms.

She could see the feed from the drone, but she left the control of the quadcopter to the former cop, concentrating on the trucks. At the moment, the video looked like a real estate commercial—gleaming water of multiple pools, neat rows of manicured trees, mazes, and a long stretch of blindingly white sand by the ocean.

"Victor Ye came up with this maneuver. A few of his crews used booby-trapped garbage trucks to break defenses during assaults. Crude but effective."

She shrugged. "What do they say? Good artists borrow, great artists steal? It's too bad Victor isn't here to appreciate the show. Don't you want to stay inside of the car? You'll be safer in here."

"I'm fine," Kowalsky said and pointed at his VR goggles. "It's easier to swing my head around with these when I'm not in a confined space. Don't want to bang my head on the dashboard."

"Your call."

"Are you seeing this? Just as we thought—two Daimyos in the front, two by the shore, and the rest of them are hanging out by the main house. Do you think they eat? Or take bathroom breaks?"

She didn't answer. As the column left the main road and headed down the private drive, a sea of corn rolled on both sides of the road.

The first truck smashed through the black wrought-iron gates, taking small arms fire from a few guards. Two Daimyo cyborgs sprinted to intercept it and close the road to the main house. The grille of the front vehicle struck the first cyborg in the chest, sending him tumbling off the road. The truck followed, swerving off the paved path and driving over the body. It then stopped, twenty tons of steel keeping the Daimyo pinned to the ground.

The second cyborg was nimbler and rolled away before the next

Peterbilt struck it. It dashed after the truck and jumped, smashing its fist through the side window of the cabin, only to find it empty. The steering wheel on the mighty vehicle spun left, engaging the emergency brake at the same time. The truck screeched, plowing through the bushes and a line of magnolias, and crashed on its left side, burying the cyborg under it.

"Two down," Kowalsky shouted, "many more to go. They are all heading toward the house, like you said they would."

The two remaining garbage trucks and the tankers sped down the winding road framed by cherry trees.

Chen glanced at the drone view. The mansion was shaped like an upside-down U, with the large square of the main house at the bottom and the wings on either side hugging a massive courtyard with a fountain in its center. At the moment, two dozen cyborgs in front of the main building looked like panicked ants under attack.

A few of them opened fire as the two remaining garbage trucks made a turn onto the last stretch of the road. The explosions took out the windshields of both vehicles and damaged their cabins but did little to change their trajectory. Both trucks plunged into the cyborgs on each side of the fountain, flinging them into the air like rag dolls. The truck on the right swiped the edge of the fountain, jumped the steps of the main entrance, and smashed into the wall, lodging itself between two marble pillars. The truck on the left careened into the left wing of the house and flipped over, crumbling a few cyborgs under its massive bulk.

"And here we go," Chen said out loud as eight fuel tankers covered the last hundred feet of the driveway and smashed into the yard. She could hear the screech and groan of metal even through the wind-shield of the pickup truck. A few of the tankers flipped over, their cisterns rupturing, unleashing thousands of gallons of flammable liquid.

"Now, Chuck," she said.

A small object detached from the drone and plunged down toward the courtyard. The picture shifted as Kowalsky zoomed the quad-copter up at maximum speed. Chen watched the black shape of the explosive charge disappear in the pool of fuel below and then detonate as it hit the ground.

It was a minor explosion first—a fireball a few feet in diameter, bulging across the carcass of a fuel truck. It burned, spitting flames around it in all directions long enough that Chen had enough time to think their plan didn't work out as they had planned. Then the fuel ignited.

It looked as if space collapsed onto itself as the air rushed into the vacuum created by burned fuel vapors. Trees snapped as they got pulled into the courtyard. The twenty-ton garbage truck that had been lodged inside the front doors snapped back into the middle of the area as if snatched by an angry god. Then, as the air that rushed to fill the empty space brought more oxygen to the inferno, the secondary explosion ripped the mansion apart, the shock wave sprinting away from the epicenter like a gigantic bubble.

"Chuck!" Helen yelled. The view of the drone spun madly as the blast reached the quadcopter. Another moment later, it hit their pickup truck.

Chen saw Kowalsky thrown over the roof and the airbag exploded in her face, blinding her. The truck skidded a few feet backward, crushing corn stalks as it went, and then stopped.

"Chuck?" Chen licked her lips. It tasted salty, and when she wiped them with the back of her hand, it came away red. "Chuck, are you all right?"

She stumbled out of the truck, looking for him. Kowalsky was lying on his back a few yards from the pickup truck, his arms thrown about, a thin trickle of blood running down his chin. She ran to him, knelt next to his head, and touched his neck, checking for a pulse.

He coughed, pushing her hand away, pulled the VR goggles off his face and sat up, spitting blood to the side.

"Are you all right?"

"Holy shit," he said in a squeaky falsetto. He coughed again, clearing his throat, and then said it again, this time in his normal gruff voice. "Holy shit, Helen."

"You scared me."

"From now on," Kowalsky said, wheezing, "I'm only referring to you as Helen the Fire Queen. Do you think they all cooked?"

She nodded.

"You think our truck still runs?"

She looked back at the pickup. The windshield was smashed and the left mirror was hanging on its wires, but otherwise the vehicle seemed to be intact. "I sure hope so. Let's get outta here."

"Can't agree more." Kowalsky grimaced as he stood up. "I have no intention of finding out one of those assholes survived somehow, and it comes here to check things out. Lead the way, Helen the Fire Queen."

33

Queens, New York

J ason Hunt scanned the dome-shaped building on the outskirts of JFK Airport. It was as large as a football stadium, its silver-gray roof glistening in the morning sun. A sign—made of large, neon-lit boxy letters hanging over the mirrored glass doors—read Ares Industries.

"I read six hostiles," he said in the microphone. "Four sentinels and two armed guards. All on the first floor. No signs of Victor yet. Can't see any heat signatures in the lower levels either."

"Same here." Helen's voice was crisp. The miniature implant spliced into his cochlear nerve made it sound as if she was speaking inside of his skull. "But I want to make another round with the drone and double-check the immediate neighborhood. Don't want to get any surprises."

"That's fine." He glanced at the back of the minivan. Martin sat on the floor, his massive bulk barely fitting between the walls. "You okay back there?"

The cyborg nodded. He hadn't been big on conversations even before the fateful fight on the bridge over the Delaware River that almost killed him. Since then, his vocabulary had shrunk almost exclusively to "yes" and "no," accompanied by an occasional grunt.

Three days ago, they had received intel that Victor Ye was going to be making the last round of inspections of the facility before its official launch. After the destruction of his Long Island mansion, the head of the Red Dragon had pushed the opening of the factory by a week, rushing to restock Daimyo cyborgs he'd lost in the explosion. Jason decided it was their best opportunity to hit it with a surgical strike before the factory floor got crowded with workers, technicians, and support personnel. They went to great lengths to leave the silo undetected as Helen cleared the way for them with the help of a military satellite and two long-range reconnaissance drones.

"Oh crap," she said, a touch of urgency in her voice, and a small graph in the corner of Jason's internal vision spiked red, tracking the influx of adrenaline. He knew what she was about to say. "Victor's limo is inbound. I'm reading four signatures: Victor himself, his giant bodyguard, a driver, and a cyborg. It must be Daimyo."

"That was to be expected." Jason took a long breath, doing his best not to allow grisly images to surface from the darkest corners of his brain. "We've talked about this. I'm ready for him."

"I wish you had a bigger force with you. Not just Martin. And we can't use the kill-code yet. We'll lose the advantage when the time comes to take down Engel."

"I understand. We wouldn't be able to sneak up on him with a bigger force, and you know it. We'll manage."

"Right." She stayed silent for a few moments. "I miss Mike on days like these."

"Me too," Jason said, watching the black limo pass by them and disappear into the parking lot in front of the building. He moved his shoulders up and down, stretching. The new armor plates were oppressively heavy, even with the extra juice from the external battery pack. "How is it looking from the air?"

"It's all clear. If he's setting a trap, I can't see it."

"Good." He clicked the start button and shifted the gear. The engine roared to life, and the minivan shot out of its parking space. "Time to rock and roll. Let's go, Martin. Helen, hit the limo."

Their vehicle zipped down the street and groaned as the grille crushed through the gate arm. He could see the limo swerve, trying not to get trapped in the parking lot. A gray streak pierced the air as Helen's drone made a suicide run and detonated on the hood of Victor's vehicle, disabling the engine. It stalled, and Jason rammed the minivan into the driver's side.

He pulled the handle and jumped out of the vehicle to find himself face-to-face with the Mute holding a Glock in his hands. He ignored two pistol shots and slapped the gun out of the giant's hands. When the Mute took a swing at him, Jason jumped, the high kick landing on the opponent's chest before the man's arm finished the hook. Mute tumbled back, rolling a few times and then stopped, unmoving, by the stairs to the building.

The doors on the limo seemed stuck, and Jason moved to the stairs, nodding to Martin, who dashed past him and disappeared into the building.

The back door on the stretch exploded, ripped off its hinges with a tremendous force, and thundered across the concrete surface of the parking lot, sending fountains of sparks. Daimyo stepped out of the car first, his motions smooth and precise, followed by Victor in full battle armor. The cyborg made a quick move, trying to sidestep Hunt on the stairs, but Jason mirrored his steps, blocking the way.

"I don't think so," he said, listening to the shouting and explosions coming from deep inside of the building. "We have some unfinished business to discuss."

"Mr. Hunt," Victor said. "It seems every time we meet, you lose a limb. I don't think replacing your head will be as easy."

Daimyo lifted his arm, and Jason ducked and rolled; the power surge dispatched from the cyborg's weapon made the air sing. The concrete steps where Jason had been a few moments ago exploded in a shower of debris.

Jason's shoulder plate opened, sending a few projectiles at the cyborg. A curved katana blade that seemed to have materialized from thin air sliced all but one. It buried itself in Daimyo's left thigh and a moment later exploded, severing the cyborg's left leg and tipping him over.

Victor charged from the flank, trying to blindside him. A few shots glanced off Jason's armor, prompting a flurry of warning signs in his internal vision. He spun, sweeping his opponent with a low spinning kick.

It was like kicking an incoming freight train, and Jason groaned from the pain radiating from his thighs where his stumps were integrated with the bionics, but Victor went down, the heft of his armor crushing the concrete of the parking lot's surface.

Jason moved toward him, trying to press his advantage, but the enhanced movement unit overrode his primary motor cortex, sending his body into another roll. A blast roared above him, the screen of his internal interface flashing amber as the armor compensated.

Daimyo, a grotesque figure with a missing leg, was crawling toward him, using his left arm for support, his torso bent at an unnatural angle. The cyborg's right arm swooshed around, bringing the deadly blade of the katana at a forty-five-degree angle, aiming to slice Jason in half.

Hunt dodged and then launched into Daimyo, tackling him to the ground.

"Watch it," he heard Helen shout, and he grunted, lifting Daimyo up as a shield just in time as the blast from a stub-nosed barrel on Victor's shoulder hit him.

Daimyo shuddered in his hands as it absorbed the energy from the blast and then went limp, the shimmering sword retracting back into his armor.

Jason catapulted the body of the cyborg into Victor and, as the man struggled to maintain balance, shot at his legs. Two small explosions shattered Victor's knees, severing his legs, and he collapsed on his back, wailing in pain and writhing on the ground.

Jason Hunt stood up and took a few steps toward him. The front guard of Victor's helmet went down, revealing the man's face distorted in agony. Large beads of perspiration were running down his cheeks, mixing with tears.

"I…will…" he started through gritted teeth.

Jason shot him through the visor, and the man's body went slack, relaxing on the ground. Hunt turned and shot a few explosive rounds into Daimyo's head as well. The cyborg shuddered as the rounds detonated and then lay still, sparks fizzling inside of his ruined head for a few seconds and then disappearing.

A large boom came from the inside of the building, and Hunt turned toward the doors, his systems looking for any incoming threats. But there were none.

"Martin's coming back," he heard Helen's voice. "It looks like he's done."

As if to confirm her words, a few moments later, the cyborg strode out of the front doors, walked past Jason, and headed back to the van.

"Did you place the charges?" Jason asked.

Martin stuck his right hand out with a thumb up, without slowing down, and then disappeared inside of the vehicle.

"He's a man of a few words," Jason muttered to himself and then louder, to Helen, "I guess we are wrapping things up. Do you have the link?"

"Yes," came a reply after a momentary delay. "He placed four charges, and I can detonate them remotely. Should be enough to bring the entire building down."

"All right."

He went back to the car and pressed the ignition button. The engine whined and whizzed for a few seconds and then, finally, sputtered to life. Jason backed the car away from the limo, turned it around, and then headed out of the parking lot.

"Hit it," he said.

"Don't you want to get farther away?"

"Do it. I want to see it."

There was a bright flash in the back and a split second later, the van shook as the shock wave rushed down the street, smashing the windows in houses and sending car alarms into a frenzy.

As Jason accelerated away, he threw a last glance at the rearview mirror. The silver-gray roof was collapsing onto itself, spewing a column of roaring fire and smoke into the morning sky.

Ares Industries, the crown jewel of Victor Ye's empire, was no more.

34

Baltimore

"This is it?" Jason Hunt asked Poznyak.

After leaving the silo compound a few days ago, the scientist and a group of workers brought a few truckloads of supplies to an abandoned farm near Baltimore. There, they had been working for the past twenty-four hours, assembling machinery and unloading a few trucks that seemed to pull in every few minutes.

Before joining Steven, against everyone's advice and his own judgment, Jason traveled to see Camp Whigs in the Nepaug Forest. Despite the rout, after Black Arrow forces left the area, many of the rebels returned to the settlement near the dam and started rebuilding it. They erected new wooden cabins where the ground was still scorched from the fires. There were a few new bunkers and an ever-expanding net of fortified positions throughout the forest. They built a small cemetery on the hill overlooking the water, and a few rows of wooden crosses bore the names of the fallen whose bodies were recovered.

Felix Strauss was one of them. When the man learned no help was coming, he and a small group of soldiers held off a large force of Black Arrow, buying some time for the bulk of his men to retreat.

Hunt wasn't sure what he was going to find at the camp. If he were honest with himself, he wasn't sure he was going to find the camp at all, despite the reports of some activity on the ground. But instead of an abandoned area or demoralized and broken troops, he found a large group of hardened men and women, determined to carry on the fight against a vastly superior foe and rebuild what they'd lost. To his shock, Darius Price was there too, working along with his men. Rallying them to press on.

Hunt stayed there overnight, helping where he could, shaking hands and answering questions. Trying to give hope. He left at the first light, picked up by a Cessna from a field near New Hartford. The pilot, a quiet young man, dropped him off a few hours later in yet another field in Maryland and disappeared without a word.

When he arrived at the farm, he found Poznyak walking along what looked like a hundred-fifty-feet-long silver space blanket stretched on the concrete floor of an empty warehouse.

"Yep. That's it. This is the same balloon that was used during prep for the infamous space jump," Poznyak said, making air quotes around the word *space*. Wearing jeans coveralls and a T-shirt with diesel stains, instead of his usual white lab coat over a suit, he looked more like a farmer than a scientist. His eyes were bloodshot and tired, and his haunted face sported a three-day stubble. "But it's going to be qualitatively different. And more dangerous."

"Dangerous how?" Hunt glanced in suspicion at the silver material. "It's not sturdy? It's been sitting in storage for many years."

"It's plenty sturdy." Poznyak reached down, grabbed a hold of the material, and lifted it up for him to see. "It's light, but extremely durable. The final jump had a target height of over thirty-six kilometers. They did two test runs before the main event. They used this balloon for the first test, and it could go up as high as twenty-two kilometers. We don't need to go up nearly that high. We need you to get to somewhere between twenty-five and thirty thousand feet. It could get you higher, but it would be counterproductive."

"How so?"

"Anything above thirty thousand, the air will be too rarefied for holographic devices to work. Twenty-five, maybe twenty-eight is the sweet spot. You'll be high enough to be flying over most commercial and military aircraft in the area, but not too high to render those wonderful stealth devices useless. To create a believable illusion, you need something to be happening. Imagine if I stick a tiny green alien somewhere on a picture of a crowded street in New York City. You might not see him unless you notice him by chance. Now imagine you have a gigantic empty screen with nothing going on. You'll see every imperfection, every crease, every rough edge. Ideally, I'd have you fly much lower, but we have to compromise between staying clear from other aircraft and maintaining invisibility."

"I see." Jason reached out and touched the fabric. It was thin and cool to the touch. That a balloon was going to lift him and Martin to the altitude of a commercial airliner seemed hard to believe. "But you said there was a problem."

"There is a problem." Poznyak let the material go and it gently floated down. "The original test used helium to fill the balloon. We don't have it. And there's no way we can find enough before the deadline."

"I don't know anything about chemistry," Jason said. "So forgive my ignorance. Is there any way to make it?"

"Helium?" Poznyak laughed. "I'm afraid not. The only feasible way to get it is to drill for it. Whatever helium we have on this planet was created from the extremely slow radioactive alpha decay. Took billions of years. We are running out of it and that's why, when we were still interested in science and space, there were projects to mine it on the moon. But that's a topic we can discuss during better times, when the war is over."

"So, what do we do?"

"We use the next best thing—hydrogen."

"I see." Hunt glanced at the technicians working on the machines by the wall. Only now it occurred to him he saw more fire extinguishers than he could count around the barn. "There's a slight chance we might go the way of the *Hindenburg*. But hydrogen is much lighter, right? At least some advantage."

"Not as much as you'd think. Most people know its atomic number is one and helium is two, so it's natural to assume it'd generate twice as much lift, but it's not the case. It generates only about eight percent more, so it's not a tremendous difference. Not enough to justify using it over helium, but we don't have any choice. You won't be in danger because of the balloon, per se. With armor and jet packs, you could bail if it catches fire."

"But everyone will know where we are."

"Right." Poznyak sighed. "You'll be sitting ducks. Well, falling ducks, since you'll be plummeting to earth. The air space over DC is restricted. The moment you pop on their radars, Engel's forces will be all over you."

"And the mission will be over before it even begins." Hunt nodded toward the technicians. "Is this how you're making hydrogen?"

"Yep. The same way they made it for the *Hindenburg*. Sulfuric acid and iron filings. No time to reinvent the wheel. But we have much better efficiencies than in 1937. We are almost done with production, and the whole setup should be ready by Tuesday evening. Then we will have four more days to test it and make sure everything works as intended. You said they are putting the new missiles on the USS *Vicksburg* on Sunday?"

"According to Rovinsky," Hunt said. "Monday at the latest. We should assume they will fire them the moment they could."

"It'll be crunch time anyway," Poznyak said. "We need to make sure the steering works. We have to test the stealth component to make sure nothing bleeds into open space. But four days should be enough."

Jason nodded but said nothing. There were too many things that could happen before Sunday. Engel as of late seemed to stop caring about the optics in favor of finishing them off. First was the attack on the silo that forced them to use Project Thor. Then, the rout of Felix's forces up in Connecticut that coincided with the strike against two of their satellites.

The irony was that the only thing keeping Engel from crushing the resistance was the satellite that no longer carried the real missile. Instead of a multi-ton tungsten rod, it had a hollow projectile that self-assembled in space and then got filled with a hardened foam from a pressurized canister. What Engel thought was their last deadly weapon was meant to disintegrate well before reaching the surface of the Earth.

"Anything we can do to keep the chances of turning into the *Hindenburg* low?"

"Apart from the obvious," Poznyak rubbed his face and blinked a few times, "not really. Sorry, I'm running on fumes. Anything that can create sparks is your enemy. Static electricity. You can't use your weapons on the platform. Don't turn your jet packs on, either."

"What about steering? Can that set it on fire?"

"No." Poznyak walked away to the set of metal shelves near the wall and, after a few moments, came back with what looked like an exhaust pipe from a moped attached to a small canister. "These work on pressurized air. The only moving part is the valve, and it's plastic. Similar principle as what they used to maneuver astronauts during EVAs, but more powerful."

"I guess there's a reason they don't use hydrogen anymore."

"Well, no." Poznyak made a face. "Your flight will only be more dangerous because we are slapping together things too fast. Not because we're using hydrogen. Prohibition of hydrogen makes no more sense than alcohol. How do you think hydrogen-based airplanes fly? They carry roughly the same mass of hydrogen on board as fuel. They use it for propulsion instead of a lift. How does that make sense? But like I said, this is a discussion for better days."

An encrypted incoming link popped up in Jason's vision, and he tensed. He opened it, expecting to hear Rovinsky's scrambled voice, but found a few lines of text instead.

They have been able to move up the schedule. USS Vicksburg *will be ready to launch on Wednesday afternoon. I'm sorry, old friend. It seems every time we speak, I bring some bad news, but such are the times. Good luck.*

"What?" Poznyak said, looking up at his face. "What's the matter?"

"We need to be ready to execute on Wednesday morning," Hunt said and sighed. "Tell me what I can do to help. The whole thing is looking like one desperate Hail Mary."

35

Rigel Compound, Upstate New York

"It's always something, isn't it?" Helen smiled.

"It is." The hologram of Jason Hunt smiled back. "But maybe we'll get lucky this time. How are you holding up?"

"I'm fine," she said.

She looked around the room. The middle area of the launch control center had been empty without Schlager. All his gear was still strewn about the small space. A few tall stacks of books by the wall. A workbench with every inch of its surface cluttered with pieces of hardware, with a soldering kit in the middle. A few rows of neatly folded shirts on a shelf. Even when she slept on their bed, Helen instinctively stayed on her side, as if expecting him to walk into the room in the middle of the night and take his spot next to her.

"You sure?"

"Yes." She chewed on her lip, thinking. Poznyak and his crew had been working around the clock for tomorrow's launch. Last time she spoke to him, it sounded like they were going to deliver on time. Helen prepared the packets of information she was going to feed to a few international space agencies that, in turn, would filter to a list of journalists following them, to make sure Project Thor's launch was spotted exactly when they needed it. Not a moment too early and not a moment too late.

She also did a few trial runs with JC to check their capability to overwhelm the sentinels that were going to be guarding the presidential motorcade. To do that without exposing the AI to the Wild West of the internet, Helen built what she called a "Faraday filter." It functioned like an informational one-way valve. She fed it with information, and JC only could get to that data after Helen was disconnected. It worked the other way, too. It slowed down the process, but ensured the AI remained contained.

"What about the rapid response team?" she asked, referring to the group of elite Black Arrow forces assigned to the White House. It was a small unit, but as the name suggested, it was capable of being deployed on a minute's notice for important operations. She reckoned an ambush on the sitting president of the United States would be deemed important.

"What about it?" he echoed. "They may be rapid, but they aren't instant. If things go well, the fight on the bridge won't be long enough for them to come to Engel's aid."

"If."

He said nothing and shrugged.

"And there are no other Black Arrow regiments near enough DC that could also spoil the party?"

He shrugged again. "You have the same information I do. It's always a possibility, but we haven't seen any, and Rovinsky's convinced the rapid response team is the only force in the city. Black Arrow barracks will be busy dealing with Kowalsky's present. There are some other teams that are doing the policing and manning the roadblocks, but those cannot be mobilized quickly and aren't meant for anything meaningful. Engel is pretty confident we won't cause trouble in the capital and, frankly, he's got a reason for it. If we were crazy enough to march on the White House, he'd have plenty of time to pull troops from other places."

"If there was no rapid response team, we could almost guarantee no interference during the ambush."

"What are you thinking?"

"Hang on a second." She fired up the computer and pulled up a search window. "Here. There's another missile silo close to Washington."

"Not sure I follow."

"You said it yourself—if there are no significant forces there to interrupt your conversation with Engel, we stand a much better chance. In that case, the RRT poses a significant threat to the entire operation. We need to remove it from the equation."

"You want to create a fake stronghold near DC in the hopes Engel sends his team there?"

"No." She brushed a lock of hair out of her eyes. "It needs to be a legitimate target."

"We don't have that kind of time. We could build something convincing enough there in a few weeks. But not in a few hours."

"It will be a legitimate target." Her skin felt hot and cold at the same time. She cleared her throat and continued. "I can plant disinformation our silos are structurally compromised, and we need to abandon them. If we move most of our personnel and show up at Engel's doorstep right out in the open, he'd have no choice but to attack before we disappear inside another bunker. That will tie up his troops and when you strike, there'll be nobody there to derail the ambush."

Jason stayed silent for a long time, his face unreadable.

"It's the only way, Jason."

"So many things can go wrong," he said.

She laughed and rubbed her face, willing the tears back. "Yeah."

"Volunteers only. Tell them now, so they have some time to think. And don't sugarcoat it. Let them know it's a desperate move."

"I will." She nodded. "And don't worry about us spooking Engel. We'll split into small groups. I'll unleash JC to create cover. We'll show up right on cue to make the juiciest, the most irresistible bait in the history of baits."

"Good luck, Helen," he said. "It's been an honor."

"You, too." She smiled. "You better not die tomorrow. You owe me. The only person who can bring Max home now is you."

She disconnected the link and sat still for a few moments, collecting herself. Then she activated the PA system and called for an urgent meeting in fifteen minutes at the entrance to the silo.

By the time she took the stairs and climbed out to the surface, a sizeable crowd had gathered. A few cars were parked next to the massive lid, and Helen climbed on top of a Humvee and raised her hand.

A wave of murmuring rolled over the crowd, and then there was silence. A sea of grim, tired faces surrounded her. There were workers from Asclepius. Soldiers from the regiments that guarded the silo. Local farmers who came to support them and stayed.

"Listen up. I'm not the one to make big speeches, so I'll just say it," she said. "I don't have to tell you things have been tough for the past few months. Hell, for many of you, it's been a tough few years. But we've persevered."

She paused, catching her breath, and then continued. "I won't lie to you. The odds aren't great. Our troops in Connecticut suffered a devastating defeat. They are recovering, but it'll take awhile before they are back to the same strength. After Freeman's troops pulled out of Albany, Black Arrow has taken over. And, as you know, two of the Thor Project satellites have been shot down, leaving us with only one, carrying the last missile. Our backs are against the wall and now we have a tough decision to make."

A short, skinny man in military fatigues, an M16 slung over his shoulder, raised his hand. "Are you telling us we are about to surrender?"

Helen recognized the face. The man was the head of the provision team that risked their lives almost daily, hunting for game, foraging in the forest, and guarding the convoys that brought food and supplies to the silo.

"No." She smiled. "We are not. Niko, you've never asked for anything after taking extra shifts. You could take it easy and not risk your life for a solid twenty-four-hour period, but you'd come right back and ask for more work instead. People voluntarily worked eighteen-hour shifts. Shared the smallest amounts of food. Protected each other. We are not the surrendering type."

There was some laughter in the crowd, and somebody shouted *That's right!*

"I cannot tell you specifics, for obvious reasons, but in a few hours, we will launch our last and most ambitious offensive ever that should determine the fate of this war. Jason will lead it." She continued, "It's our last hope, and if it fails, there's a great chance the rebellion will be crushed. Many of us will die or be imprisoned. And those who survive, will have to go into exile. And this is where I come to ask you for a huge favor. To give Jason a fighting chance, we will need to draw Engel's rapid response troops from Washington. And the only way to do it is to give him a bait he won't be able to refuse."

"You want us to be the bait?" Niko asked.

"Yes." She kept the man's gaze. "My team and I will plant a story with the right sources that will reach Engel and his advisors that we are abandoning the compound and making a run for another silo in Maryland. We will create a narrative that this place is compromised after the two strikes and ready to collapse. Small groups would leave from here and make their way to a rendezvous point. Once there, the groups will merge as they make the last push to the new site. Engel's rapid team would be the only logical choice to strike us in time. That would give Jason an opportunity to ambush Engel and his forces, while Leonard Freeman's men will secure the capital."

"And if he fails?"

She shrugged. "We'll be out in the open, fighting an overwhelming force. We'd spent a lot of time and money prepping this site before anyone moved here. The new silo has been abandoned for many years, and even if some of you reached it, it would be unlikely to provide any shelter. Most of us will die or get captured."

Helen saw Niko look down at his boots for some time, as if considering what to say.

Finally, he lifted his head and looked her in the eye. "Where will you be, Ms. Chen?"

"That one's easy." She sat down on the Humvee and patted the warm metal of the roof. "Right in here. Riding next to you. But I recognize it's an enormous risk. We have one hour until we need to leave. I want you all to take some time and decide if that's something you can do. Think it over. Be honest with yourself. Discuss it with your loved ones. If you can't, we'll understand. No questions asked."

"We don't need an hour, Ms. Chen," Niko said and turned to the crowd. Whistles and shouts of approval sounded in response. "We'll go."

36

Baltimore

"If you say it'll work, it'll work," Jason Hunt said, putting down what looked like a long backpack made of smooth plastic on a workbench.

"It'll work," Poznyak said. "I wish we had more time to test things before using them. There's a reason for procedures."

Hunt shrugged. "Desperate times, desperate measures. I suggest you hit the sack. Big day tomorrow. You'll need as much rest as you can get. Now, if you don't mind, I want to make a call."

"Sure." Poznyak gave him a nod and turned on his heels. "We'll run the diagnostics on the chute one more time and wrap it up. I'll see you in the morning."

Hunt left the scientist and walked toward the office built into the farthest corner of the warehouse. It was a small, surprisingly clean space with two square windows cut into the sheetrock walls that gave a view of the entire floor. A simple aluminum desk and a hard plastic chair were set in one corner. A rusting file cabinet with a bent side stood by the door. Thick stacks of invoices and purchase orders of a now-defunct vending machine company were neatly piled in the corner.

He straddled the chair, resting his elbows on the desk, and dialed the link. A moment later, a window opened in his internal interface and Helen's face appeared in his view.

"Hey," she said. "I've set up a projector for you."

"Thanks. All ready for tomorrow?"

"As ready as it can be." She gave him a reassuring smile. "We'll get it done."

"That's what everybody keeps telling me."

"Then maybe you should listen. I'll leave you now," Helen said. "But don't make it long. We have to be going soon. You have ten, fifteen minutes, tops."

"Got it."

She gave him a wave and disappeared from the view. Another moment later, Rachel's face appeared in his vision.

"Hi."

"Hi," he said. He watched her for a few moments, absorbing every detail. The pitch-black color of her hair. The shape of her lips. "How are you holding up?"

"I'm fine." She shrugged. "It sounds like we are about to march toward DC."

"Is there any way I could convince you to stay behind?"

"No." She flashed a smile. "I know I have a lot of catching up to do, but I don't think I'll be a burden. I'm sure Poznyak's team could use a hand. If everything else fails, I'm able-bodied. I can carry things and do whatever else is necessary."

"Do you remember the night in Fort Lauderdale when we went out for dinner? To celebrate your job offer?"

"Vaguely." She gave him an apologetic smile. "What about it?"

"What you said about new technology and how it gets integrated."

"No." She shook her head. "Remind me."

He tilted his head, the long-forgotten images rushing through his mind. The table at the La Buena Vida restaurant. The yachts, moored by the peer, rocking in a breeze. The smells of sea and oiled wood. "You gave me a speech?"

"Oh?"

"Well," he chuckled, "first, I gave you one. That the augmentation tech would never get past amputees. That everything else would be a fad, like plastic surgery."

"And what did I say?"

"You gave me this spiel about progress and shamed me into submission."

She laughed. "Sounds like me."

"Yeah."

"But why do you ask?"

"Forgive me for getting all philosophical, but I hear that's what often happens to men on the eve of life-and-death events. You have a better feel for where the future will be. I couldn't see what you saw, and now here I am, half man, half machine, and perfectly content with the fact."

She nodded but said nothing.

He hesitated before proceeding. So far, he kept Rachel in the dark regarding JC's role in bringing his wife out of the cryogenic sleep. Part of it was because he didn't want to overwhelm her even more than she already was. But there was something else. A nagging thought he couldn't quite put into words. Despite all the evidence and multiple conversations about JC with Helen and Max, and Steven, he still wasn't buying into the idea of the program being sentient.

Somehow, on the eve of what might as well become the last day of his life, he wondered if this was another, what he called, "Fort Lauderdale" moment. When a new force was about to become a reality that would reshape the world as he knew it. Last time, Rachel saw it coming a mile away while he scoffed at the idea. He was spectacularly wrong then. He could be wrong now. And if another seismic shift was under way, this time he wanted to be prepared for it.

"What do you think of AI?" he asked. "Do you think it's possible for a sophisticated program to develop into a self-aware, sentient being? And I'm not talking about something that can pass as intelligent. The Turing test and all that. I mean something self-aware to the point you'd need to consider moral implications when dealing with it."

"That's a strange question."

"Strange how?"

"I don't know." She shrugged. "You are about to go off to a battle that will decide our future. We are going to march off toward the enemy as bait. And yet, you want to talk about technology and artificial intelligence."

"You're right." He sat up straighter, lifting his elbows off the table. "I guess it's a topic better left for some other time. We can talk about it if I come back. I'm sorry. I'm terrible at saying goodbyes. There are a lot of things I forgot how to do. For the past few years, this war has been all I know. If it ends tomorrow, I'm pretty sure I'll be lost. I never could understand why some soldiers who survived the horrors of deployments into some of the most terrible spots on earth would come back home, stay for a while, and then sign up for another tour again. And again. I think now I know. That's the only life they understand."

"We will talk about it *when* you come back. Not *if*." She smiled. "It's been a long road, I'm sure. I wish I had been there for you, but I wasn't, and we can't change that. But I know tomorrow you'll be victorious. And when you come back, there'll be much to do. Communities to rebuild. People to help. There's no doubt in my mind you will find your purpose. And then we can sit down in a nice place, have some good food and expensive wine, and philosophize about the future tech, and how AI will change the world."

"It'll change the world, huh?"

"I didn't say that," she said, chuckling. "You'll have to come back to finish this conversation. Go get some sleep. You'll need it."

"I love you, Rach," he said. "Be safe."

"I love you, too. I'll see you soon. And Jason?"

"Yeah?"

"Be careful." She blew him a kiss. "I'll be waiting for you."

He terminated the link, stood up, and pushed the chair under the table. Then he went out to the wide expanse of the warehouse. Poznyak, despite his promise to get some sleep, was still up, talking to a group of techs as they watched something on a computer monitor.

There wasn't much he could do to help, and he went back to the office, grabbed the plastic chair, and went outside. There, he put it next to the wall of the warehouse and sat down, resting his head against the cool brick wall.

It was dark, the stars blinking in the sky above him. Somewhere among them was the Modi satellite that carried the fake missile. If it worked, it could help them strike the decisive blow against Engel and turn the course of the war, or maybe even end it. If it didn't, none of them would live to see another day.

Jason closed his eyes. Despite the late hour, he wasn't tired, and his implants keeping his chemical balances at optimum levels were only half the reason. He wasn't scared or excited either, he realized, despite the stakes being higher than ever in his entire life. For now, he was content. No matter what happened tomorrow, he was at peace. After all, his entire journey until this point wasn't defined by how much he hated Alexander Engel. Or by how much he wanted to defeat the evil conspiracy trying to strangle the world.

Sure, he felt responsible for his father's cause, whose torch he had been carrying for many years now. The cause he adopted as his own. He owed it to the people who followed him. And to those who no longer could. But more than anything, he risked it all to rescue the woman he loved. And now, no matter what happened tomorrow, he knew he did. Rachel Hunt was living, breathing proof that all the struggle, all the pain and blood he spilled had not been in vain.

"Hey there, big fella," he heard Poznyak's voice. "Are you all right there?"

He opened his eyes to find the scientist standing at the doorway. "I'm fine, Steven. More than fine. And I wanted to thank you for it. I thought you should've been sleeping by now."

"Sleep is overrated. Besides, we'll have to start pumping gas in the next thirty minutes. No rest for the wicked." Poznyak smiled and looked up at the night sky. "It's not quite like in the city, is it?"

"No."

"Did I ever tell you when I was a kid, I spent quite a bit of time on the farm?"

"I had no idea."

"Yeah." Poznyak crossed his arms and leaned against the wall, his eyes searching the stars above them. "Don't miss much about the place, to be frank, but I do miss the stars."

"I grew up in the city," Hunt said. "But my dad used to take me places. He liked to show me the constellations. Told me stories about them. Some from the myths. Others he came up with himself."

"Orion," Poznyak said. "Rigel. Is that the connection?"

"Yeah." Hunt smiled at the memory. The face of his father as he told him the story. The bond he felt to his old man that night as they watched the sky together. "My father told me the story of the fearsome hunter who fought evil. I think he liked we shared the name. Hunter. Hunt."

"Poetic."

"Right." Hunt chuckled. "Though I read the Greek version later and didn't quite like it that much. Got stung by a scorpion."

Poznyak laughed. "I suppose as far as myths go, we can pick and choose how we want them to end."

"Sure."

The scientist reached into the pocket of his jeans coveralls and pulled out a small rectangular object. "I'm not the superstitious type. But before tomorrow, I don't think this will hurt."

"What's that?"

"Brandy. The cheap kind." Poznyak shrugged, took a small sip, and offered him the flask. "To victory."

Hunt took it and brought it to his lips. "To victory."

"Now," Poznyak said, taking the flask back. "Go get some rest. Doctor's orders."

37

Washington, DC

*J*ason Hunt had never been to space. But looking down at the constellation of lights generously sprinkled over the dark land visibly curving at the horizon was the next best thing. A massive balloon was drifting at twenty-eight thousand feet outside of the no-fly zone around Washington, DC after it took off the empty field near Baltimore, and silently drifted over the next few hours toward its destination. A few dozen hologram devices attached to it in a hexagram pattern rendered it invisible to the naked eye and Helen, with the help of JC, scrambled its radar signature. Jets of compressed air, controlled by an onboard computer, corrected the balloon's course without leaving a telltale heat sign for everyone to see. Jason and Martin were secured facedown to a small, flat, wooden platform with a six-inch barrier running around that separated them from the void below. It wasn't the most comfortable of settings, and Jason kept fidgeting this way and that to relieve his stiff and sore muscles. The massive bulk of Martin next to him hadn't moved once during the entire flight.

"We are in position and ready," he said, peering over the edge of the platform after checking his coordinates. "How do you copy?"

"Clear." Helen's voice coming through the link was calm and crisp. "Initiating the countdown sequence."

Before he could stop himself, Jason looked up at the sky. It was silly, he knew. There was no way for him to see the missile. His interface marked the area of the sky with the satellite, but even on the highest magnification, all he could see was the blackness of space. The piece of deadly machinery orbiting Earth at seven thousand miles per hour was camouflaged against far more advanced optics than his. He turned back to the ground below.

"We have the launch."

He felt a painful pang in his stomach. There was no turning back now. Somewhere over a hundred miles over the surface of the planet, a missile separated from its carrier, its vernier thrusters steering it into position. Then, they would separate, and the main propulsion engine would activate, accelerating the missile toward its intended target.

So many things could go wrong, he thought. Engel could take the goddamned Marine One, like Price had predicted. Head straight to Joint Base Andrews, instead of the Pentagon's bunkers. Poznyak's design had never been tested and might not stand up to the harsh environment of the vacuum. The chemical in the filler could have expanded less than perfectly, making the missile unbalanced and throwing it off course. They might have miscalculated the strain the missile would experience during the entry. It could break apart into a million pieces in the upper layers of the atmosphere. Too soon to cause Engel to flee the White House. Or the primary engine that stayed up in orbit, unused for decades, could misfire. Just because two launches worked as intended—no, *especially* because the first two launches worked as intended—this launch could go completely off the rails. They could also spot the launch too late. Or too early. Or not detect it at all.

"How are we looking?" he asked out loud, shaking his head, trying not to spiral into the dark well of doubt. There were things that would be in his control a few minutes from now. A missile hurling from space wasn't one of them.

"So far, so good."

He could hear his own breathing rustling inside of the pressure suit and wondered if Martin could hear his.

"No jets have been scrambled and all the relevant radio traffic appears to be normal. The RRT has left Washington and are heading our way. Estimated contact in ten minutes."

"Be careful."

"Are you still sure you want to broadcast the entire thing?"

"Yes."

"Okay." She cleared her throat. "Remember, the transmitters don't need to slow down as much as you do, so they'll hit the water about fifteen seconds before you hit the bridge. It might give Engel a bit of a head start. Not enough to pull back as long as we time it right, but enough to look for the incoming trouble."

"I understand." Jason checked the clock in the corner of his interface. "Six minutes until the show starts. They should pick up the atmospheric entry any moment now."

He glanced down again, looking for the black snake of the Potomac slithering its way through the city of lights around it. Then he ran the diagnostic on the jet pack strapped to his back. Everything glowed a steady green, and he closed the system, satisfied. The flight down was too complex of a maneuver to be done manually, and both his and Martin's engines were going to be controlled remotely by JC. Somehow, that part of the mission worried him more than facing Engel's army on the bridge almost thirty thousand feet below. A red line in the corner of his vision produced a small spike and then started to climb up. The adrenaline.

Jason drew a sharp breath, trying to calm down, but the line continued its slow ascension. He smiled inside of the pressure suit, aware that it must have looked manic. It didn't matter. Years of struggle and sacrifice were at stake today. His parents. Rachel. His friends who no longer were with him. His own limbs. Everything in his life led to this moment and now, in a few seconds of a raging firefight, he was about to write the conclusion to this bloody saga. The red line plateaued and went down. One way or another, it was going to end today, he thought. He was ready.

"And we're off," Helen exclaimed in his ear, her voice taut with tension. "I'm picking up massive chatter everywhere. They've detected the launch. Get ready."

Jason pressed a button on the edge of the barrier, releasing the fasteners around his body. Martin, next to him, moved for the first time, doing the same. The locks that kept the ledge in front of them upright clicked open, flattening the side of the raft.

"On my mark," Helen said. "Three, two, one, go."

Jason pulled at the edge and hurled himself into the darkness, vaguely aware of Martin plunging next to him. The stars below him shifted and turned a few times as he spun around. The thrusters on his back fired, arresting his spin and correcting his trajectory. He knew better, but he still expected the roaring of the wind. Instead, he heard nothing except his own rugged breathing and an occasional gurgling of the fuel lines feeding his jet pack. The flickering stars far below him winked and went out—the darkness spreading from the heart of the capital in all directions like a blob of black ink in clear water. He blinked, disoriented, before an artificial grid reappeared in his vision, enhancing his view.

"JC took down the power grid," Helen said. "And you are reaching terminal velocity now. Prepare for decoupling."

There was a gentle push on his back, and he saw two dark, slim objects shoot down ahead of them: one from him, and one from Martin. He saw a quick flash of small engines and then the objects disappeared into the dark, heading for the still invisible bridge.

"The package is on the move. Shit."

"What is it?"

"There are four sentinels, Jason, not two. Two groups. Two limos."

"The more the merrier."

"I've marked one of them. JC calculates it's a fifty-two percent chance to be Engel's limo."

"Flip of a coin." He laughed. "Unbelievable. What's your gut telling you?"

"I think she's right."

"That's good enough for me."

"We might not be able to take control of both groups of sentinels. Not in the time we have. We'll take over the ones in the back first, block his ability to retreat. If we can get the others, it'd be a bonus."

"That's okay, Helen. We stick to the plan. I trust you."

"Parachute deployment in five seconds. Get ready."

The thin line of the bridge over the black band of the Potomac was visible now, approaching fast. He could see the cavalcade now—a slithering snake of flashing lights, its head making its way onto the bridge, its tail whipping around the Lincoln Memorial.

There was a light push into his back and then a hard pull on his shoulders as his parachute deployed, arresting his speed. A few brief moments later, it disengaged, whisking away his pressure suit with it, and Jason plunged toward the bridge again. Hot air hit his face, and he heard the roar of the jet pack's engine. It whined as he fell the last few hundred feet toward the hard surface below. Then there was a hard snapping sound as his feet struck the concrete of the bridge, in front of the motorcade, sparks flying in all directions as the leading cars of the convoy swerved, trying to avoid the collision. Out of the corner of his eye, he saw the massive bulk of Martin crashing into the hood of the leading car like a multi-ton comet. Then sentinels opened fire.

38

Washington, DC

Two projectiles hit the dark waters of the Potomac on both sides of the bridge and disappeared under the water. After a moment, they bobbed to the surface and opened up their rugged shells like flowers in full bloom, releasing hundreds of miniature video drones in the air. They swarmed around the bridge, forming a loose sphere a quarter mile in diameter and shone bright projector lights onto the surface of the bridge. Every square inch of the bridge, illuminated like the world's biggest stage, was now being transmitted in high definition to every TV station in the country.

Another moment later, two dark, large shadows trailing fire and smoke struck the concrete surface of the bridge like large bolides, sparks and debris shooting in all directions.

Jason rolled sideways as the heavy sentinel in front of him opened up, two fat turrets on its ugly, squashed head spitting fire. He shot at its spindly legs, watching it fall to one side, the turret swinging as it fell, trying to track him. He jumped as the road disintegrated under

209

his feet and landed on top of the turret, unloading a flurry of armor-piercing rounds from a shoulder cannon. The sentinel heaved under him like a rumbling volcano before an eruption and then stopped moving, its outline turning gray in Jason's tactical overlay. Neutralized.

He saw Martin rip off the turret of another sentinel and push the dead hunk of the machine in front of one of the lead cars, a black SUV, trying to make a break for it. They collided with a sickening crunch, the lead car flipping over and landing on its side, its wheels spinning.

There was a roar of an engine and one limo smashed into the SUV, pushing it to the side and getting through the clearing. Martin and Jason shot at it, a large explosion ripping out of the front axle of the car as it skidded to a stop, sending a fountain of sparks ahead of it.

Another limo made a run for it, but Martin was too fast—a silver streak connected between his shoulder and the underside of the vehicle. The explosion lifted the limo up in the air, like a rearing mustang, and then it crashed down with a mighty thud, its wheels askew, smoke and flames coming from the engine.

"Jason." Helen's voice cut through the cacophony.

An SUV with Black Arrow markings skidded to a stop a dozen yards away from him, a machine gun spitting fire through its open window. He shot a fragmentation grenade into the opening and rolled away behind the husk of the dead sentinel for cover.

"I took down the remaining two sentinels. We neutralized support helicopters. Kowalsky's present is tying up the Black Arrow at the barracks. And 82nd Airborne Division units loyal to Price are engaging Engel's forces near the Lincoln Memorial and on the other side of the river in Potomac Park."

"How are they doing?"

He heard Helen chuckle. "They are handing it to Engel. Big time. Black Arrow is no match for the 'death from above' boys. The tide is turning."

"RRT?"

"Contact in two minutes, but Leonard sent some reinforcements that might intercept them. Fingers crossed."

"Stop." The sound of Engel's voice, amplified by the PA system, echoed across the river. The shooting ceased, plunging the bridge into an almost unbearable silence, interrupted only by the crackling of an engine fire on the burning stretch. The back door of the limo opened and Engel, clad in full battle gear, stepped out onto the road. A split second later, two shimmering figures of Daimyo assassins followed him, a curved sword extending out of their right hands.

"Not so fast," he heard Helen say.

The figures froze in mid-step and then collapsed like marionettes whose strings had been cut.

Jason motioned to Martin to stay as he saw the cyborg inch forward at the sight of the president. "Enough!"

"Black Arrow units are all down," Helen breathed into the comms. "The National Guard is moving in to apprehend whatever's left of the mercs. The 82nd has blocked all access roads to the bridge. He knows he's cornered. You can take him now."

"Wait," Jason said as Martin moved another inch.

"I'm here." Engel threw a quick glance at Daimyo and opened his arms wide.

A long, curved blade seemed to have grown out of his right wrist, and Jason suppressed a shiver. The man's armor was unlike anything he'd ever seen. It shimmered like on Daimyo cyborgs, but also had a liquid mercury look to it, similar to Martin's plates. But unlike Martin's armor, it was the color of silver, tinged with blue. Engel's face plate was an impenetrable mirror—reflecting the burning carnage around them. A window with a view of the apocalypse.

"Isn't it what you wanted? A duel for everyone to see? A fight to the death under the unblinking eye of a thousand video cameras? To crush my image? To humiliate me?"

"Yes." Jason took a few steps forward and stood in front of the man. "But I can settle for an unconditional surrender. Tell your dogs to stand down, lay down your weapons, and give yourself to justice. Accept the consequences."

"Justice." Engel scoffed, and his blade traced a tight circle in the air with a deadly whoosh. "I'm not the only one who should remember the consequences."

"What are you doing, Jason?" Helen's voice was tense. The sounds of automatic fire and a loud explosion almost scrambled her words. Engel's rapid response team must have made contact. "He's baiting you, and we don't know what that suit is capable of. You and Martin should work together."

Jason muted the incoming link and motioned to Martin to step back. The blade in Engel's hand whooshed in a flat arc, going for his neck, and Jason fell back as the tip of the katana sliced the air an inch away from his skin. He shot the man in the chest, a burst of uranium-tipped armor-piercing explosive rounds ripping into the shimmering plates. They burned, tight concentric ripples radiating from the point of impact, and Engel stumbled back, crying out in pain.

Jason rushed forward, pressing his advantage, only to be greeted by a blue pulse out of Engel's shoulder. It was as if a freight train hit him at full speed. He flew back a few yards, his vision covered in amber signals, each vying for his immediate attention, and fell on the back of the dead sentinel. Another moment later, Engel was on him, the blade cutting at a forty-five-degree angle across his chest.

Jason rolled, avoiding the blow at the last moment, the armor of the heavy sentinel giving way under the blade like butter under a hot knife. As Engel lifted the sword for another strike, Jason propelled himself forward, catching his opponent's wrist and unloading the entire cassette of the uranium-tipped bullets into Engel's armpit. It severed the limb, blood and gore spraying the concrete as Engel fell backward, awkwardly catching himself with his left hand. Something foamed at the stump as his armor struggled to close the wound and stop the bleeding.

Jason stood up, taking a few steps toward the fallen opponent, and then lifted the severed arm with a blade. The plates on Engel's chest moved, opening up a strange-looking twin barrel, but Jason was too quick. He jumped forward, the blade in his hand writing a figure eight in the air as it sliced through the barrels and then Engel's left shoulder.

The man screamed. There was a blue spark in his chest, and then something went off with a low, reverberating rumble. It hit Jason like blue lightning, momentarily blinding him and overwhelming his systems.

When his vision returned, the first thing he saw was Martin shaking his head like a swimmer who came up for air, getting the water out of his ears.

Then, he looked down at Engel, aiming a gun out of his forearm plates at the enemy's chest. The man was still alive. The explosion burned a black hole through the middle of his chest armor, the white of the bone briefly visible through the opening, before blood-tinged foam covered the wound. Engel's left arm, though still attached to the body, was cut halfway through, the sealer bubbling out of it. The armor, no longer shimmering, now looked matte, listless, like the paint of an abandoned car that had been left out in the sun for many years. Blue arcs of energy ran down on different parts of Engel's body and when they did, the man shivered and moaned in pain. A moment later, the visor on his helmet went down, baring his face. He coughed and choked as it did. His skin was pale and covered in soot, a long cut running across his forehead.

"Kill me," Engel snarled. He coughed again, a trickle of blood running down his chin. His teeth, white as sugar, were covered in dark blood, too, making him look like a vampire after a feeding spree. "Kill me now."

Jason lowered his hand as the barrel of the gun retreated behind the armor plates and smiled. "I don't think so. You'll live. But it's over, Alex. There'll be an investigation. There'll be a proper trial. And if the jury decides death should be your penalty, then so be it. But the days of lawlessness are over. The system isn't perfect, but it's still better than whatever the hell you and your cabal have to offer."

"You fucking coward." Engel spat, his face twisted in rage, pain, and disgust. "A hypocrite. Lecturing me as you are about to level everything in a mile's radius of the White House. Thousands of people will die so you could prove a point. To humiliate me. If you expect me to keep mum about Project Thor or somehow pin this on me, because I used to control it for a hot second, you're delusional. I'll tell everyone who's willing to listen. I'll show evidence. They'll never—"

There was a loud boom above them, and the night skies were illuminated by a series of bright streaks that each split into hundreds more, like the world's biggest fireworks. A few moments later they disappeared, leaving a few glowing trails that soon vanished.

A line of text appeared in his vision. Helen must have overridden his communication logs.

82nd Airborne took care of the RRT. We're good.

Jason smiled, closed the text, and then pointed at the sky. "Nobody's leveling the White House. That was what you ran away from. Fireworks. The best show in town."

He stepped aside as he watched the National Guard units seal the bridge and load Engel into an armored ambulance. A massive palm touched Jason's shoulder, and he twisted around, startled, only to see Martin. To his shock, he saw the cyborg's face plate was down, revealing the man's plain, pockmarked face.

"I'd like to go home now," the cyborg said, his voice surprisingly quiet. Almost timid. "I'm tired."

"Me too, buddy." He reached out and put his hand on the giant's shoulder. "Me too."

JFK Airport, Queens

$\mathcal{H}$elen Chen squinted against the bright sky as she watched an UH-1N Iroquois helicopter appear over the airport. It was still far, first only a dot to the naked eye, but it grew in size as it made its final approach toward the helipad. It had departed from the USS *Gerald R. Ford* aircraft carrier of the Carrier Strike Group 2 a few minutes ago after receiving a transfer of the Russian prisoner. A small yacht that belonged to a Cyprus company with a tenuous link to the Kremlin government delivered him to the ship. Despite Darius Price negotiating Schlager's release, the operation of turning over the man who smuggled a weapon to space via a Russian rocket was a delicate matter neither side wanted to advertise.

Hunt and Chen had arrived at the airport an hour ago in a bullet-proof Defender, followed by two Suburbans with members of Jason's tactical support team. They drove through a checkpoint unchallenged, as their presence had been pre-cleared, and parked right near the landing zone. The area by the helipad was empty save for the few airport workers who tried their best not to stare at Jason. She couldn't blame them. In his full battle gear, the man looked like a comic book character that somehow stepped off the page onto the hot tarmac.

"It's such a strange thing to see a navy helicopter landing at JFK," she heard Jason say.

"I don't understand. Why couldn't they bring him to the tower?"

"There are still some rogue Black Arrow units around the city. Most of them have been mopped up by now, but not all. I don't think any of those that are still around have any surface-to-air capabilities, but I didn't want to risk it."

The loud roar of the helicopter drowned out all other noises and a second later, Chen tucked her face into her elbow, protecting her eyes from dust and flying debris. One of the full-sized doors on the fuselage slid open, and Helen ran toward a stumbling figure climbing out of the cabin.

"Max." She buried her face into his chest, squeezing him, and felt his arms wrapping around her in a grip so tight it made it hard to breathe. He smelled of sweat and machine oil and sea, and it was the best scent she'd ever smelled.

"We've won, haven't we?" he asked into her hair. "We beat them."

"Yes," she said, not letting him go. "Darius is president. Engel is in custody and the newly reorganized US Army is cleaning up the remnants of Black Arrow. And now you're home."

"It's nice to be home," she heard him say and let go, looking up at him. His face was covered in a shaggy beard and his lips were chapped. There was also a fresh scar running over his left eyebrow and his left eye was bloodshot, the skin under it yellow and blue, bearing the evidence of what must have been a nasty bruise.

"Who did this?" she asked in a calm voice, pointing to his face.

"You should see the other guy," he joked, but then, seeing her face, turned serious. "Rough seas. You have no idea how much it sucks to be on a small boat in choppy waters in the middle of the ocean. It's safe to say we won't be going on a cruise after this experience."

"Hey, brother," Jason said, stepping closer. "It's good to see you back."

Helen stepped back, and the two men embraced.

"You okay, man?"

"Yeah." Schlager looked around the airport. "It was anticlimactic. In the beginning, it was scary as shit. I will not lie. Especially for the first two weeks right after the capture, as they kept me in a solitary cell and a guy with dead eyes visited me. Those interrogations were exhausting. Same questions over and over and over again for hours on end. But they never touched me. The food was atrocious, though, so I'm dying for a proper burger or something."

"Come on then," Helen said, pointing to the limo. "We can talk on the way to the tower."

"It fucking worked, didn't it?" Schlager said as the Defender cleared the checkpoint, turned on the strobe lights, and picked up speed. "I saw the fireworks on the net."

"It did." She smiled.

"That was the worst part of the ordeal," he said, a shadow crossing his face. "Not knowing if it was going to work. They jammed everything. I wouldn't have even known how long they had me locked up if not for my implants. Most of my stuff didn't work at all, at least anything that could have connected me to the outside world. Even internal diagnostics were glitching."

"When did you find out?"

Schlager rubbed his hands together. "I started suspecting something was up when they moved me. There were too many things happening at once. First, they drove me somewhere. Then I was on a train for a while. And then finally the yacht. They blindfolded me most of the time unless we stayed somewhere for the night. By the time I smelled the sea, I was convinced they were going to release me. I figured if they wanted to ghost me, it wouldn't be so elaborate. But the first time I could access the network was when they transferred me to the carrier."

"Darius moved heaven and earth to get you released," Hunt said. "He put on a lot of pressure."

"For which I'm grateful, but enough about me though," Schlager said. "Is everyone okay? From what I read on the news, it sounds like it was a big shoot-out. I saw some clips. It looks like a movie."

"We lost a few men," Helen said. "About a dozen people were wounded. Unfortunately, a few Secret Service agents were killed as well. But it could have been worse. Luckily, it was lightning fast."

The convoy got on Van Wyck Expressway and, a few minutes later, took the ramp to the Belt Parkway. The road, normally choked with traffic, was almost empty. A few military vehicles with US Army markings were parked on the shoulder every few miles. A few servicemen stood around the cars, observing the flow of traffic, their assault rifles slung across their chests.

"You okay?" Helen asked Schlager as the car crossed the Manhattan Bridge and headed onto Canal Street.

"Yeah." He turned back from the window to face her. "I can't believe this is over. It's just surreal, that's all."

"Which part?" She smiled at him.

"The part where we get from JFK all the way to the city in less than fifteen minutes." He leaned over and patted Jason's shoulder. "Do we get to keep these flashing lights, or do you need to return them at some point? I feel like we've earned them. Saving the world has got to count for something, right?"

They shared a chuckle as the cavalcade pulled up to the corner of Broome and Sixth Avenue. The car slowed down and then came to a full stop. Helen pulled on the handle and swung the door open.

"What are you doing?" She saw the confusion on Schlager's face. "Why are we stopping a block away from the tower?"

"Come on." She beckoned and stepped out of the car into a hot summer afternoon. "I want to show you something."

"Okay." He followed Chen and stood next to her, his fingers finding hers. "Jason, are you in on this, too? What am I looking for?"

"Don't involve me in this," Jason replied from the front seat. "This is all Helen."

"This." She pointed at a semi-trailer parked alongside the road. Two men wearing bright-yellow work jackets were standing on either side of the back of the vehicle.

"The truck?" There was even more confusion in his voice now.

"It's not just a truck," she said, suddenly finding it hard to speak. "It's a promise. I didn't make that promise, but I wanted to keep it."

The way his fingers crushed hers, she knew he'd understood. She waved to the two men by the truck, and they rolled the back door up, revealing a car parked inside of the trailer. It was a striking dark-green coupe with slick helmet wings and a pair of large Zeiss headlamps.

"I present to you the 1930 Gurney Nutting Speed Six Coupe. Commonly known as the Blue Train Bentley."

Schlager stood there for a few seconds, unable to say anything, and then walked toward the trailer, stopping a few inches away from the car's front grille.

"It's...magnificent."

"Yes."

"How did you do it?"

"Let's just say Diego Flores no longer operates a large cartel in Bolivia. Kowalsky and Latham helped." She shrugged. "Chuck's still pissed about it, though, as he got a flesh wound during the op, so if I were you, I wouldn't bring it up when you see him. Play it cool."

"He got shot?" Schlager spun around to look at her.

"Eh. It depends who you ask. If you ask Kowalsky, then yes, he was shot. Was this close," she brought a thumb and an index finger close to each other, "to bleeding to death, but bravely fought and survived through pure grit and perseverance. If you ask me, I'd say it was a graze, but who am I to judge?"

"Thank you." He leaned in and planted a kiss on her cheek.

"I think Mike would have wanted me to do that," she said softly. "He gave you his word, and he wasn't the kind of guy who broke his promises."

40

Orion Tower, Manhattan

The observation deck of the Orion Tower looked like a mix between a nightclub and a dinner reception. The laser lights pulsated with the rhythm of the music, the thumping of a subwoofer shaking the crowd. A score of waiters navigated the floor, skillfully balancing trays full of champagne and hors d'oeuvres. Small groups gathered, cheered, and drank, and then dissolved like schools of fish migrating from one place to the next.

It had been oppressively hot most of the day in Manhattan, but in the afternoon a fearsome storm descended upon the city, choking it in humidity as raindrops sizzled on hot asphalt and deafening the residents with squalls of rolling thunder. It battered the streets for over an hour until it finally quieted, leaving a thick fog that devoured most of the buildings.

By the time the night fell over the streets, it seemed as if the tower, along with a few other skyscrapers, was an island, floating over a gray stormy ocean that went on as far as the eye could see.

Jason Hunt pushed his way through the crowd, smiling and shaking hands and getting pats on the back. Some stopped him to take a picture, and he dutifully posed, grinning on demand for the cameras.

"Here you are," Rachel said, shouting over the music. She leaned over the bar and planted a kiss on his cheek. She wore a plain black T-shirt and a pair of dark jeans, her hair pulled into a tight ponytail with a rubber band. Along with two other volunteers, a young man and a woman in her forties, both from Poznyak's Asclepius crew, she was manning the bar for the party. "What would you like to drink?"

"Surprise me," he said, glancing over the rows of labels without registering them. "Something smooth and stiff, and make it a double."

"All right." She turned around, surveilling the shelves, and then plucked a black bottle with sharp corners off the top row. "The Macallan M Black. Will that work?"

"Sure." He shrugged. "Make it neat, please. The advantage of having an internal filtration system is the ability to enjoy stiff drinks without consequence."

"I don't know if that's an advantage." She winked at him and poured a double shot of whiskey into a crystal tumbler and then slid it across the bar. It left a wet trail on the dark wood that sparkled under pulsating lights. "Sounds more like a curse to me."

"I don't know." He raised a glass to salute her. "I haven't decided yet. Thank you."

"I'll see you after the party," she said, turning away from him to tend to the people arriving at the bar.

"You bet."

Jason walked past the counter and looked around. In the farthest corner of the deck, there was a lone, skinny silhouette leaning against the window, a glass in his hand.

"Max?" he said, joining his friend.

"Jason. What have you got there?" His friend nodded at the tumbler in Jason's hand. "Something interesting, I hope?"

"Macallan. You?"

"Macallan."

They shared a chuckle.

"How predictable. Where's Helen?"

"She went downstairs to change." Max stretched his neck, surveilling the crowd. "You know how she is. It took me a week to convince her to wear something nice for five minutes, but now that she's indulged me, she wants to be back in jeans and a T-shirt. She should be back soon."

"Are you guys doing all right?"

"Yeah," Max smiled, "better than all right. I'm the luckiest man in the world."

His friend glanced around, pulled out a small box from his back pocket, and opened it. A ring was nestled on top of the black velvet. There was no diamond or embellishments of any kind. A simple band of polished metal.

"Holy shit, Max."

"Yeah. I've tracked the tool she used to hack the New York Stock Exchange, and had it melted," Max said, putting away the box. "It's not the same device she used, but close enough."

"That's great. When?"

"I don't know." Max shrugged. "Whenever. Who cares. As long as she says *yes*."

"You know she will. That deserves a toast." Jason offered his tumbler and Max extended his, the soft clink of the crystal almost inaudible in the cacophony of the music. "To the luckiest man in the world."

He sipped on his whiskey and turned to the window, looking down at the clouds. The billboards normally covering the grime of the streets in garish neon lights mutedly shone below the surface of the fog, like some exotic fish in the treacherous depths of the ocean. Looking to lure the unsuspecting prey into the jaws of quick and gruesome death.

"Why the sulk, then?" Schlager said.

"How do you mean?"

"Isn't it obvious?" His friend glanced at him and then returned his gaze to the streets below. "We've defeated the evil empire. Engel is rotting in custody. Victor Ye is dead. A man who seems to care occupies the Oval Office. We are alive, and your wife has been miraculously returned to you. Your best friend is about to get married. I'd say most people would be in a celebratory mood. And yet I see a frown on the front of that big noggin of yours."

"There's a giant party going on." Jason made a sweeping gesture. "We are celebrating."

"Right." Max nodded and took another sip of the Macallan. "There is, indeed, a giant party going on. And yet here we are, like two pimply teenagers on prom night with nobody to dance with. And you can't even get properly drunk."

"I'm happy," Jason said, swirling his drink.

"Like hell you are. Talk to me."

"It looks good on paper," he said. "It does. But not in reality. If anything, this is worse than when we first started."

Schlager took a small sip of the whiskey but said nothing, his eyes scanning his old friend.

"What now seems like ages ago," Jason said, "right after Rach got an offer from Asclepius, I took her to dinner. There was this place in Fort Lauderdale she and I liked, and we went there to celebrate her new job. It's nice. You sit right on the marina. Good food. Nice music. I remember being torn."

"Because of Engel's connection to the company?"

"Some of it, sure," he said. "But I remember we had this weird conversation about how the world was not going in the right direction. I was in one of my philosophical moods. And I wasn't sure then, but I thought augmentation technology was another fad. Something that would only divide the world even further."

"Has it? We have embraced the technology. I know," Schlager reached out and touched Jason's shoulder, "some choices were made for you. But we all followed, to some extent."

"Yes," Jason said. "Because we have the means and, by definition, we are in a very select minority. And now, since the theft of the technology, this is going to be yet another form of control. Another tool for those who pull on the strings from the shadows. Too many people can make it now. We can't dictate low prices anymore. Big corporations will collude as usual and keep prices artificially high. I'm already hearing about some oversight committees to regulate the tech sold to consumers, which to me sounds like a stamp of approval that could be used to manipulate who gets the augs and who doesn't."

"But more people making it also means more competition, and competition is a good thing. And we've kicked Engel's ass," Schlager protested. "Restored order. I hear Guardian Manufacturing is filing for bankruptcy next week. The feds have seized Ares Industries, whatever was left of it after yours and Martin's visit. We scattered Black Arrow to the wind. Its leaders have been arrested. The United States Army is restored. I could go on and on. If there was ever a decisive victory, this is it."

"All true. And that is why we are celebrating. But, trust me when I tell you, this is a temporary respite. Engel may have lost, but he's also shown what's possible if one was willing to go far enough. I'm sure there are people out there who are learning from his mistakes as we speak and planning their future moves. Corporations rule the world already and in some twisted, perverted way, we have helped to usher in the future we fought so hard to prevent. Helped them to see how to do it right the next time. And with our technology now in the open, it'll only get harder and harder for us to beat them back again. This is going to be a new arms race."

"We have a head start. And we won't stop fighting. One thing I've learned since we went after Engel is nothing in life is black-and-white. There's always collateral damage. There's always something you'll regret later. Things that will get worse because of the actions you take. People who will get hurt. It's easy when all you are trying to do is to work from nine to five. But when you are trying to change the world, you don't get to complain. All you can do is put the things you've done on the giant cosmic scale. If it tips to the dark side, then maybe you're the wrong guy for the job. But if it tips to the light, then it is good enough for me. And as far as I can tell, it tipped all the way."

Max downed his drink. The music changed, and a slow country song replaced the fast beat. A soft baritone sang of things lost and found. Of a long way home. Of love that never went away. Max patted Jason on the shoulder. "Cheer up, man. I love you, brother. Now, if you'll excuse me, I'm going to find my girlfriend and ask her to marry me. I strongly suggest you do the same."

"I'm already taken care of in that department," Jason quipped.

"Shut up. You know what I mean."

"You're right." Jason finished the rest of the whiskey and glanced back. "I think I'll go, too."

He pulled Schlager into a hug and then let him go, watching as his friend pushed through the crowd and then retraced his steps back to the bar.

"Here for another round?" Rachel asked, smiling at him from behind the counter.

He looked at her, taking in her slim figure. The tiny wrinkles around her eyes. There was a glint to her eyes he missed so much. She stood there as he always remembered her—relaxed, confident, with a mischievous half-smile. Ready for anything life could throw at her.

"No." He extended his arm and took her hand into his. "I'm here to take my wife home."

41

Almada, Portugal

As she watched the red-colored cables of the Ponte 25 de Abril hanging over the sparkling azure waters of the Tagus River, Helen Chen couldn't help but find it eerily reminiscent of the Golden Gate Bridge in San Francisco.

A steel suspension bridge, named after the date of the Carnation Revolution that saw the overthrow of the authoritarian regime of Estado Novo, stretched for almost a mile and a half, connecting Portugal's capitol Lisbon, and, on the other side, the significantly smaller town of Almada.

Helen crossed the bridge and arrived in Almada the night before. She stayed in a small rental apartment on the first floor of a sleepy townhouse. In the morning, she took a taxi to the coast and spent an hour playing tourist. First, she walked around the Sanctuary of Christ the King, the large, eighty-feet-tall monument overlooking Lisbon. Then, for some time, she sat on the bench, watching a steady flow of cars crawl over the red-colored bridge. Now and then, a train would rumble through the lower level, the soothing sound of its rhythmic clanking floating over the water.

At ten o'clock, she walked down to a small, dusty, asphalt path running alongside the cliff and stood there watching the waters of the Tagus below. She knew she had a decision to make, but as she watched the white petals of the sailboats on the water, her mind wandered.

She spent the entire trip from New York as if in a trance. Her body went through the motions of rolling the luggage, checking in, and then going through customs once she landed. She was like a swimmer, treading water over the great white shark circling in the dark right below her. Pretending that as long as she didn't look down, nothing was going to happen.

"Hello."

Helen turned, startled, seeing a woman standing in the middle of the road. She was petite, her olive complexion accentuated by a simple white blouse. She seemed relaxed, her posture at ease, her hands resting in the side pockets of her light denim shorts.

They'd met in person before, of course. Helen still remembered the fear as the woman overpowered her in the Orion Tower. The ruthless precision of every move she made. The surprising strength of her small hands. But now, in broad daylight, she could see her properly for the first time.

Jill Cooper was a striking woman. A blunt bob of jet-black hair with a few silver streaks framed her face, a perfectly symmetrical oval with a set of big, dark-brown eyes. A short nose of an aristocrat. Full, sensuous lips. Even her rather short stature seemed elegant and refined. Like a sculpture in a museum.

"Hello, Jill," Helen said.

The woman waited, without saying a word, and then walked closer, until she stood at the edge of the cliff, looking at the Tagus.

"How's Elizabeth?"

"She's good," Jill said, her eyes never leaving the river. A light breeze played with her dark hair. The warm air smelled of saffron and roasted chestnuts. "It's difficult, building a relationship after so many years, but we are trying. I'm grateful I have this chance."

Helen nodded.

"I see your relationship status has changed too."

"It has." Helen touched the ring on her left hand, turning it this way and that, a new habit she found comforting.

"Congrats." Jill turned away from the river and met Helen's eyes. "I saw the fight on the bridge. I guess, most of the world did. What a brilliant idea to make it televised. Psychological warfare at its finest. It seems you were able to put the information I'd provided to good use."

"It worked as advertised," Helen said. "Apparently Engel wasn't keen on having an army of almost-impossible-to-destroy cyborgs without a kill switch. We'd wrestled away control of his toys before. He wanted to make sure if it happened to Daimyo cyborgs, we couldn't turn them against him. And something tells me he never fully trusted Victor Ye either."

"Can't say I blame him. I'm glad I could help. There is some poetic justice in how it all played out." The woman turned back to the water again. "Engel had an unbeatable army and controlled the media. And yet, at the end, it's what destroyed him. A collapsed army and the spectacle in the spirit of the best Hollywood action movies."

"You are a strange one," Helen said. "A philosophizing assassin?"

"It's hard to explain what my life has been to those who don't know, Helen. I know what I've done. I know *who* I am. There's nothing I can do to change the past, or right the wrongs. All I can do is to move forward and try my best not to repeat the same mistakes. I don't think I'll ever be able to redeem myself, and I am at peace with it. But it doesn't mean I'll stop trying. One step at a time. Hopefully, helping you and Jason was one of those steps."

They stood there for a while, the silence growing heavier by the moment. Neither of them was willing to break the spell.

"Andrew and Audrey Hunt," Helen said. She could see Cooper's shoulders tense for a few moments, but then she relaxed again.

"Yes. I had them killed. And many others. I remember every name and every face. Men and women. Young and old. Politicians, soldiers, corporate bigwigs, CEOs. Husbands and wives. Parents. Brothers." She turned around and met her eyes. "Sisters."

"Mary Chen," Helen said, before she could stop herself, the name rolling off her tongue like the first pebble of a mighty avalanche. "You killed my sister. It wasn't a suicide."

"I did. It was my specialty. Creating a story that would have most cops fooled. She was an obstacle in Engel's scheme. He wanted to acquire her company, and Mary stood in his way. If it wasn't me, it would have been somebody else. I'm sorry. I wish there was something I could do or say to make your pain go away, but it doesn't work that way. Things like that cannot be undone."

Helen moved back from the edge of the cliff, keeping Cooper in front of her. "Don't try anything stupid. I have a loaded drone above us that will blast your head right off, if you as much as flinch."

The woman shrugged and slowly took her hands out of her pockets. "I'm unarmed. I knew what this conversation was going to be. What else could it be? It's not like we are two best friends, trying to catch up. Besides. Secrets like these cannot stay buried forever. Sooner or later, they would come out. Authorities would never find me. But the Witch? It was a matter of time. I could tell you my life story and at the end maybe you'd understand why I did what I did, or maybe you wouldn't. But I won't even try, because the result is the same. It won't bring your sister back. Or anyone else."

"You knew I came here to kill you?"

"Kill me?" Cooper tilted her head. "No, I didn't think you were coming here to kill me. I thought you were coming here to confront me. How it played out after that was the real question for you. But sure, I realized dying today was a distinct possibility."

"But you came anyway?"

Cooper shrugged. "This was going to happen whether I liked it or not. I wanted it to be over with. Do it on my terms. Now. Do what you will."

Helen stared at the woman, her heart racing. She wasn't bluffing—a new-generation hunter drone was hovering up above them at an altitude of one hundred yards. It was equipped with a laser-guided hypersonic weapon that was linked to Helen's cranial implant. Any move that the computer deemed aggressive and a bullet, traveling at Mach 5, would cover the distance between the muzzle of the drone's weapon and the back of Cooper's skull before the woman could blink, let alone react.

If she had been honest with herself, Helen didn't know what Cooper's reaction was going to be when she arranged for the meeting. She wanted to confront her about the Hunts and her sister, and see her reaction. Part of her hoped Cooper would deny her involvement and try to spin the story. Maybe even attack her. That would make the decision easy—strike her in self-defense. Leave the scene with no regrets. Never look back.

But now, looking at the woman calmly standing in front of her, Helen desperately wanted to be angry. Instead, all she felt was a profound sense of loss and sadness.

"What do you think I should do? Let you go?"

"I think…" Cooper said, her words so quiet, Helen had to strain to make them out. "I think you need to do what brings you peace."

Helen opened the drone window, the view of Cooper's forehead behind the red crosshairs filling up her vision. She saw Cooper lift her face to the sky and close her eyes. A small red button appeared in Chen's vision. All she needed to do was reach for it. It would have been so easy. Not even a gesture was needed. Just a thought. A hole would appear in Cooper's forehead and the woman would tumble down the cliff, and Chen would disappear, never to be seen again. A kaleidoscope of faces raced in front of her. Mary, Hiroko, Eugene. Mike Connelly. Would they want her to pull the trigger? To spill more blood, however justified?

She stared at the red button for another moment and then closed the window, swiping the battle interface away.

"I better never see or hear about you ever again."

"You won't," the woman said, her eyes still closed.

From where Helen stood, it seemed she was simply enjoying the warmth of the sun on her face. Perhaps, Helen thought, it was *exactly* what she was doing.

"Goodbye, Jill."

She turned around and started walking up the hill without looking back. Her hand found the ring on her finger and turned it this way and that, its weight comforting on her skin. The former assassin was right—she needed to find what brought her peace. As she climbed the uneven path, overlooking the strikingly blue water below, Helen Chen knew exactly what it was. Home.

42

Orion Tower, Manhattan

Rachel woke up with a start, her face covered with a sheen of sweat, her body tingling from the tips of her toes to the back of her skull. She stayed immobile for a few seconds, catching her breath, listening to the rhythmic beat of her artificial heart. An adrenaline spike peaked on her internal vision and was now descending to its base level, the entire graph fading from her view. There was still a dull ache in her chest and a pulling sensation in the back after the surgeries. The base of her head, where the cranium implant was installed, was heavy.

The pieces of a nightmare still lingered in the dark corners of her mind, like some slippery tentacles moving just out of reach as she tried to recall them. There were fragments. Small pieces of a jigsaw puzzle. A bottomless void of a pitch-black room. A foot-long needle floating over a closed eyelid. An invisible cage.

She blinked a few times, and they disappeared, defeated by the soft morning light filtering in through the window.

Rachel pulled the blanket down and shivered as cold air rushed over her naked body. She glanced at the scars on her chest from the triple transplant. They were still itchy at times, but they'd lost the angry red color of the first few days and now were white and pale, almost invisible. What would take years under normal circumstances was done in a few weeks, thanks to the speeding effects of the nanobots circulating through her body.

She picked up the bathrobe from her nightstand and threw it over her shoulders. Then she walked to the window and looked down at the city below.

The heavy fog had disappeared overnight, and the sky was clear, save for a few long wisps of cirrus clouds in the west. The sun was still low, coloring the buildings as far as she could see in copper tones. There were a few sailboats going down the Hudson, eager to take advantage of the fair weather.

"You're up early," she heard and turned around to see Jason get up from the bed. The metal of his artificial limbs shimmered and sparkled as he moved.

He walked over to her and scooped her in his arms, lifting her off the floor. By now she knew the metal of his bionics was the same temperature as the rest of his body, but it still surprised her every time she touched it.

"How was last night?" he asked with a grin.

Her finger traced the scar running from his chest up to his shoulder, where the artificial arm fused with his flesh. "It was strange."

"Strange?" He frowned but didn't let her go. "Is it because of my augs?"

"No. Nothing like that. It was great. It's just I'm not used to being, you know…" She trailed off, not knowing how to phrase it.

"What?"

"Being intimate," Rachel said. "On some level, I guess, I knew it's been years."

"Yes." He carried her away from the window and laid her on her back across the bed. "I guess we have a lot of catching up to do."

She shivered as he pulled the robe off and closed her eyes, giving herself to the moment. He kissed her, and she kissed him back, their bodies merging into one, moving with an ever-increasing rhythm. Soon, nothing mattered anymore.

"I think I should change my name," she said, as they lay on the bed side by side, resting. Her naked thigh was pressed against his, where the flesh met the metal, but to her skin it felt uniform. Warm and alive. If she hadn't been looking, she wouldn't know there were two separate parts. One human. The other one a machine. "I don't think Rachel suits me anymore."

Jason propped himself up on an elbow to look at her but said nothing.

"You're quiet."

"I assumed you were going to explain where it was coming from," he said. "You are one of those people who always plan things out before they do something, and I'm guessing this wasn't a spur-of-the-moment decision either."

She locked her fingers under her head and stared at the ceiling. "I died, for all intents and purposes. Sure, you can argue I was asleep, but you know it's not true. You didn't even know if it was going to be possible to wake me from that sleep. As I was lying in that chamber, waiting to pass out and listening to the murmur of the liquid pouring in, I was prepared to die. It's not wrong to say I was dead for many years. I feel like Rachel Hunt is no more. She's still there, I suppose, but we can't pretend something like this doesn't change a person. There's a different world from what I remember. It's hard to even begin to describe how different. And you have changed a lot."

"I'm still the same."

"No, you're not," she said, "and I don't mean your body. Everything you've been through while I slept away has changed you. You are not the same Jason with chubby cheeks and a ponytail I left at our place on Broome Street. The guy who said augmentation was a form of plastic surgery. He was a wealthy man with a hippy heart and a paci-fist, and you are a hardened soldier and a leader and inspiration to millions of people. It might not be obvious to you because you've lived it, but it's obvious to me. Like when you see somebody's kid after a long while. Trust me. You're not the same person. You can't be. And that's okay."

He ran his steel fingers through a crew cut. "I guess you're right. What do you want to call yourself then?"

"I was thinking since I was reborn in June, maybe I can call myself that. June. Not the most original name, I know, but I feel like it suits me. It's short. Compact. Complete. And I can keep my middle name. What do you think?"

"June," he said, as if tasting the word on his tongue. "I guess it'll take some time getting used to it, but I like it."

"Good." She stood up. "I'm going to take a shower."

"Okay. I'll see you later, then." He stood up as well and started getting dressed. "I need to take a trip to Brooklyn. Steven wanted to talk to me. They've gotten most of the equipment back from the silo, and we need to figure out what our priorities are. He's got these two guys he hired, and he's been talking about synthetic brain tissue nonstop for the past few days. I'm not sure if I'm fascinated or mortified. But his pitch is it'd be the last step to make humans immortal."

"Fascinating. It sounds like Steven. I'd be begging you to take me with, but I have a few errands to run myself. I'll join you in the afternoon." She leaned in and placed a soft kiss on his lips and walked toward the shower. "I can feel you staring."

"Wasn't even going to deny it. It's a magnificent view. Bye…June."

She stepped into the shower and turned on the water to its highest setting, letting the hot jets bite into her skin, massaging the knots out of her muscles. She stood there for some time, as the sweet soreness still lingered.

"June," she said out loud, keeping her tongue on the top row of her teeth after it hit it on the last syllable.

She turned off the shower and stepped outside, her skin glowing with heat. She put on some fresh underwear, a pair of jeans, and a simple T-shirt. Then she sat in front of a computer terminal, activating voice controls.

"Email," she said.

A window popped up on the screen, a cursor blinking on the address line.

"Whom would you like to send it to?" a disembodied voice said.

"Delgado," she said, and gave computer the address. "Subject line: Deus ex machina."

The cursor jumped into the body of the email, and June opened her mouth, ready to dictate, but then closed it. After a moment's hesitation, she turned off the voice control and pulled out an old-fashioned keyboard. Her fingers hovered over the soft keys for a few seconds and then typed a brief message.

She hit Enter, sending the cursor to the next line, and signed the email.

June Camille Hunt

She stared at the blinking cursor and then hit the backspace a few times, deleting the last name. She cocked her head, looking at the two names, considering.

June Camille

"No," she said out loud, and her hand returned to the keyboard, deleting both words and then signing the message in two decisive strokes, her index finger stabbing at the keys with force:

JC

ACKNOWLEDGMENTS

Acknowledgements (and a bit of a backstory)

It's hard to describe the feeling of finishing a novel, let alone a series that consists of six books and two short stories. I started *The Blueprint* in the summer of 2013 and now, as I'm writing these words, it's October of 2022. For the past nine years, I've spent a lot of time alongside Jason Hunt and his loyal friends, figuring out how to defeat Alexander Engel and build a better world than the cabal had envisioned for humanity. You'll be the judge of how it all turned out.

Those characters now live (and die) in their own world, with its own history and its own rules. I know some people say doctors have a god complex. If such a complex exists, they are looking for the wrong bunch of people.

It's been a long journey. And not just writing the Upgrade series. The first time I remember trying to write something, I was still in first grade (I think). My mother read a short poem to me. She'd always been one of those strange people who know a lot of poetry by heart and, often, annoyingly so, as I thought at the time, recite parts of them in conversations.

I have no recollection of what the particular poem was or what it was about. However, I remember being so struck by the beauty of how the rhyme worked, I immediately wanted to create something like that myself. It wasn't the first poem I'd heard, but there was something that plucked the right strings, and I was off to create what was undoubtedly a masterpiece.

While the text of my first stab at writing is lost forever (for which I am grateful), I remember there was something about the moon and the clouds, and possibly the rain, though I can't be sure. But then again, a lot of my early writing had lots of rain, so it's a safe bet the poem had it, too.

I was a voracious reader. I devoured everything I could get my hands on, and poetry was my first love. An introduction to the magic of what a skillful wordsmith could do. My brief relationship with poetry was shuttered, however, when my father gifted me a small book that contained a collection of short science fiction stories. *From father to son*, he signed it on the inside of the jacket of the book.

It blew my mind. There was a multitude of different worlds out there, universes even, where brave men and women battled aliens, traveled through time, and colonized exotic planets. Poetry? What poetry? I wanted to write about blasters and gigantic spaceships jumping through wormholes. And how a young lad of humble beginnings became the ruler of the galaxy and saved the girl. *Rendezvous With Rama* and *Space Odyssey* and *Foundation* and many others completely turned my understanding of what's possible upside down. Like most kids, I gobbled up Alexander Dumas and Mark Twain, Jonathan Swift and Jack London. And yet, nothing consumed me as much as good science fiction.

By the time I was in high school, I must have written at least two dozen short stories and one, semi-completed novelette about the colonization of a hostile planet by a brave crew of space explorers. The novelette famously (or infamously, depending on whom you asked) hijacked a physics lesson when the substitute teacher overheard me reading it to a group of my classmates during recess and pretended he didn't hear the ringing bell. He let me finish reading the entire thing. In his defense, it was one of the last lessons before the summer break and there was not much to do, anyway.

I continued to write throughout college. Ah, the college years! The time when we think we know everything about the world and scorn at older generations who understand so little. That was a period when I wrote some weird, dream-like short stories my like-minded twenty-something philosopher friends called Dali-esque, in a nod to the surrealist painter.

The idea for *The Blueprint*, that later transformed into a series of books, had been in the back of my mind for a long time. When the original *Matrix* movie came out, I discovered the incredible (and unknown to me at the time) genre of cyberpunk. It fascinated me not only because of a novel premise, but because there was a fantastical mix of cutting-edge science fiction and the world that could be just around the corner. What they call in the TV land "Next Sunday A.D."

Intrigued, I went back to the roots of the genre—William Gibson's *Neuromancer*. And while I didn't enjoy Gibson's writing style, I loved the premise. Specifically, because I thought some version of a cyberpunk world had such a high chance of manifesting itself in real life.

What interested me, however, was the *how*. How could the reality of today transform into the dystopian world where mega corps ruled the world and cybernetically augmented soldiers did their bidding? What nudges would it need to move from the realm of possibility into reality?

There were a lot of books and movies that were set in the not-so-distant world full of rain, swords, and garish neon lights, but none I could find would tell me a story about how it got there. I wanted to write a story (or six) that would explore the transformation. The metamorphosis.

Looking back at how much I've written for most of my life, it's strange *The Blueprint* turned out to be my first fully fledged novel. I started writing it arguably at the worst possible time, too. It was after the birth of my son and one year since I launched my company, which at the time teetered at the brink of failure. Spare time was nonexistent, and I wrote most of the novel on the subway. I typed away, crammed between cranky commuters (if I was lucky enough to score a seat) and angling the monitor of my laptop away from prying eyes as the R train shuffled me to and from the office. On those days when seats were not available, I daydreamed about the plot, took notes on my phone, and gawked at people, looking for something I could use for my characters.

Despite my determination to finally write a first full-sized novel, I'm not sure I'd be able to accomplish that if not for a good friend, David Longshore. A towering intellect and a fabulous writer himself, he once wisely told me to stop polishing the same chapter, looking for perfection that didn't exist, and just "finish the darn thing." I wish he was still around to cheer me on the completion of the series, a feat I thought impossible a few years ago. I'm sorry you can't share this achievement, my friend. And I hope wherever you are, it's a warm, sunny place where you can see the ocean full of magnificent ships you loved so much.

Along the way, I have been lucky. I met Stephen King's first editor, Mike Garrett, when I finished the first draft of *The Blueprint*, and he gave it a few passes, teaching me more about the craft in a few back-and-forth emails than I thought possible. I've met the most fabulous designer, Jeroen ten Berge, who gave the series its distinct look and became a wonderful friend.

And the research for the topics covered in the book was absolutely delightful. Not all, but a lot of technologies and tools described in the books are real, and I tried my absolute best to make descriptions of science as accurate as possible.

I have many people to thank, so, in no particular order, here it is:

I'd like to thank Oleg V. and Alex B. for educating me about hacking and providing a fascinating glimpse into how real-world breaking into sophisticated systems works. I'd also like to extend my sincere thanks to Andrew Ackerman for input and some fantastic stories about the life of a special forces soldier.

To Wesly Farris, for giving me a glimpse into the inner workings of the military and always willing to help with research. To Faith Williams, the best editor any author could wish for. The reason the series is readable is that she caught a gazillion typos and inconsistencies in the plot line. Neill Thorne did a fabulous job narrating the series and gave the characters their unique voices. To Jeroen ten Berge for the design.

To my writer group, which is a great support net that keeps us all motivated and excited to share our stories.

To my wonderful readers, whose every email I always try to answer. Your curiosity and support made writing this series a fantastic journey.

To my wife, who always serves as the sounding board for all my writing projects and keeps me going. And last, but not least—to my son, who makes it all worth it.

JOIN THE UPGRADE SERIES

Thank you for reading DEUS EX MACHINA, the last book in THE UPGRADE series. I hope you enjoyed it.

If you enjoyed this book, please take a moment and leave an honest review. Reviews are important for authors and help us sell more books and thus spend more time writing new stories you can enjoy. You can do that here:

Leave a review

And, of course, don't forget to join the series to learn about upcoming releases, exclusive free content, and more. You can do it right here:

Join The Upgrade Series

Thanks again for reading and hope to see you soon!

ALSO BY WESLEY CROSS

THE UPGRADE SERIES

BOOK 1. THE BLUEPRINT

BOOK 2. VERTIGO

BOOK 3. THE LOOP

BOOK 4. SPARE PARTS

BOOK 5. FATA MORGANA

BOOK 6. DEUS EX MACHINA

ROGUE (A short story)